One SERIOUSLY MESSED-UP WEEK IN THE OTHERWISE MUNDANE & UNEVENTFUL LiFE of ~~SAM TAYLOR~~ JACK SAMSONITE

TOM CLEMPSON

One SERIOUSLY MESSED-UP WEEK IN THE OTHERWISE MUNDANE & UNEVENTFUL LIFE of ~~SAM TAYLOR~~

JACK SAMSONITE

atom

www.atombooks.net

ATOM

First published in Great Britain in 2011 by Atom

A CIP catalogue record for this book
is available from the British Library.

ISBN 978-1-907410-55-0

Typeset in Melior by M Rules
Printed and bound in Great Britain by
Clays Ltd, St Ives plc

Atom
An imprint of
Little, Brown Book Group
100 Victoria Embankment
London EC4Y 0DY

An Hachette UK Company
www.hachette.co.uk

www.atombooks.net

Dedicated to Matilda and Theo,
for encouraging immaturity.
To Joe, Amy and Katy, for informing it.
And to Laura, for putting up with it.

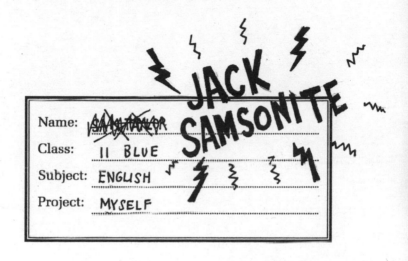

Name: ~~SAM TAYLOR~~ JACK SAMSONITE

Class: II BLUE

Subject: ENGLISH

Project: MYSELF

inTRODUCTion

TO NOT READ THIS COULD SERIOUSLY DAMAGE YOUR HEALTH!

Seriously. The crap that I have written down on these pages is probably the most important stuff you will ever read in your life. Maybe not as important as 'Danger 50,000 volts' or 'Trespassers will be shot', but, in terms of importance for the well-being of your future existence, this is up there. Trust me.

I know it all sounds kind of melodramatic and like I'm up my own arse, but I can assure you that is not the case. I know this because someone once told me to 'always write your introduction after you've finished – that way you know exactly what it is you are introducing'. So that's what I'm doing right now. That is how I know that, by some fluke chance, whilst I was documenting one week of the monotony that is my life, something kind of unbelievable actually happened.

Now here I am, sat in the bed of a beautiful girl, and my face is beaten to a pulp. Despite first impressions I'm actually a gentle soul – mild-mannered, quiet and a bit of a hypochondriac. Not sure why I just told you that though, I've just ruined a bit of upcoming character development. But maybe I needed to write that in case you don't actually continue reading. Maybe I need you to know the kind of person I am in case you put the book down right now. You can, you know. I don't care. In fact I dare you not to read! I almost want you not to read any more. But I warn you once again – your future happiness hangs in the balance.

Enjoy.

MONDAY

1st Period
Physics

Nob-ache.

Seriously bad nob-ache.

I don't actually have nob-ache right now, but, as an almost-sixteen-year-old boy, involuntary and unwelcome wang-ons take up about 78% of my waking (and un-waking, for that matter) life. Therefore, nob-aches are a large part of who I am and should not go unmentioned in a project entitled 'Myself'. Especially as, when I was suffering from the aforementioned debilitating affliction about two hours ago, it occurred to me that to start a story with the word 'nob-ache' would be unbelievably cool.

'I've got nob-ache' is actually how I wanted to start it but, unfortunately, as I don't presently have any such ache, I didn't want to start this whole thing off with a lie, so I had to settle for the single home-made word 'nob-ache' and then go on to explain why, in these rambling and incoherent opening paragraphs. Not a great start, but it did allow me to use the word 'nob-ache' at least seven times, so it's not all bad, I suppose.

'Sam?'

Shit, the teacher's talking to me, better pretend to be making notes . . .

The 'teacher' whose Science lesson I have been writing through is called Jane Monroe. She vaguely resembles a mole, in a cute kind of way, so obviously not especially attractive, but, given that she is only one of about three female teachers under the age of forty in our school, the general consensus amongst most of the male students here is that she's 'worth a go' or that she's a 'five pinter'. Obviously most of the guys at my school are total dicks – not only are they all completely desperate for any form of sex with *anybody* other than their left hands, but I very much doubt that any of them would still be standing upright after five pints, and, if they were, their nobs certainly wouldn't be. I think the term 'five pinter' should really be replaced by 'I would do her in an instant as long as there was no chance of anyone ever finding out about it, and if they did find out then I would have to make up an elaborate excuse as to why I did it, like, "I didn't know what I was doing! I'd had FIVE PINTS!"'

'Yes?' I reply to Five-pints-moley-face Monroe with a carefully balanced tone of innocence and deep interest and concentration.

Please don't come and see what notes I'm making. Please, please, please . . . !!!

'I *said* pens down,' she says, eyebrows raised in an impotent gesture of sternness. She's such a timid little thing that even when she shouts it's kind of cute. I don't want to give her a hard time though, so I guess the pen is going down and I'll catch up with this later . . .

2nd Period
English

Well, there you go – 'Sam', that's my name. I was kind of hoping to use a pseudonym, something cool and mysterious, but I guess it's too late thanks to old Moley-face catching me off guard.

I'm in my English lesson now and although I'm not supposed to be doing my homework during the lesson I'm not going to feel too bad about it, considering the homework I'm doing is actually for this class. Another factor playing a part in the me-not-feeling-bad department is that we're nearly fifteen minutes into the lesson and we are still waiting for our teacher, Dave Kross, to arrive. If this were any other class, with any other teacher, half the students would have seen this as an opportunity to take off.

But not this class. Dave Kross is without a doubt the coolest teacher who ever walked the earth and I don't think I know a single person that doesn't agree with me. (Considering he's the one who'll be marking this paper, maybe I'll get a good grade for brown-nosing.) Seriously though, without wanting to sound too gushy and pathetic, he is a good guy. I don't mean he's 'cool' and 'crazy' and 'down with the kids' and likes to manipulate us, I mean he's a genuine, down to earth bloke who makes us feel like friends rather than students. He even refuses to jump the queue in the canteen like all the other members of staff and instead lines up with all us kids – he's a proper good guy. And also, seriously, I really DO want to get a good grade for this work. I know I sound like I don't give a shit, what with my blatant lack of respect for decent grammar and wotnot, but here's the thing – this exercise is categorised as 'Creative Writing', so that's what I'm doing, I'm being creative with my own laziness! And if everything works out, then my creative laziness will get me good enough grades to get to film school, where I can make creatively lazy films for the whole world to see.

So there you go, I have inadvertently gone and given my main character (myself) motivation for this story – I need to get a good grade. Shit. Not only is that extremely obvious, it's also a complete cliché! And here's me trying to be original. I truly am a dick.

Anyway, here I am (a dick, as we have recently discovered), in Dave's English lesson (our school is pretty laid back – we call the teachers by first names and we don't wear uniforms), and so far I'm the only person with my book out. How much of a swot must I look? I've noticed a couple of people start to panic as they've seen me – head down, writing away furiously – and are clearly worried in case I'm working on some last-minute homework that they might have forgotten about.

'Jack,' says Cole, who's sat beside me, shoving my arm, trying to get me to respond.

'Jack!' he barks, obviously unaware that I'm writing down everything he's doing.

'Jack, you twat!'

Cole's a twat and he's got no nob.

By the way, my name is Jack now. According to Hollywood it's the coolest name available for a man. Have you noticed how about 70% of all action heroes in Hollywood are named Jack? I mean the characters, of course, not the actors, which is weird actually because thinking about it there are barely any actors named Jack . . . Nicholson, Palance . . . who else? (Hey, they were both in *Batman* . . . weird.)

3rd Period
Biology with Eleanor Wade

I've changed my mind. My motivation in this story is no longer to just get a good mark for writing it. My new motivation has a name and I call it 'Eleanor Wade'.

There she is – Eleanor, Eleanor, Eleanor . . . Woof! Sat one row in front of me and one place to the left is the most perfect example of a female I have ever encountered. She actually makes me look forward to Biology. (This is where I turn to face the camera and whisper, 'I wouldn't mind doing a bit of Biology with her!', sounding a little less cool and a little more creepy than intended.)

'What the hell are you doing?' Cole just asked.

'Nothing,' I lied.

'What did you say about "doing a bit of Biology"?'

'Shut up!' I pleaded in whispers.

Clive Cornish may be a dim-witted, wiggy-haired Science teacher but he has the hearing of a spry kitten (kittens probably have good hearing, right?). Plus Clive Cornish is a short wiry thing with a lady's voice and heavy nipples who likes to compensate for his femininities by hurling out detentions

like they are sheep on Facebook – and I was never really
into that whole 'throw a sheep at someone' thing. If he
keeps us late we'll end up with no afternoon break, and my
bottom needs an afternoon break! Not for shits, mind you,
although I probably could do with one, but I'm talking
about farts. My stomach is gurgling like I just drank a
genuine grown-up coffee-shop coffee (does that happen to
other people or is it just me?), but if I unleash the raging
beast here it would be just my luck that everyone would get
just enough of a whiff to make them feel sick and then Cole
would take great pleasure in loudly blaming me, whether I
was guilty or not.

'What did you say about doing Biology?' Cole repeated,
whispering this time, which is just as obvious as shouting
when he shuffles himself to within two inches of my ear.

I warningly motioned towards Clive Cornish with my
head, eyes and eyebrows. (Does that motion have a name?
You know, where you clench your teeth and raise your eyebrows in a 'Not now!' kind of way? It should do. It's not
really a glare and it's not a nod. Lets call it a 'glod'.) But sub-
tlety is just not in Cole's nature.

'Were you talking to an imaginary camera again?' he
whispered with an eager grin, ignoring my intense glod. (I
like it!)

'Yes,' I admitted unashamedly, hoping to shut him up and
avoid an inevitably severe mocking.

'You're a bummer!' he exclaimed, failing to keep his laughing outburst to a whisper. 'I thought you were trying to quit.'

*Oh Jesus, he's going to crucify me. And he's going to do it
loud enough for Eleanor to hear.*

'Is it because you like kissing boys?' he asked, unable to control his stupid snigger.

Here we go. Luckily by now I am familiar with the techniques required to placate the giggling moron. (Why am I friends with him?)

'No, you idiot,' I replied out the corner of my mouth, not looking up from my writing, 'it's because I like kissing old ladies' bottoms.' I deadpanned.

'Cole?' comes Clive Cornish's nasal voice, bringing Cole to sudden silence. We're done for! He heard us! Goodbye, play time. I mean break time! (Why do I still do that? It's been five years. I haven't had 'play time' since primary school!) Hang on . . . Clive's face . . . the waiting . . . he's not telling Cole off, he's waiting for an answer to something. He must have asked a question! Is Cole smart enough to work this out? Please, Cole, do not say 'Sorry' – say anything, anything to do with Biology, say 'Enzymes', say 'Photosynthesis', but if you say 'Sorry' he'll know you're guilty, you'll be signing your own death warrant . . .

I'm furiously writing all this down, pretending to be deep in my work. Cole has been silent for way too long. Everyone is beginning to turn and look. Speak, damn you, speak! Wait . . . his mouth begins to open . . . he stutters . . . a word begins to form on his lips . . .

'Vulva?'

Shit!

No . . . wait . . . Cornish is blushing! He stutters, too . . . he . . .

'No, Cole,' he mutters sheepishly, face bright red, 'anyone else?'

A dozen sniggering hands shoot up into the air.

'Yes . . . Eleanor.'

'The Natural History Museum?'

'Thank you. Yes, it is on display at the Natural History Museum in London.'

Must – keep – writing . . . anything to keep me from laughing.

Last Break

We're sat outside in the tennis courts with our backs against the mesh fence, both pretending to be doing homework when we are clearly here because of the bouncy girls swinging their rackets. Jerry Lee Lewis's 'Whole Lotta Shakin' Goin' On' is going round in my head and the sun is warming the back of my neck in a soothing kind of way.

'Whoa!' whispers Cole without moving his lips as Caroline Baker bends over, awaiting the delivery of Victoria Jones' serve.

Things aren't looking too bad for this afternoon, after all. We just managed to avoid a Clive Cornish close shave by the skin of our teeth, I've been to the toilet and let out a whole bunch of hardcore farts, and people keep congratulating Cole for saying 'Vulva' to Cornish with no repercussions whatsoever. Plus, I don't want to tempt fate, but I did a pretty good job of avoiding a mocking from Cole.

'Not bad, Mish Moneypenny,' I said to camera.

'Cut it out,' muttered Cole.

Cole is never going to understand my habits of speaking to camera or humming my own soundtrack. He's not a movies person, he's a motorbikes and beers person. Why *am* I friends with him?

I smelled her before I even heard her voice. Eleanor has just walked past behind us and I really wish I could turn around to see her without looking like a perv.

'I know,' she said as she passed, 'I wish I could just pick him up and put him in my pocket.'

Of course in my head she was talking about me, but in actual fact I think it's more likely she was talking about the kitten that one of the Art teachers had been playing with at lunch (don't know why).

I suppose I should take some time to explain who Eleanor Wade is. Eleanor Wade is not Sarah Carmichael. Or, in other words (without having to explain who Sarah Carmichael is, too), Eleanor Wade is a proper girl, a nice girl, a girl who actually has some control over the opening and closing of her legs and mouth. She is not the most popular girl in school, not even in the top ten, which for me is some kind of a miracle. I can't understand how she doesn't have every filthy sports freak and rich boy trying to get into her knickers – she is absolutely perfect! Unfortunately for me, though, Sarah Carmichael got herself a new boyfriend two weeks ago, which means every arsehole with a hard-on is on the prowl for other prey, and I know it's only a matter of time before these brainless dipshits figure out that Eleanor is possibly the most beautiful and charming girl in school. When that day comes the competition will be too great, Eleanor will be fed up and jaded with every boy trying to get with her, and my chances will be blown. That is why I have to act fast. However I have to be careful, because whilst I don't even register on the popularity scale, I am not completely unliked – as much as I would like to be invisible, I somehow attract attention, people do notice me, and when the predators spy me seasoning potential prey they will pounce without a moment's warning. I have to move fast, effectively and completely below the radar.

The best thing I have going for me is the fact that most people don't even consider Eleanor when they are out on the prowl because she never seems to go out with anyone. There was one guy, back in Year 8, who she went out with for three horrifying weeks. His name was Scott Saloon (could never work out if the name was cool or twattish, so just to be safe, to make sure we eradicated any subliminal association with anything as masculine and cool as a cowboys' pub, we decided to rename him Scott Salon, like a ladies' hairdressing place not to his face, obviously, else he'd batter us), she dumped him, he declared she was a lesbian, and now he is a dedicated follower of Sarah Carmichael.

Now . . . there is a very small possibility that Scott Salon was not actually spreading a spiteful rumour when he proclaimed Eleanor a muff-diver, but was actually stating a fact. However, the unhealthy collection of R-Patz pics pasted all over Eleanor's exercise books last year gives me eternal hope. (Please don't think I'm actually someone who uses people's abbreviated cock-names like J-Lo and LiLo, I'm only using R-Patz because I can't actually remember his real name. The only thing I can think of is Robert Patrick, but I'm pretty sure he's the bad guy in *Terminator 2*.) Shame that she is attracted to such a pretty boy as R-Patz (sorry) and not someone with a more geeky Woody Allen quality to him. Still, R-Patz is closer to my league than, say, the women's rugby team. I suppose if she wasn't so beautiful you would class Eleanor as a geek – she's hyper-intelligent, always does her homework on time and hardly ever shows off any skin. (Which drives me insane! In a good way. I think the ones who don't show it all off have a lot more mystery and appeal to them than the ones who paint it orange and flaunt it for the builders.) Yes, Eleanor does seem like a fem-nerd, but on the other hand her sharp yet classy fashion sense and bubbly affability seem to contradict any theories of geekdom.

And there she is . . . Eleanor Wade and a couple of friends have just sat down on a patch of grass to the left of the tennis courts. She makes my insides warm and squirmy, and I'm sorry to say that I find it hard to take my eyes off her (which makes it all the more difficult trying to write this stuff down). She leans on one arm and her thick, dark, curly hair separates around her shoulder, teasingly revealing her skin, like a miniature strip show for the easily satisfied. She's not super-sized and she's not super-skinny. In my opinion she suffers from the Mummy Bear syndrome – she's 'just right'. (Is it Mummy Bear's porridge that's 'just right' or is it Baby Bear's? I don't know. Should be Mummy Bear – she's the one in the middle, right?)

Hopefully I have painted an accurate description of Eleanor (flawed perfection) and by now you're probably getting a pretty good idea of what kind of person I am (a flawed nobody) and you are probably thinking the same thoughts that haunt my insomniac sleep – *she's way out of my league*. But I do have one trump card up my sleeve – I

MAKE ELEANOR WADE LAUGH! I haven't spoken to her that many times, in fact barely ever, but the times that I did I always managed to evoke at least a few giggles. This is possibly my proudest achievement in life. Eleanor Wade laughs at me – mostly because I fall over quite a lot and talk complete gibberish whenever she's around, but there's definitely affection hidden somewhere in those laughs. You know those dating shows where the bimbo claims to prefer a good sense of humour over body or looks and then she goes and picks the dim-witted firefighter or football player over the jolly little librarian? Well, Eleanor seems like the kind of intelligent being that *would* go for the librarian.

The way to a girl's heart is surely through her funny bone. I just hope I get there first.

My radar has just picked up my worst fear – a predator. Zack Pimento is sat at the opposite end of the tennis courts with his gang of pretty-faced clones, and his gaze is locked firmly on Eleanor.

Get your eyes off of her, you slimy pervert!

I can see the filthy thoughts filtering through his head like shit through a sieve. He's not gazing at her longingly like I do, he's leering at her like a filthy animal that has picked up the scent of meat.

This is it, Zack – I may not have had a problem with you in the past (other than you being precious and arrogant), but now it's war. I have gone my *entire* school life without having a single girlfriend and you have had at least three, despite the fact that most people think you like boys! I am not about to let you swoop in with your designer clothing and million-dollar grin and take the girl of my dreams just for you to have a bit of fun with before you discard her like a fisherman discards a tiddly fish that doesn't live up to his standards. Well I'm going to make sure that this tiddly fish doesn't get reeled in by your cheese-baited rod. Try all you like, but I will do everything in my minuscule power to ensure that she gets hooked on my cheese-baited, NO, love-baited (Christ, that's even worse!), my *special*-baited rod (I'm beginning to wish I hadn't bothered with the whole fishing metaphors thing now). Whatever. She's my tiddly fish and I'm going to eat her up before you even—

I think I better just stop. You get the gist of it anyway.

TUESDAY

The Bus Journey In

I was far too distraught after witnessing pretty boy Zack leering over my destiny to go to the final lesson of yesterday (History). I was even too distraught to go to the library and do some more writing. But to the library I did go, oh yes I did, and in that library I concocted a cruel and devious plan. After schemes of biological warfare, kidnap and death threats brewed like poison in my cauldron-like skull, I finally settled on a plan, a plan that would put Zack out of the picture, whilst simultaneously leaving my conscience entirely guilt-free . . . almost.

For some unknown reason I have taken it upon myself to write a little accompanying piece for this story. Like this one, I have written it in the first person, but, unlike this one, it is a fictional piece. It focuses on a fictional character named 'Zed', who decides to confess his deepest darkest fantasies about a girl that he wishes to 'taint'. He writes these confessions in the form of a letter, which lists in great detail every degrading act he has imagined practising on this innocent girl – acts so eye-wateringly sick that I couldn't dare bring myself to include them as part of this project. In fact I feel ashamed to have written such a perverse piece of fiction and I have the unshakable urge to get rid of it as soon as possible. I must fold this sick piece of filth up until it is a teeny weeny nubbin of paper and throw it away from my person . . . if it happens to land in Eleanor Wade's bag and if she happens to assume it is, in fact, from Zack, then it can't be helped.

OK, OK, I know it sounds malicious and devious, but at no point have I written the names Eleanor or Zack on that letter. I have merely based a character on the person I believe Zack to be, and apart from the letter Z the only thing that could possibly lead Eleanor into believing that the letter could be to *her* from *Zack* is if she too believes it to be an accurate representation of the way Zack feels about her. If so, then I have done nothing but highlight (and possibly exaggerate) the truth. If not, then she will just assume that one of her friends has played a joke on her – no harm done, right?

On the flipside I have also come up with a fairly decent plan to ensure that Eleanor and I have the chance to get better acquainted. I could let you in on this plan, but it would be far better storytelling if I leave it for you to find out later. (Don't worry, this one is a genuinely innocent plan with no poetic licence on the truth.)

I have spent most of this morning's insanely long bus journey mulling over what conclusion I can bring to my English assignment. It's entitled 'Myself', so, kind of obviously, I should finish it with a nicely rounded and succinct summary of who I am, who I see myself to be, how I think others see me and what kind of category or group I fit into. But for the life of me I cannot decide which group I belong in. I can't even think of a new category to file myself into. It's kind of sad. The more I think about it the more it is freaking me out – I have no redeeming personality! The whole world seems to get riled at the idea of being labelled, but at least they know where they stand. I am an average guy, from an average background, in an average family with an average income. I am a nobody! A nobody, stuck on the never-ending bus journey to a nobody's school.

Seventy-two minutes and counting. That is the worst thing about living out in the sticks – it takes for ever to get anywhere. Three hours of each day is wasted on the school bus. THREE HOURS! That's fifteen hours a week. That's sixty hours a month! That's about six hundred hours a year (accounting for holidays, etc.), which means that in my five years here at this school I have spent over four solid months just travelling to and from school! My youth is drifting away in the sands of time and I'm wasting it on a twatting bus!

I'm getting off. I mean it! Right now, I'm getting off!

The Hard Walk In

I'm off.

I think maybe I had a little panic attack. Luckily I didn't get off right in the middle of nowhere, I'm not that messed up. I got off at the bottom of town, which is only a mile or two away from school, so with twenty minutes left before school starts it's no big deal. In fact it's a good idea – with all the early morning traffic the bus has to go through as part of its winding route through the centre of town, I'll probably end up getting to school before it. Although that would be a lot more likely if I got up off this bench I am sat on and stopped writing. But I think I'll wait here just a few minutes more. See, the bench I am sat on is situated at the start of the footpath/cycle track that begins at the Drive Thru then runs alongside the canal and eventually leads straight to school. Cole and our friend Tim use this path to get to school every day, so I'll stick around for a while in case they haven't already gotten this far. Since they're both usually a couple of minutes late, I can probably expect to see them appear around this corner any second now.

This is pretty cool actually. Why haven't I done this

before? I've been riding that bus for five years. If I'd gotten off fifteen minutes early each day I would have saved . . . Screw it, I can't be arsed working out the minutes, hours and days thing again. Basically it would have been a whole lot better. Anything to get off that bus a bit sooner. I hate stepping through the school doors when I've just been sat in that filthy tin can for an hour and a half and am suffering from long-journey syndrome (bed hair, dead legs, drool-mouth and general zombification). Plus, since there are no adults on our bus to maintain any degree of civilisation, the dickwits on the back seat constantly get away with smoking the entire journey, so I spend the whole day stinking of tobacco and getting dodgy looks from any teacher that gets too close. A few of the braver/stronger/swottier kids complain to the driver every now and then and that usually puts a stop to it. Once, after waiting ages for someone else to complain but no one having the guts, my asthma got so bad that I decided to throw caution to the wind and go complain to the driver, except by the time I was halfway down the bus I realised that that nob-face was puffing on a cancer stick, too! Dickhead.

Oh yeah, and speaking of dickheads there's another unwelcome long-journey syndrome – nob-ache. Full-on, ball-numbing, pant-ripping nob-ache. I mean it. Eighty-six minutes of unaccountable erection, cramped up in one position, in seats as comfortable as a concrete pillow and enough leg room to give an umpa lumpa a serious case of deep-vein thrombosis. It's no merry-go-round. Plus then I have the whole joy of figuring out a way of getting off the bus whilst hiding the raging Beast of Boneville that is trying to break its way through the fly of my jeans (a carefully positioned school bag is usually the only answer until you get the chance to wrangle the monster and harness it in the reliable grip of Old Mr Waistband). It's moments like these I thank Jehosifer that I go to a school that doesn't wear uniforms. What must life be like for those sorry sons of bitches who have to live with the puny defences supplied by Mr-100%-Cotton, weak as shit, thin as tissue paper school TROUSERS?!

I'm assuming this whole nob-ache thing is common among adolescents and you grow out of it by adulthood (at least I seriously hope so, I really do not want to be concluding this project by pigeonholing myself as a 'Pervert'). I see far too many grown men wearing cotton trousers BY CHOICE for nob-ache to be a lifelong affliction. No one would wear such flimsy nob protection if there were a possibility they might suffer a huge ninety-minute boner as a result of sitting in a seat. No, choosing the correct clothing for the lower region is as important to us guys as the right body armour is for a warrior about to march into battle. The first line of defence is snug, robust, elasticised underwear. This helps ensure that the evil is kept flat against the pelvis, rather than charging straight ahead as if about to take part in a jousting contest. The next line of defence is undoubtedly a thick, hardwearing, heavy-duty pair of jeans – something that's got a fighting chance should the first defences fail (which, if the beast approaches from the wrong angle, they are liable to do). The jeans must not be too baggy or a circus tent situation will be a very likely outcome. Nor must the jeans be too tight, or one of two outcomes will be your downfall – 1: the beast will stay flat against the hip, but will be as obvious as a shotgun in a gymnast's leotard; 2: the beast will tackle the denim head-on and will more than likely lose the battle, resulting in a loud 'snap' followed by a howling scream of agonising pain (not sure if that would actually happen). When picking the fit of a pair of jeans you must always think Mother Bear (or Baby Bear, still don't know). One more piece of wisdom I have learned these many years on the battlefield – at every available opportunity it is essential to reposition the evil stick to point diagonally upwards. A surprise down-the-trouser-leg attack can be disastrous, resulting in a visible lump, a severe limp and the near-impossible task of repositioning (like trying to unsheathe a four-foot sword from its scabbard in a three-by-three toilet cubicle).

I'm quite sure that for people who do not suffer this horrific disability, this all sounds very petty and puerile – why not just think about Margaret Thatcher, Winston Churchill or any other British prime minister? Of course, what these people clearly do not understand is that, yes, in the big scheme of things this is fairly petty, but 95% of the time there is nothing sexual about it. The willy has a mind of its own! You could be quietly considering complex chess manoeuvres when suddenly an unprovoked attack of the trouser-snake renders you incapacitated for sixty minutes. (And no, it has nothing to do with 'pawn' – pah! Get it? 'Pawn'! No? Sorry.) I guess the whole nob-ache thing is just another symptom of growing up, along with spontaneously wet armpits when you're not even warm, or having a face full of spots when you've been washing five times a day and eating nothing but salad and steamed vegetables. It is these evil manifestations of puberty that cause us teenagers to get bullied by the popular wankers (who are mostly evolutionary freaks who are immune to all the above), to spend all our hard-earned cash/lunch money on rip-off quack remedies, and to lose all traces of self-esteem we may have once had. These are the things that grown-ups forget about when they laugh at us for claiming that life is tough.

Anyway, getting off the bus early is clearly a good thing. On the plus side it means I get some exercise and fresh air (good for the spots), which also relieves any 'stiffness' acquired on the long haul. On the negative side, the long walk means awakening the (until now) dormant waterfalls under my arms. However, this problem can be remedied by carrying a fresh T-shirt and a can of deodorant in your bag at all times.

'Oy, numpty!' bellowed Cole cheerfully, just as I had given up waiting for them and begun to get off the bench with my bag in front of my crotch, purely out of precautionary habit. 'What happened? They throw you off the bus for being such a numpty?'

By the way, obviously I'm not writing this all down whilst actually walking, it's about twenty minutes later now and once again I am sat at a desk, but hopefully everything is fresh enough in my memory.

Although I couldn't see him, I knew Tim must be somewhere behind Cole (he's quite small and Cole's quite big) because a) Cole was showing off and being a prick (which he

always does in front of Tim), and b) I could hear Tim
sniggering.

'Yes,' I replied.

''Appy days!'

There was no need for Cole to say ''Appy days!' here, he
just likes to shoehorn it in as often as possible, along with
'numpty' and 'Calm down, dear!' It's one of his least endearing qualities.

'Aren't you bored of saying that yet?' I moaned.

'Calm down, dear! Too much of a numpty for insults?'

'No, I'm just fed up with you and every other idiot saying
things like "Calm down, dear" and "'Appy days" and
"numpty". It pisses me off. Insult me as much as you like,
doesn't mean anything coming from a nud-fuggler like you,
but at least try to do it without using the same bullshit
phrases that Connor Clarey and his nob-face army all use.'

'Jesus, we're only having a laugh, you big . . .' Cole struggled to think of an insult of his own, '. . . stupid frickin' . . .'
here it comes . . . 'nincompoop!'

Even with Cole's limited cerebral abilities he somehow
always manages to say the right thing when under pressure.
OK, so nincompoop isn't a completely original insult, but
it's quite possibly the funniest one I can think of. I tried hard
not to laugh, but my attempts were futile, which only made
it seem even funnier, until it became one of those stupid
moments where everyone ends up laughing uncontrollably,
like the finale in an episode of *Digimon*.

It's true, though – the whole calm down, dear, 'appy days
stuff – I can't stand the way Cole and Tim are so quick to
jump on the bandwagon with anything popular. (When

those Scoubidou things were popular, Cole and Tim collected them. When they were out of fashion, Cole and Tim ridiculed the kids that still collected them. In Year 9 Tim actually bought himself a pair of Ugg boots off eBay. Apparently he was THIS close to wearing them to school before his mum told him he was wearing girls' shoes. This year they're harassing their parents for iPads.) It shames me to know that my friends are barely any different than every other arsehole around. I'd like to think they had something more unique about them, but as each year passes they lose more and more pieces of who they once were and become more and more like everyone else, to the point where I think to myself, 'If I had only just met these people, I would probably hate their guts.'

The Most Annoying Fad Phrases

3. **Legend! (has replaced 'Nice one!')**
2. **Sack That (has replaced 'Screw that for a laugh')**
1. **Mint (has replaced 'Sweet!' As if *sweet* wasn't annoying enough, they then had to go and get specific)**

I think that fads and fashions are possibly one of my biggest hates. They can turn me off anyone or anything. Take, for example, The Killers – I used to love The Killers! I had some import CDs that my uncle brought back from America, along with a load of other stuff, most of which was crap, but The Killers soon became one of my favourite bands. And the best thing of all was that no one over here had even heard of them. They were *my* band.

'What sort of music you into, Jack?' I remember Matthew Lilly asking.

'I'm really into a band called The Killers right now,' I mentioned.

'The Killers? Who are they? They sound shit!' was his response, which was clearly the plan all along, no matter what band I said, just to make the girls around us laugh, to make him look dominant and me look stupid.

I didn't care though. In fact it pleased me that no one had a clue who they were. It meant the music had no stigmas attached. It was my secret. But then the dreaded day came – the stereo was on in our Art lesson and so far it had been churning out all the usual garbage, but then, as I was washing my brushes in the sink, I thought I heard a familiar tune. I turned off the tap and there it was – *my* music blaring out the speakers. At first I assumed that someone had put a CD on.

'Is this The Killers?' I called out, trying to find out who had put it on, but the only response was a cocktail of blank stares, frowns and 'I don't care' shrugs. That's when I realised it was much worse than one other person having my album – it was on the radio! It was being shared with millions of listeners all over the nation! Those bastards!

Of course it wasn't long until they were everyone's favourite band and 'Somebody Told Me' was playing over and over in every shop, every common room and on every MP3 player. Even Matthew Lilly had one of their T-shirts and was claiming that he had discovered the band years ago, way before everyone else. That was the point that I threw my albums out – they had been irreparably tainted. Since that day I have not allowed myself to get too attached to any bands. I've tried my hardest to only like shit bands that will never become popular, but, well, they're mostly shit.

Nuggets

As we strolled into the school grounds I saw two things that made me feel that today might be a good one – a) my bus was running late and was only just pulling into the bus bay at the same time as us, and b) Zack Pimento was chatting with one of his girly friends (who was walking on his left), and his lecherous eyes were checking out some Year 9 girl on his right. This doesn't mean that he's not going to go after my Eleanor, I know, but it does mean two other things – a) he seems to leer at *most* girls so it is unlikely that he has singled Eleanor out as his soul mate and will therefore not be putting 100% of his efforts into her, but will probably spread his 'charms' amongst a few different possible applicants, and b) seeing his slimy perving makes me feel a whole lot less guilty about slipping that note into Eleanor's bag on our way out of school yesterday.

Last night I was beginning to feel anxious about the whole thing. I felt guilty for stitching up Zack, who in all honesty isn't a major arsehole; I felt deceitful for trying to trick someone who I am supposed to respect and wotnot (Eleanor); but worst of all I was feeling *extremely* paranoid that someone might have seen me put it in her bag. I had

dropped the note through the top of Eleanor's bag whilst half
the school were bottlenecked in the entrance hall in the big
rush to get out through the two double doors and home. It
had seemed like a good time to do it because it was so mad-
busy that no one would notice a few tugs on their bag and
no one was going to waste time to see what other people
were up to when they only had one thing on their minds –
'Get home, get home, get home!' But after I dropped the note
in her bag I realised that Helena (a friend of Zack's) was
walking right behind me! I'm sure she didn't see anything
but the moment kept playing over and over in my head until
it became crystal-clear slow motion, revealing a sly sideways glance from Helena the moment the note left my
fingers. Of course in reality I hadn't even seen Helena's face,
she could have had her eyes shut for all I know, but my paranoia has ways of making me expect the worst of a situation.

'Chin-tickler!' blurted Tim as we walked through the
entrance hall discussing new and original insults.

Tim had been suggesting this little nugget for the past
eight minutes but had yet to receive any response, good or
bad, from either Cole or myself, so every forty-eight seconds
or so he would excitedly blurt it out, trying to sound like he
had only just come up with it but actually sounding like a
Tourette's sufferer with an extremely feeble vocabulary.

'I still think butt-nugget's a good one,' said Cole, sounding almost philosophical about the subject. 'Or maybe
cock-nugget. What do you reckon?'

'Chin-tickler!'

'Well,' I mused, 'cock-nugget has a nice ring to it, but if
you're wanting it to catch on you need something that

doesn't have an established swear word in it already. People like insults that they can use in front of teachers and not get bollocked because the teacher doesn't have a clue what it means.'

'True.'

For some reason Cole wanted to come up with an insult that would catch on and eventually be used by everyone in the school and beyond, which, for me, defeats the whole purpose of coming up with *your own* insult, but hey.

'So butt-nugget, then?' confirmed Cole.

'I like it, but it's still not going to catch on in front of teachers, it's too descriptive, too self-explanatory, you need completely brand new words that they just won't have a clue about.'

'Like "twat",' laughed Cole.

What Cole was referring to is that, somehow, two years ago, Clive Cornish was the only living human to not realise that 'twat' was a swear word, and for two whole months we managed to get him to use it almost every single day in substitute for the word 'twit'. Burned into my memory for eternity is the time that Cornish told Tim to, '*Go to the principal's office and explain to him why you're being such a silly little TWAT!*' then Cole laughed sandwich out of his nose and fell off his stool. Christ, I nearly shat myself. Unfortunately someone must have tipped him off because Cornish never used the word again after that day.

'What about gruff-nugget?' I suggested.

Cole looked at me as if I had discovered the cure for cancer.

'Fuuuuuck!' he whispered in breathless awe.

I knew that one would appeal to him. 'Gruff' is the word that Cole claims to have 'invented' for the patch of pubic hair that sits between your balls/fanny and your butthole, like the beard of Billy Goats Gruff (an appendage I am still yet to discover/grow on my own body).

'Chin-tickler!'

And so we settled on the phrase 'gruff-nugget', which Cole claims is a perfect word to describe the uncomfortable attachments to the 'gruff' the day after eating crunchy peanut butter. I'm sure we could have done better but we had to leave it there whilst register was being called and I had to have a very important chat with a girl called Alice White. She is to be a pivotal part of my plan to woo Eleanor, which, if all goes smoothly, could be in full swing by this afternoon.

Almost 1st Period
Almost Geography

Talking to Alice White was not an easy task for me. My mouth dried up, my pits did the opposite, and I didn't have a clue where to put my hands or eyes. You see, Alice is one of these people who seems to bring out all the symptoms of 'pathetic loser' in me. She has this thing called 'hotness' and I appear to be severely allergic to it. If I'm having a conversation with someone like Cole or Dave Kross I am absolutely fine – my words flow free and articulately and I'm barely even aware that I have any parts of my body other than my mouth. But if you stick a pretty girl in front of me then I am guaranteed to dry up like a monkey eating sand.

Still, at least she was nice to me! Alice has sometimes been a bit of a bitch to me in the past (along with lots of other people), but since we both started Theatre Studies lessons she has lightened up a bit (along with lots of other people). I have no idea what triggered this change, but have chosen not to question it. Maybe she is growing up and therefore considers people's feelings a bit more (does that happen as people grow up?), and everyone else is probably just following her lead. Although, whilst I *am* grateful that these charitable folk can now bring themselves to acknowledge me, I can't seem to forget how they were all so happy to walk all over me just a few years . . . no, *months* ago. I'm sure that some of them have genuinely changed and have matured a bit, but I will never be able to bring myself to completely like them. I still notice some of them picking on other kids in school. It's not like in the films where they choose one kid to bully and keep going until he cracks, in fact I don't even think they realise that they are actually bullies at all – have you ever met anyone who genuinely believes that they are a bad guy? They mostly just think they're being funny.

Anyway, I spoke to Alice (with difficulty), told her my plan, and she agreed to help out. Nice. I just hope it works.

1ˢᵗ Period
Geography

Geography . . . Now here's the stupid thing, one of the stupidest, in fact . . . I actually *chose* to take this subject! What was going through my head two years ago when I opted to take it as an exam subject, I do not know. I actually volunteered myself to undergo four hours of torturous hell each week. What was I thinking?! Clearly I hadn't thought things through. I have a faint memory of mildly enjoying the lessons at the time, but that was when we had Bernie Firth teaching us, who actually made the subject seem vaguely fun! But I clearly hadn't considered the possibility that I could end up with one of the other zombie teachers for the two years of GCSE purgatory. The worst-case scenario actually happened and I am now stuck with Maggie Driskell (Pisskell/Dismal/Drizzle, take your pick) droning away at me about some mind-numbingly dull drivel. With her complete lack of enthusiasm and her monotone drawl, I think she even manages to bore herself.

My only saving grace, the only reason I ever bother

turning up for the lessons at all, is that I get to share this hideous experience with Em, who is possibly the funniest girl ever born with ginger hair. And sometimes we actually manage to transform the dullest lesson in the world into one of the funnest (for us two, at least). Through carefully monitored research we have discovered that one of the best ways to liven up the snore-fest is to create our own dialogue to other people's actions (it's a bit like turning the volume down on the TV and making up your own words). Thankfully one of the classroom windows looks out on to the playing field so we usually have a wide variety of exer- cising fools as unwitting players in our audio-dubbing activities. Although the best 'audio dub' we ever did was when Em played her 'Get By in French' MP3 lesson on her iPod, creating the illusion that a chirpy Frenchman's voice was emanating from the melancholy cluster of droopy flesh that is Maggie Driskell's face (probably one of those 'you had to be there' moments). I don't think that I've done a very good job of conveying the high calibre of Em's comic genius, but, trust me, she's funnier than a fart in a bath.

Surprisingly, though, Em and I are like chalk and cheese. Em likes to go out and party, I like to stay in and watch films; she smokes and gets shit-faced, I'm a health freak and a scaredy-cat; she burns joss sticks and incense oils, I have asthma. The only similarities we really have is that we both dislike the majority of our school peers and we both have a twisted sense of humour.

Em's Top Three Prominent Features

3. **Ginger**
2. **Pokey-out ears**
1. **Flared nostrils**

I love that Em is funny looking. I'm kind of prejudiced when it comes to fit girls. The fit girls are the arrogant bullies who made my life a misery for three whole years and will soon end up working in the supermarkets, trying to raise enough money to support the baby they are trying to raise by themselves because they were so busy looking hot and getting accidentally knocked up to realise that they had lost all control of their lives. I have clearly given this too much thought.

I'm trying to write this all down as it's actually happening (except for the dialogue – I can't talk and write at the same time), but it's getting pretty difficult as Em and I are desperately stifling our laughter . . . we're watching John Deaks (unfortunate surname) shuffling uncomfortably in his seat at the other end of the classroom, whilst we quietly pretend that he has secretly shat in his pants. The sad thing is, as the minutes tick by and he seems to get increasingly squirmy and uncomfortable, I'm beginning to think that we might actually be right. He does look like the kind of person who could shit himself.

Oh crap, Saggie Dismal has got her textbook out. This can only mean one thing . . . one of my greatest fears of all time . . . one by one she is going to make us read aloud in front of the entire class! This fear ranks fourth in my list of school-time dreads, only after . . .

1. **Arriving at school naked from the waist down (thankfully never happened)**
2. **Being called up to the front of the class when I've got a massive hard-on (also never happened)**
3. **Arriving at a lesson and remembering that I have forgotten to do a very important piece of homework that the teacher is proceeding to collect from everyone else (has happened probably about three or four times)**

Fifth on the list is sitting down in a classroom full of people, getting my books out, the teacher coming in and THEN I realise I'm in the wrong lesson (that has also happened, but only the once. Never again).

Here we go. Dismal has got the hell ball rolling and Amy Norvich is reading the first paragraph in a nice clear and confident voice. Bitch. How can she be so calm? Doesn't she know that every single person in the room is looking at her, noticing every imperfection in her face, body and clothing? Doesn't she know that the entire room is silent except for the sound of her own voice and everyone is waiting for her to cock up so that they can laugh at her? It's a cruel world and Amy Norvich seems to be immune. She's not normal.

I'm doing my calculations . . . one, two, three, four . . . seven, eight, nine people to go . . . no, eight people to go before it's my turn to humiliate myself and there's eighteen minutes left of the lesson. The fact that Dismal is the cruellest taskmaster when it comes to reading aloud may, for once, be in my favour. Whereas most teachers will make you read a paragraph or two, maybe a whole page if the writing demands it or if the reader seems happy to do so, Dismal seems to enjoy messing with people's heads. Sometimes, even if the reader is doing fine, she'll cut them off after just a paragraph (like she just did with Amy), but other times she will let you read for *pages*, even if you're dying up there. I think she likes to see people suffer. It's probably the high-light of her week. She once left me to read for over FOUR pages, even though in the first paragraph I completely mis-pronounced the word 'analyse' then, in a futile attempt to correct myself, proceeded to stutter the first two syllables over and over and over again. I'm just hoping that the six people before me all get long sentences so that the lesson is over before it gets to me.

Kevin Jones is up now and he is . . . MY GOD! He must have had about THREE lines! Lucky bastard! That means there are only five people to go and there are eleven minutes left before the bell. I can feel myself heating up with nervous adrenalin already. My only hope of survival lies in the fact that Mike Peters is up before me and he seems to get almost as nervous as I do, so naturally gets as long a sentence in the hot seat as me, so maybe he'll end up reading until break time. Probably not though, he's dyslexic, which doesn't buy him any sympathy with Dismal, but she does get fed up of repeatedly having to read words for him, and sometimes lets him off lightly just to save herself the hassle. Plus, being dyslexic kind of gives him a Get Out of Jail Free card with the rest of the class, who seem to cut him a bit of slack when it comes to laughing at his cock-ups. I, on the other hand, have no such excuse – I am simply shit.

Five people to go and I'm starting to feel sick. I take a

quick puff on my inhaler. My right foot is jiggling around uncontrollably. Maybe I could go to the toilet. No, it'd never work. She'd smell my fear and make me read extra. Crap, my stomach is beginning to churn like mad. Another puff on my inhaler. If I don't throw up then I might crap myself. I'm beginning to feel bad about laughing at John Deaks now. My breathing is starting to tremble, which means, when I speak, my voice will wobble and crack like I'm about to cry. Calm down! My handwriting looks like I'm riding on TWO buses!

OK, the trick is not to think about it. Focus on something else. Em's hand has just clutched tightly on to my leg to stop it from jiggling around. I stop, but her hand stays. Oh shit. She may not be the girl of my dreams but I am still a virgin and a man, and any physical contact is an absolute novelty. Don't think about it. Focus. FOCUS!

Find something to look at! A square of carpet, a chair leg, a—

HOLY SHIT!

I CAN SEE RIGHT UP SALLY KIRK'S SKIRT! Jesus Christ! Her knickers are almost see-through! Look away. Look away! I can't! This is the furthest I've ever been with a girl! *Em, let go of my leg, for Christ's sake! I'm beginning to get—*

'Jack . . . continue, please.'

Oh dear god.

2nd Period
Maths

It's all over. I am now sat in Julie Quill's Maths class. The Geography lesson is done and no amount of writing will ever be enough to explain what exactly I just went through. But I'll give it a go . . .

'Jack? Continue, please,' repeated Saggie Dismal as I desperately flicked through the pages of my textbook, without a clue as to where we had gotten up to. Em quickly pointed at a paragraph on some page and I hastily began to read.

'P . . . p . . . plate . . .'

What the hell is this word?!

'Plate . . . tech . . .'

'Standing up, please, Jack,' said Dismal coldly.

What?

No!

Shit!

Nob-ache! I've got nob-ache!

Everyone's going to see!

Stall her. Quick, think of something clever!

'Huh?' I said, with the composure of a drunken worm.

'Standing, please,' she snapped, like the evil old cow that she is.

'Oh, right . . . yeah.'

Stall! Stall! STALL!!!

I took my jacket off, pretended to lose my place in the book again. People were already beginning to laugh. Shit. Em showed me where we were again. Shit shit shit! The dozy class, who had gradually lost interest in any of the readers, were now fully alert again and hanging on every clumsy, panicked move I made.

'In your own time,' drawled Drizzle impatiently, getting a tittering laugh from the class.

Bitch.

OK, this was it, I couldn't stall any longer. Was it still there, standing to attention? Had it died down yet? I couldn't tell. I was numb with fear. I could see my entire future, as the subject of school mockery for ever more, flash before my eyes. I could hear the wang-on-related insults being hurled around in my head. *This is it – the second I stand up my life as I know it is over*, I thought, as I slowly rose from my seat and prepared for the entire class to burst into a fit of hysterics.

'Plate . . . tecotis . . .' I began.

'Tectonics,' corrected Dismal, with a sigh.

'Plate tectonics . . .'

What the hell was going on? Not so much as a snigger! I had been in two minds about where to hold my book. Instinct told me to hide my face behind it, but it wasn't my face I was so worried about hiding. I went with instinct and now, head carefully hidden behind the pages of the book, I imagined the entire class to be staring at me in slack-jawed horror. I was preparing myself to hear the sharp snap of Dismal's voice saying, 'Out! Now! To the principal's office!' but it didn't come. I carried on reading, hands shaking, voice wobbling, heart in my throat, and I was messing up almost every other word, yet still there was no laughter! I quickly glanced down to my jeans . . .

Phew! It wasn't half as bad as I thought it was. It had felt like it was poking out half a mile but, in fact, as far as I could see, it was just a barely noticeable bulge. But something had to be wrong – not having a boner has never saved me from the mocking laughter of school kids before. Something strange was surely afoot.

Suddenly Dismal's harsh voice interrupted my monotonous mumblings and I nearly jumped a mile.

'Emma?' she said.

Em stood up and carried on reading the next sentence. I couldn't believe it! What the hell had just happened? Am I the luckiest man alive? How did I survive that?!

'Jack?' said Dismal, interrupting Em and snapping me out of my hypnotic state of disbelief.

'Huh?' I replied, my heart suddenly rocketing back up into my throat. Maybe I hadn't been so lucky after all. I stared at the dull-faced witch and waited for her to calmly send me out of the class for indecent exposure.

'You can sit down now.'

This time the class did laugh, just a little snigger though. I quickly sat down and felt my face turn beetroot-red. I raised my book and tried to hide behind it again as Em continued reading. Over the top of my pages I could see that some people were still looking at me. I tried to figure out what expressions they bore on their silly little faces – it wasn't disgust, it wasn't pity, it wasn't sly mockery . . . What the hell was it? It was a look that no one has ever given me before. For the life of me, I could not understand. All I knew was that something was very, very wrong.

After the bell rang and we all began packing our books away it took a moment for Em to say anything.

'Are they new jeans?' she asked, in an oddly blunt kind of way.

'Er . . . yeah, pretty new,' I lied, trying to sound as casual as possible.

Blame it on the jeans. Blame it all on the jeans!

'Why?' I stupidly asked without thinking.

'Oh, nothing,' she said with a shrug.

'OK,' I said, eager to finish the conversation, even though it was obvious Em wanted me to beg for more information.

Neither of us said anything as we picked up our bags and left the classroom. Then, as we entered the hallway full of shuffling morons, she said it.

'They make your nob look huge.'

I gave her a look of puzzled surprise as I tried to assess whether or not she was being sarcastic. She was baiting me, she must have known it was a hard-on and she probably thought it was all because she had put her hand on my leg. But then she did something that gave the whole game away – for the first time in my life I saw her blush!

'What?' she said defensively. 'You've got a huge nob. It's kind of hard not to notice.'

I couldn't believe it. She was being sincere! She honestly

thought the bulge in my groin had been natural flaccid girth!
I was speechless.

'Well, it's true,' she shrugged, turning a deeper shade of
scarlet.

Holy crap. This was brilliant. How many people had
noticed? How many people had thought the same thing as
Em? Was that why no one was laughing? Were they gaping
in awe at the unofficial size of my willy? Was that the
expression on their faces? Were they actually impressed?

Christ . . . I'm going to be a legend . . .

2nd Period
Maths – the Comedown

Em's comment had made me feel pretty good (in a fraudulent kind of way) and, as I swaggered my way through the halls to this Maths lesson, I couldn't hold back the funky music that boomed between my ears ('*She give me money! When I'm in nee-ee-heed . . .*' – well, actually it started out as that '*Macho macho man!*' by the Village People, but I had to switch to something more . . . macho). And do you know what? Even though I was riding a lie, for the first time in my life I actually felt kinda cool!

I wasn't sure if it was my imagination, but, as I entered my Maths lesson, I could have sworn a number of eyes flitted fleetingly at my crotch. They did! In fact . . . Sally Kirk! She wasn't just glancing. She was full-on *staring*! But at what? I had no semi. In fact I felt positively shrivelled. She nudged her friend and she stared too.

Have I been rumbled? Can they see that there's nothing to see?

Not comfortable with being treated like eye candy, my heart began to race. I slipped my inhaler from my pocket and . . . oh, bugger. The moment of realisation hit me at exactly the same time as it did Sally Kirk. My not-entirely-un-penis-shaped inhaler had been inadvertently prolonging my legendary status by sitting in just the right part of my left pocket, at just the right angle. In removing my phantom penis from my pocket, holding it to my mouth and giving it a long hard suck, I fear I may have broken the illusion. Sally Kirk gasped in silent giggles and quickly revealed the truth to her friend. '*Blah blah blah, not his nob, blah blah blah, INHALER!*' was all I managed to lip-read. My short-lived legendary status was diminishing through Chinese whispers, just as quickly as it had arisen.

I had been *this* close to being a hero.

It was nice while it lasted.

3rd Period
Theatre Studies

Theatre Studies. This is where it begins. This is where we start the ball rolling on the whole wooing of Eleanor Wade (mmmmmmm . . . Eleanor Wade . . .).

Fingers crossed.

Each Theatre Studies lesson always kicks off with improvisational and warm-up activities. 'Warm-up activities' pretty much translates as '*making a complete tit of yourself in front of everyone else*' and usually comprises a series of demeaning rituals supposedly designed to help eradicate any inhibitions of public performance (not an easy task for me, considering the last chapter). Needless to say, these warm-up activities do very little to boost my self-esteem and usually have me rocking myself to sleep at night, cringing in disgust at the hideously pretentious guff that I subjected myself to. For example, today's warm-up involved everyone running around the stage, flapping our arms in the air and shouting out, 'Wooooooooo-woooooooooo-woooooo!' – something that will no doubt haunt me for many nights to come. I suppose it goes without saying that after five minutes of Theatre

Studies I had lost any sense of bravado or coolness I had managed to stockpile during my five minutes of fake-huge-nob status.

We are currently sat in an unorganised scattering around the auditorium, whilst our teacher, Connie Decker, sits cross-legged in the centre of the stage and reels out a whole load of dull crap about the upcoming theory work we have to complete before the end of the year. Now, whilst describing my surroundings using words like 'auditorium' and 'stage', I fear that you may actually be picturing a theatre – how wrong you would be. What our 'theatre' (and I use the word very lightly) actually consists of is a large room with black walls and some large wooden step-like things at the back. The large wooden step-like things have a total of three deep tiers and along each row is a line of cheap plastic school chairs – welcome to our 'auditorium'. In front of the auditorium is a floor – welcome to our 'stage'. In fact the only thing remotely theatre-like about our theatre is the tiny wooden room that is perched at the top of some ancient scaffolding at the back of the auditorium – welcome to our 'lighting box'. There is no green room, no backstage, not even any wings. If we want wings we have to carefully position some huge black screens (or 'flats') to the left and right of the stage so that when we do a performance we actually have somewhere to exit/enter the stage from, rather than just walking to the edge of the room. The sad thing is, once upon a time this was actually a proper theatre that made respectable productions that the general public used to pay to see, but, due to budget cuts throughout the entire Art department four years ago, everything diminished by 75%.

The four Theatre teachers were reduced to one, the huge theatre got taken over by a new canteen and we got left with the old backstage area, and the average Theatre Studies grade dropped from an A to a D. We are now lucky if our productions fill just half the auditorium with non-paying students. My entire life is cursed.

Connie has now sprung to her feet and, hold on, I just have to quickly explain one more thing – she is not a stuck-up camp luvvie man like they have in the films, she is a big old lesbian (I say big and old because she is both old (sixty-ish) and big (taller and wider than me) and I say 'lesbian' because she is a lesbian). She is now pacing back and forth as she speaks, swinging her arms in front – 'Clap!' and then behind – 'Clap!' She's wearing a long black knitted jumper and black Lycra leggings, which makes her look like a kid in one of those massive bumblebee outfits, only without the orange stripes – maybe a Christmas pudding. I suppose you've guessed by her clothing that she also isn't one of these energetic, bright-orange hair, eccentric types who loves big musicals. She is, in fact, a chin-stroking arty type who prefers serious (boring/depressing) theatre. I'm not sure which kind are more annoying. I suppose at least the flam-boyant type wear clothing that doesn't always blend in with the black walls. Does she wear it because she's a gloomy depressive or because she thinks it makes her look thinner? Either way it looks weird, especially if you insist on wearing tight leggings and clapping your hands – her legs look like water balloons with hiccups.

We're all sat here, some of us sorting through notes (some of us just pretending), silently waiting while she acts like she's thinking long and hard about what we should do next, when we all know full well exactly what we're going to do next, because it's going to be the same as what happens at the beginning of every new term.

'Emma,' she chirps, beckoning Em with a chubby finger.

'Woop-di-doo,' mumbles Em as she gets out of her seat next to me and makes her way to the stage.

Connie has arranged two chairs, side by side, in the centre of the stage. She sits in one and motions for Em to sit in the other. She (Em) does. After a moment of silence Connie bursts into character, swings an arm round Em and begins an unconvincing Cockney accent. Oh dear. I can feel Em's inner cringe radiating through the room (she has serious problems with people who cross 'the comfort zone', and with Connie's death breath I don't blame her).

'Sawww . . . cam 'ere offern, do ya?' bellows Connie in a terrible, clichéd, gum-chewing impression of a gruff London geezer, who sounds more Australian than Cockney.

Em acts disgusted, a little too convincingly.

'What . . . to the bus stop?' she replies, completely deadpan.

It gets a big laugh.

'Yeah, I ain't sin you 'ere bifaw.'

'Yes, well, I normally drive,' she says in an upper-class snoot, removing the arm from her shoulder as if it were a rotten rag. 'My car is in the garaaage this morning and I am forced to use . . . (she shudders) . . . public transport (she nearly retches).'

Another big laugh.

Connie's face is inches away from Em's, leering straight at her, but Em hasn't so much as glanced at her.

''Ow you larkin' it then – the, er . . . public transport, as you call it?'

'To be honest I'm not enjoying the . . . clientele.'

Connie suddenly claps her hands together so loud that everyone but Em almost leaps a foot in the air.

'Next!' she shouts.

This confirms my prediction – the first activity of a new term is always 'Next'. 'Next' is an improvisational exercise where, one by one, we all have to spontaneously write ourselves into the scene until the entire class is taking part in one big, made-on-the-spot, piece-of-crap play. The cue for the next person to enter the scene is whenever someone claps their hands. Sometimes the person with the biggest guts/ego will nominate him/herself to go up next, or sometimes we'll go in some kind of order. Today we go in order of seating – left to right. Andy Gay Clay is up and he bounds on to the stage in his usual, over-enthusiastic, luvvie way and pretends to be someone . . . wait for it . . . it's going to be clever . . . and original . . . he's going to be someone waiting for a bus! How does he come up with these incredible spontaneous works of genius?! Twat.

(Again, I don't have anything against gays – Johnny Macmahon in my Art class is gay and he's one of the coolest people I've ever met – in fact I don't even know for sure that Andy Gay Clay *is* gay. I do, however, have something against twats, and Andy Gay Clay is definitely one of those. The twat.)

There's another five people to go before it's my turn. Aha! I bet you think I'm nervous. Well, I'm not! I'm not sure if it's because everyone else is making a complete arse of

themselves, or because I'm confident on stage (unlikely), or
if it's because I'm acting and I don't have to be myself (probably), but speaking in front of people in the theatre doesn't
scare me like it does in the classroom. No one is watching
me, Jack Samsonite (what a cool name! Or is it too wanky?
I can't decide), they're looking at a character – someone
completely different, made up, not real. I know it sounds
like a load of arty toss but unfortunately it's true – acting is
like a breath of fresh air because I get to be someone other
than gobshite me. My chest is thumping, but with excited
adrenalin rather than fear, and . . . I better go, I'm up any
minute now . . .

3rd Period
Theatre Studies – Improvised

Wow. It couldn't have gone better if I'd planned it (which I didn't, this wasn't part of my big plan). In everyone's eagerness to be ready for our cues, a bunch of us had left our seats and were waiting at the side of the stage. Whilst I was rapidly racking my brains for something original but not too over the top to bring to the scene (bus stop removal man, Tourette's sufferer, pimp), Eleanor tapped me and Alice on the shoulders and suggested the three of us go up together. She chose me! She could have tapped anyone on the shoulder, but she tapped me! It made sense though, really, seeing as I am one of only a handful of normal people in our class (in that I'm not extremely serious about being the world's greatest actor, yet I'm not there to mess about and be idiotic either – I'm not one of the prima donnas who are all, 'Look at me! Look at me!' and neither am I REALLY REALLY shy, which some of the class are and it makes you wonder why they chose to do the subject in the first place).

Alice and I quickly agreed to Eleanor's proposal, then the two of them looked to me for an idea for our entrance.

CLAP!

I quickly shoved Eleanor into a chair and began dragging her backwards on to the stage as if she were reversing in a wheelchair. Alice followed on, not sure what we were doing.

'Aaaaaargh!' I shrieked, inspecting Eleanor like a doctor and pointing to her crotch. 'No! Nurse, I said to remove the patient's SPECTACLES!'

It got an impressive roar of laughter from everyone (including Eleanor and Alice), which I feel kind of cheap about because it was a gag I nicked from a birthday card – I hate people who steal other people's jokes and pass them off as their own, but this was an emergency. Anyway, we carried on with the scene, pretending that Alice and I were paramedics whose ambulance had broken down so we were having to use the bus instead.

'That was *mental*!' laughed Alice as we stumbled off the stage in hysterics. Everyone congratulated us, begrudgingly, for doing so well, then we all returned to our seats, only this time Eleanor and Alice both sat with me – a Jack sandwich! I felt a great pressure to be charming and funny, but opted to clam up and take a puff on my inhaler instead. Smooth.

3rd Period (still)
Theatre Studies – the Plan

Well, now I'm worried that I may have over-hyped the brilliance of this plan for you and am thinking that I probably should have revealed it earlier because, after the success of our warm-up activity, it really doesn't seem so special any more.

Oh well . . .

As you know, the whole purpose of the plan was to get me better acquainted with Eleanor. As you don't know, the next few months of Theatre is 'Group Project Assessment', where the class will be split into two groups to work on separate plays. So far I have done reasonably well in my mission to wriggle my way into Eleanor's life just in our standard lessons, but think how much easier it would be if I were in a group with her – half the number of people, half the distractions and, considering the unequal boy-girl ratio in our class, probably only one or two other males to compete with. And it just so happens that, this term, fate is on my side . . . Allow me to explain.

Firstly it all begins with one random decision by Connie –

Who will be the team captains? Each term, when it comes time to split the class into two groups, Connie picks two random people to captain a team and they, in turn, pick their teammates, just like a game of football. Except, thanks to my ingenious deductions, I have, erm, deduced that these 'random' choices by Connie are not so random at all, oh no, because I have cracked her code and I have spotted a pattern hidden away in her supposed 'random' decisions – they aren't random at all . . . they are reverse alphabetical! Which means today's captains will randomly be Chris White and . . . wait for it . . . Alice White! (No relation, in fact there seems to be a lot of racist incestual surnames going on in our Theatre class – two Whites, one Whiting, one Whitely and one Chalke!) After this afternoon's improvisation it seems kind of obvious that Alice will pick Eleanor and myself to be in her team, especially Eleanor (even though the two of them don't really speak to each other outside of the theatre, they do seem to have a mutual respect for each other). But I wasn't to know that when I laid the plans this morning, and even if I *did* know it I'm far too paranoid to assume that anyone would choose to pick me for anything. So that's why I spoke to Alice this morning and told her that if she should by any chance get picked to be a captain in Theatre, I would be really honoured to be on her team. I just had to hope that I was right and that she would pick Eleanor as well.

I truly am a cunning little fox.

So here we are, all sat on the floor/stage waiting for Connie to finish sifting through the stacks of paperwork in her bag. Everyone is chattering away to each other except for me, whom—

What did he just say?

'What did you just say?' Alice asks Andy Gay Clay.

'Apparently . . .' he whispers in an overly dramatic way, with one hand cupping his chubby, goateed mouth from the side and giving his lips a good lick, 'we're going to be doing a FULL CLASS production!' He finishes with a wide-eyed glare of excitement.

No! A class production? But the fates are supposed to be on my side! We can't be doing a class production! We need to be in smaller groups! We need to be forced together into tight little teams of trust!

'We need to be intimate!'

Shit. I think I just said that out loud.

'I wasn't talking to you.'

Andy Clay is giving me funny looks. Everyone else probably is, too.

Act like nothing happened. Head down, write, write, write!

'What was that about?' someone whispers behind me.

'OK, everyone,' calls Connie. (Phew! Saved by the lesbian.) She's pacing around us in circles, rubbing her hands together. 'It's time to make plans for our practical.' She annunciates the last word in a typical phlegm-fuelled actor-like way so that you can hear the spit crackle on her tongue. 'We're going to try something a little different this term.'

No . . . *please* don't say Andy is right! Please don't say we're not going into groups! Please don't say we're not going into groups!!!

'We're not going to be splitting into two groups.'

SHIT! Crap shit crap and shit! Crap crap crap!

Shit!

Andy Clay turns to Alice and raises his eyebrows with excited smugness.

Piss off!

'Instead we're going to try something a little more . . .'

Clay begins to quietly clap his hands in overwhelming anticipation.

'. . . intimate.'

All eyes turn to me. They look at me like I'm some kind of magical, time-travelling futureboy.

I shrug it off.

Connie continues, 'We'll be splitting up into three groups.'

What? No . . . YES! That's . . . YES!!! That's even better! That's only about five or six people in each group! That's even more intimate!

'. . . and the group captains will be . . .'

Oh god, what if I was wrong? What if she really is going to pick people at random? Oh crap, I'm going to be sick.

'. . . Alice White!'

YES! YES! YES!!! You bloody genius!

'. . . Eleanor Wade!'

What? No. NO! NOOOO! What have I—

'. . . and Jack Samsonite!'

I . . .

    I . . . . .

        I . . . .

Kill me now.

3rd Period (still)
Theatre Studies (again) – Plan B

It's all over. The lesson has ended. I am still here. In the theatre. And I'm a dick. I'm an absolute cocking cock of a dick. Cock! What have I done? Why did I say anything this morning? Why did I try to make a plan? I should know by now that nothing ever goes my way. I should have planned for the absolute opposite and then maybe things might have worked out. Amy Whitely's glandular fever may have just ruined my life. If Amy Whitely had been at school then she would have been next in line instead of Eleanor. Eleanor was never meant to be a team captain! And neither was I! And if Amy Whitely hadn't spread her glandular fever (the kissing disease!) to three other people in our class then I wouldn't have been next in line! Fate is a sick and twisted son of a bummer and I hope he dies soon. I normally like to think that we're in control of our own destinies but it's times like these that I wonder if I should just give up trying at everything and let the powers-that-be take me on whatever messed-up little merry-go-round freakshow of a life that they've hilariously concocted for me.

Sod it. That's not the way to think. I'm not a negative person. I'm not giving up now. Eleanor is destined to be with me and I'm not going to let a stupid little thing like fate get in the way of that. So Plan A has failed, time to think of a Plan B – the mother of all Plan Bs. Who's to say this cock-up isn't going to turn out to be a good thing? Just because it wasn't in my plan doesn't mean it's a terrible thing. Standing up in front of a room full of people with a semi-erection wasn't part of my plan either but that didn't turn out so bad. Maybe Eleanor heard the fake news that I have a fake huge willy and hasn't heard that my willy is fake and is now irresistibly drawn towards me? No, of course not, she's not that kind of girl. I want her to like me for me, not my fake huge nob. Does that make me sound like a girl? How come no one else seems as sensitive about these things as me? Then again, girls are supposed to go for the sensitive type who isn't afraid to cry, right? Strange that they always seem to go for the insensitive types who like to make other people cry, then. Either girls are complete idiots or they have really bad judgement. Maybe I should go bully some little kids and the girls will think I've got issues and am therefore a deep and sensitive guy who needs mothering. Stupid girls.

Anyway, back to Plan B, which, by the way, now includes trying to find a way to get Em to stop hating me. Perhaps I should explain . . .

The three team captains were stood in the middle of the stage (Eleanor, Alice and me), and Connie pulls three straws from her bum. (Seriously! I don't know where they came from! She just stuck her hand behind her back and the next thing I know she has these straws in her hand (and Lycra leggings do not have pockets – yuck!). I was going to have to pull one of those manky pieces of plastic from her hand. Vomit!)

'Longest straw goes first, shortest straw goes last,' she explained as she stepped towards us.

I ended up with the long straw, but it didn't make any difference to me if I went first or not – the one person that I really wanted on my team was already the captain of another.

'Jack goes first,' Connie announced to the class.

Obviously I pick Em, right? My eyes search through the horde of idiots to find her face when something attracts my attention – Zack Pimonto. Yes, *that* Zack – Zed – I can't remember if I already mentioned that he was in this class, but he is, and he was staring straight at Eleanor and pointing intently at his own chest. A quick glance towards Eleanor revealed that she was looking back at him, and, get this, she was *smiling*! Smiling! Smiling at the cheese-dick who leers at her when she's not looking. Smiling at the arrogant piss-face who tries to go out with half the girls in the school. Smiling at the only other guy in school who seems to show an interest in the girl of my dreams – and he's better looking than me.

She's going to pick Zack! They're going to be best friends! He's going to show her his sensitive side (which I've seen before and it's all an act), they'll begin to bond and within two weeks they'll be seeing each other! By next month he'll have stolen her virginity and in five years they'll be married! My entire future happiness hangs in the balance here, and the only insurance I have against eternal misery is to ensure

that Zack and Eleanor don't end up in the same team/love-
less marriage!

It suddenly occurred to me that if I, Futureboy, cannot
control my own destiny, then I was just going to have to
mess around with other people's.

The name seemed to just fall from my mouth.

'Zack,' I said.

And in one instant I had murdered their marriage and all
their unborn babies. (Oh no, that sounds horrible. Just for
the record, I was being insensitively poetic, I don't actually
murder babies – unborn or otherwise. In fact I'm quite a big
fan of babies. I used to be one myself.)

The class seemed to gasp silently in shock. I wanted to
explain to them that I am not actually a baby-killer, but then
I realised that they were not shocked by the words inside my
head. (How could they be? Honestly!) No, it was the word in
my mouth that had shocked them, almost as much as it had
shocked me. The silent gasp of surprise was followed by an
awkward pause, where everyone seemed to be thinking the
same thing – *surely this is a mistake!* I was supposed to pick
Em! Everyone knew it. I knew it. She was my best Theatre-
Studies friend. When Zack finally shuffled his way across
the stage he didn't do such a good job of hiding his disappointment. I could feel Em's cold and solemn stare boring
into my skull. I plucked up the courage to look her in the
eyes and gave a small nod of my head and pointed my
finger – 'You're next.' For some reason she didn't look too
ecstatic.

'Andy,' said Alice.

Andy clapped his hands in a little explosion of camp

excitement and trotted over to Alice's area. (He has to be gay!) I know I keep referring to him as Andy Gay Clay, but he isn't actually gay (or so he claims). There is no way anyone would consider this to be possible if it weren't for the fact that he was constantly lusting after Joanne Jones, who he asked to pose wearing nothing but a fig leaf for his photography project (she refused so he used his cousin instead – yuck!) and who he tearfully tried to snog when he got drunk on cider at Jane Dowley's birthday party last year.

Anyway, it was Eleanor's turn to pick a player and I was telepathically willing her not to pick Em. The moment between when her mouth opened and when the words actually came out seemed to happen in slow motion and I knew inside what that word was going to be because my good luck had run out for the day.

'Helena,' she said.

YES! No, DOUBLE yes! Not only was it not Em but it was also not a boy – it was Helena Bloom, a thin, shy, over-acting-type girl!

'Emma,' I said without hesitation, struggling to not shout her name with excitement/relief.

But my excitement didn't last long when I saw the icy expression on Em's face. She spent a lifetime slowly packing things into her bag, then folding her jacket, then whispering something to James Harfield sat next to her. Finally she plodded towards Zack and me with very little enthusiasm, then continued to have a pleasant little chat with Zack whilst completely ignoring me.

I know I'm a male and that males are not supposed to

understand the opposite sex in any way whatsoever, but my carefully honed spidey-senses were definitely picking up the subtlest hints of I-ABSOLUTELY-HATE-YOU-RIGHT-NOW!

I don't think even a fake huge nob can save me now.

Last Break

We each picked the final members of our teams, making three groups of four. Zack was constantly pestering me to pick Katy (abnormally wide face) Dorma the entire time I was choosing, which I'm assuming means he fancies her, too. Pervert. I seriously considered picking her, not to shut him up but to ensure that he had someone nearby to fall in love with so that he didn't continue to chase after Eleanor. It turns out that I couldn't bring myself to do it. I'd already picked one arsehole to be on my team just to ensure a non-Eleanor-bond – there was no way I could put up with the arsehole's gobby little gossiping friend too. Plus, two of them would result in mutiny. I like to be on a team where everyone is fairly equal-minded so that there's less arguing and conflict. Zack and Katy are both outspoken, opinionated, bossy rich kids who always want to get their own way. If they were on a team with me and Em we'd spend the entire time arguing, them against us. I ended up choosing Carly Chalke as our fourth member. She's not great at acting but she does seem like quite a hard worker, she's always enthusiastic in an understated kind of way and she's good at doing costumes and props and stuff. Plus, she's reasonably quiet and seems like she won't fight for creative control (in other words she's a pushover). It's not like I'm intending to be the dictator of our group and boss everyone around, but it's always easier to have someone on your team who prefers to take orders rather than give them.

We're supposed to be given a topic for our group productions so that we can go away and write something ready for production at the end of term, but Connie seems to think that that isn't enough pressure, so she's given us an ice-breaker task first – a two-minute mime to be ready for next lesson! How much spare time does she think we have? We had ten minutes left of the lesson to quickly brainstorm ideas and arrange a time to meet for rehearsals. We desperately batted around a few pathetic ideas (window cleaners, tennis match audience . . . you get the idea – so far so shit). We finally settled on the idea of a bunch of strangers in a lift. Not sure what we could do with that but it's a start. None of us could make our schedules match for any time other than the lunch break immediately before our next Theatre lesson on Thursday. It was either that or stay behind late one day. Sod that. We'll pull something out of the hat, I'm sure. If it's shit then it's shit, it's not as if we're being marked on it or anything.

As the lesson wound down I tried to explain to Em how I had intended to pick her first but accidentally said Zack's name instead, but for some reason she thought I was making it up, which made me mad – she's so untrusting.

We continued the rest of the conversation in complete silence.

4ᵗʰ Period
English Literature

Once again I am sat in my English classroom waiting for Dave Kross to arrive. Although this is the English classroom, and Dave is our English teacher, I'm not actually in my English lesson – this time it's English Literature. I've been working from this timetable for over a year and a half now and still I have to double check whether I'm supposed to be having English or Lit. It gets a tad confusing, especially as half the class are exactly the same people from my English lesson too! And even when I have checked the timetable I still end up getting my Lit books out in my English lesson and my English books out for my Lit lesson. It's all jolly good fun.

The classroom door has just opened, the class volume has decreased by 73% and Dave has entered the room approximately four and a half minutes late. Whenever Dave is less than five minutes late he always receives a sarcastic round of applause (the kind a barmaid gets when she smashes a tray of glasses) and today is no exception. (I probably should note that, although I have been to a pub a couple of times I have never actually seen a barmaid drop a tray of glasses, nor have I seen a waitress do it – my reference is drawn purely from the movies, like *Groundhog Day*. I look forward to experiencing it in real life in the near future.)

Dave takes a bow, he pulls a few books from his bag, pauses, returns them to the bag, then pulls out the correct books for this lesson (nice to know I'm not alone). He picks up the whiteboard marker and we already know what he is going to write – *English Lit*. He claims it's so that we don't get confused about which lesson we are in, but I think it's more so that *he* doesn't get confused. However, there are still a few people switching books. It's become a kind of start-of-lesson game to watch and see who has made the 'wrong book mistake' (today is a cracker – five people plus Dave).

'Shakespeare!' bellows Dave cheerfully, placing the marker pen on his desk. Apart from a few girls who almost jump out of their skins, the entire class groans on cue.

'New term, new subject,' he explains with an *I don't make the rules* shrug. 'Guess which play.'

'*Macbeth*?'

'Oooh, you're lucky this isn't a theatre else I'd be throwing you out. No.'

'*The Tempest*?'

'Nope.'

'*As You Like It*?'

'For so many reasons, no.'

'*Much Ado About Nothing*?'

'NO! Come on, last guess.'

'Oooh *Hamlet*!'

'Nope. You are all officially idiots.'

'*Romeo and Juliet*,' says Em.

Dave touches the tip of his nose and points at her.

'*Romeo and Juliet!*' he repeats, 'On the ball as always, Miss Ball.'

Once again everyone groans (it's a common thing when Dave gets into his *play on words* and innuendos).

'Groan away, groan away . . . but you'll all be groaning on the other sides of your buttocks by the end of this term' – no groans this time because it doesn't make any pissing sense – '*Romeo and Juliet* is quite simply the greatest piece of literature that is ever likely to weasel its way into your pathetic Sonic and Mario lives, I shit you not.'

'Yeah, if you're a girl,' adds Scott Salon, to a lukewarm response of mild amusement from about three members of the class.

Ha! Crash and burn, you arrogant prick. He pretends that his ego isn't knocked by the lack of laughter and continues to sit in his ever-rehearsed wanker's pose (lounged across his seat, elbow resting on the back, left leg outstretched in front, right leg crooked up on the seat beside him), but if you look carefully you can see his ears burning bright red and his left foot wiggling nervously from side to side. I hope he's dying inside (not literally). He isn't exactly a Bad Boy, trying to cause trouble, he just likes to think that he and Dave have some kind of amazing buddy-movie comedy banter between them, but in reality Dave has the amazing comedy banter and Scott is just a tosser.

'That, Mr Saloon,' begins Dave, a killer insult surely brewing, 'is word for word the exact same remark that Old Farmer Bigot made in 1908 right before he had sex with his cousin and his brain fell out of his rectum.'

'At least he was having sex, which is more than I can say for some people,' says Scott, with a cocky grin.

'Oooooooh,' chimes the rest of the class.

'Yes, he was,' agrees Dave, 'but that was nearly one hundred years ago. Unfortunately today that attitude will only attract women of that same era, so, er . . . have fun pulling on Friday night, Scott.'

'I will,' Scott jokes back, confidently.

Wait for the punchline, Scott, wait for it . . .

'The, er, cemetery is two miles that way.'

Bullseye! Dave strikes again. It's by no means one of his best, in fact it wasn't very good at all, but still it receives raucous laughter from the entire class, turning Scott's cheeks a deep shade of beetroot.

'Any more sexist, shallow or generally stupid comments before we start?'

'Women can't drive,' says Steven Parker, to mixed reviews.

'Ladies,' says Dave, addressing the room, 'you're on your own.'

Predictably all the guys laugh and all the girls protest.

'The first line of the play, please, someone?'

There's an embarrassing silence. Everyone thinks they know the answer, but no one wants to say it in case they're completely wrong. Scott has a smug smile on his face and is looking around at the class, shaking his head, as if to say *I expected more from you*, but I don't see him offering up any answers.

'Come on, guys,' says Dave, 'I know you're not all completely ignorant.'

Still no one answers. Maybe not everyone does think they know the answer. Maybe it's just me! I'm going to have to pluck up the courage to raise my hand.

'*Two households, both alike in dignity*,' Em says glumly.

I quickly pull my hand back down (good job too, my answer would have been completely wrong).

'. . . *In fair Verona, where we lay our scene*. Thank you once again, Miss Ball, you absolute goddess,' adds Dave. 'Now, can someone else tell me what that means?' He repeats the first line and waits for an answer.

'He's kind of saying,' says Zack, clearing his throat, 'this is where the story is.'

'Exactly! Simple as that. Not every single line written by Shakespeare has some deep hidden meaning, sometimes they're just words. The only difference between this collection of words and the collection of words on the front page of today's paper is the fact that Shakespeare actually thought about what words he was using and . . . another difference?'

'It rhymes,' says someone somewhere.

'It rhymes!' repeats Dave, slapping the back of his hand into his palm, like a TV lawyer trying to get his point across to the jury. 'Think of it, if you will, as the introduction to a comic book, you know the little yellow box in the top left corner? *Meanwhile, back on the ranch, Clark is dyeing his nylon tights.*'

The whole class nods in amused understanding, but I get the impression that half of them have never picked up a comic book in their lives and don't have a clue what Dave's talking about.

'*From ancient grudge break to new mutiny, where civil*

blood makes civil hands unclean. From forth the fatal loins of these two foes a pair of star-crossed lovers take their life; Whose misadventured piteous overthrows Doth with their death bury their parents' strife. The fearful passage of their death-marked love, And continuance of their parents' rage, Which, but their children's end, nought could remove, Is now the two hours' traffic of our stage,' says Dave, reciting the entire introduction with impressive fluidity.

In fact he says the words with so much passion, meaning and understanding that something that would normally take a few readings to understand seems to make perfect sense the first time round. Who would have thought that this tubby little Glaswegian could narrate Shakespeare as well as any RSC player? He pauses for dramatic effect, as if allowing time for the words to bore deep into our brains.

'Bloody brilliant,' he says bluntly. 'Excuse my French, but that's what it is – I mean what an introduction. Absolutely – bloody – brilliant. It's still powerful today, but back when he wrote it, it was a WHAM BAM car crash of an introduction. The audience would have been knocked for five and left gasping for more. One word to describe that introduction . . .'

Dave spun round, pointed straight at me and I realised that I was supposed to provide that one-word description. Pen down. (I'm now writing this in the safety of my own home.)

'Ummmmmmm . . .' blood rushed to my face, 'short?' I said pathetically.

'Short, punchy, yes.'

He span and pointed at someone else (apparently he wants lots of 'one words').

'Rhyming?'

'Yes, it's rhyming, as we already said, but why?'

'For emphasis, so it sticks,' I heard myself saying.

'Exactly,' agreed Dave (phew!). 'The rhyming underlines its importance. It's like highlighting it in Day-Glo pink. More words.' He spun again and pointed at another victim.

'Original,' said Jessica Henry, confident that she was saying exactly what Dave wanted to hear.

'It's amazing, isn't it?' He revelled in genuine excitement. 'Even now, after hundreds of years, it still strikes you as being original. Why is that?'

Jessica Henry was stumped. So was everyone else for that matter.

'Think about it,' he prompted. 'Forget about the rhyme and the language and the rhythm, what is it about that introduction that sets it apart from any Hollywood blockbuster in the past twenty years?'

'It gives away the ending,' said Zack effortlessly.

Bastard!

'It gives away the ending! Not only that, it tells you the whole bloody story! More importantly, this is a romance with a major twist and this introduction goes and gives it away in the first fifteen seconds! Not only do we find out the story, the twist, the end . . . we also find out that there's no happy ending. How un-Hollywood can you get? Name one single film in the history of films that has ever done that.'

American Beauty? Kind of? I wasn't going to say it though, else I'd sound like a know-it-all wanker.

'*American Beauty*,' said Zack.

Bollocks!

'Trust me to have the world bleeding authority on films in my class. Yes, Mr Pimento, thank you for successfully ruining my point.'

The class chuckled and Zack's little group of followers all smiled at him proudly.

Zack had just outsmarted Dave Kross.

Bollocks! Bollocks! Bollocks!

I quickly tried to think of another film that had done it, but decided that if I did then it would just seem desperate, like I was trying to muscle in on Zack's glory. *Sunset Boulevard*! Don't say it though.

'*Sunset Boulevard*,' called Scott Salon.

BOLLLLLLLLOOOOXXXXXXXXXXXX!!!!!!!!!!!!!

When the hell had Scott Shitting Salon ever watched a black and white film? In fact when had he ever watched a film that didn't star Steven Seagal or Jason Statham? Then I noticed Helena Bloom sat next to him and I put two and two together.

'All right, all right,' said Dave above the roaring laughter, shaking his head in shame, 'maybe we'll skip the introduction for now.'

Of course! Another film that did it – *Romeo and Juliet*! They made a film of it. It's a cheap shot but since the class is in high spirits already I'll get away with it, it'll be the cherry on top, the last insult . . .

'Or *Romeo and Juliet*!' I yelled.

Oh balls.

4th Period
English Literature –
Never Speak in Public

What had I done? The entire class died down, no one laughed. Not even Dave.

'No, I'm not sure that one really counts,' he said apologetically.

Dear god, please could you fix it for me to have the ground do that opening up and swallowing thing I've heard so much about?

Face back in my book (but not actually writing), I tried to go along with it, as if I knew it was a crap call, smiling like a twat.

I *am* a twat.

'Since we have a class full of smart-arses intent on making a fool of me, let's skip to the end. The last line of the play, someone, please . . . ?'

Screw that.

Half the class decided they knew the end of *Romeo and Juliet* and they all attempted reciting it, resulting in an ungodly monotone drone of a dozen murmuring fools.

'Guys, that was just *beautiful*! Have you ever thought of having your voice boxes removed? It would really complement your style. Maybe the odd lobotomy here or there . . .' Then, over the laughter, he continued with the final line: '*For never was a story of more woe than this of Juliet and her Romeo . . .*'

Once again he left a pause for the words to resonate, then repeated the line.

'*For never was a story of more woe than this of Juliet and her Romeo . . .* So, my smart-arse movie buffs, tell me, into which Hollywood genre would this be pigeonholed in modern cinema?'

Everyone sensed a trap and no one dared answer.

'Come on! It's not a trick question. If you went into your local Blockbuster, what section would you find *Romeo and Juliet* in?'

'Romance,' said Zack with a shrug.

'Correct, but what genre is it really?'

'Tragedy,' I said.

'Tragedy,' confirmed Dave. 'Thank you, Jack.'

How come everyone else always gets called Mr this or Miss that, but he only ever calls me by my first name? Is that a good thing or a bad thing? I've never been able to work it out. Maybe he forgets everyone else's first names, or maybe he can never remember my surname.

'It's a romantic tragedy, but a tragedy nonetheless,' continued Dave. 'Why would it not be part of the tragedy genre in today's cinema?'

Long pause . . .

'Because they don't make them any more?' I said tentatively.

'Exactly. The genre is going the way of the Dodo.'

A dozen arms shot up in the air, no doubt desperate to contradict Dave's claim, but Dave ignored them and carried on.

'Maybe once in a while one might pop up, usually in independent or European cinema, but as far as mainstream box-office cinema goes, tragedy no longer exists. Why? Because Hollywood is obsessed with happy bloody endings. Who doesn't like a happy ending? They liked them in Shakespeare's day too, but they could also enjoy a good old tragic ending. They loved seeing people worse off than themselves! And that last line of the play, in rhyme again, it's almost saying – "and just in case you didn't notice, this is a very tragic story!" *For never was a story of more woe than this of Juliet and her Romeo.* As if we hadn't noticed! It's like he was rubbing salt into the wound. I can't think of a more tragic story.'

My hand went immediately into the air.

What was I doing?!

'Yes, Jack?'

'Well, at least they fell in love,' I argued, with a blushing shrug.

Dave didn't look convinced.

'All the more tragic that they *died* then,' he said. 'They had this entire beautiful future ahead of them and it got ripped away.'

Now it was my turn to look unconvinced.

'Yeah,' I replied, 'but at least they died knowing that they loved each other. It would have been a whole lot more tragic if they had both loved each other, but never did anything about it and *then* they died.'

'Jack,' began Dave, a sarcastic comment brewing, 'if you had written that story then I think Romeo and Juliet would have been *happy* to kill themselves at the end . . . along with half the audience!' He allowed time for the class to have a giggle before continuing, 'Don't you think it's more tragic that they died when they had so much to live for? So much love lost?'

'At least they had something to lose,' I added. 'Or maybe you just can't remember what it's like to be a teenager.'

Someone else joined in, but I couldn't see who.

'Better to have loved and lost than never to have loved at all,' they said. Who was it? The way our classroom was laid out, with all the chairs and desks lining the walls in a U shape, prevented me from seeing who it was sat four or five seats down on my left. They sounded a little bit like . . .

'What the hell is this, prove Dave wrong day? Even the new girl is picking on me! I had higher hopes for you, Miss Wade.'

Miss Wade? Eleanor? What?

I tipped my chair back as far as possible (one more inch and I'd be on my back) and, sure enough, just a few metres away from me sat Eleanor in all her radiant beauty. My Juliet . . . in my Lit lesson!

I don't know what she was doing there – I don't care, just as long as she's staying. THREE subjects together now – Theatre, Biology and now English Literature. That's six lessons a week together! See what I mean about there being a flip side to every downer?

Nobs

I shall now discuss with you something very close to my heart – my top three nob names. Now this is a tricky one because, although I am a big fan of the words 'cock' and 'dick', I prefer to use them as name-calling insults rather than in reference to the male member. So, with that in mind . . .

3. Nob. Obviously. I love this word. Of all nob names I probably use this one the most. It's brilliant – punchy, compact, versatile – ideal for any occasion.

2. Willy. Most guys are obsessed with using power words to describe their little tiddlers (prick! cock! dick! truncheon!). 'Willy' goes against the grain. It seems to be a word reserved solely for those under the age of eight. Except for me. I feel almost unique in being the only person I know to still use the word. It has a certain comic element to it ('Ouch! You hit my *willy*!'). Plus, with a little bit of reverse psychology and double-bluffery, it is my belief that girls probably

assume that, if you are confident enough to use such a tiddly and wimpy name for your nob, you must be hung like a hammock.

1. Penis. It is blunt. It is to-the-point. It is the official, universal term for the nob, yet no one uses it. The word seems to make everyone cringe except for doctors. Unfortunately it does not have the same raw impact as 'vagina' . . . Whilst I'm at it I may as well go all the way – my top three lady-bits names: 3. Fanny (funny); 2. Minge (for a similar reason to 'willy' – women like to make up sensual and delicate names for their flaps, like 'velvet curtains', or they go for something cute and childlike, like 'furry front bum', whereas 'minge' manages to sound repulsive without going to the extremes of 'beef curtains' and 'hairy axe-wound'); and 1. Vagina (obviously). It has an inexplicable shock value when a man says it with confidence ('Ouch! You hit my *vagina*!'). As with cock, dick and prick, all other flap-names are best used as insults.

Tuesday Night

I tried recapping the rest of this afternoon's events whilst I was on the bus home, but it was just too bumpy. I'd manage to write maybe one or two words before my pen would shoot across the page and scribble through everything I had just written. Kind of frustrating. After half an hour it began to make my blood boil with infuriation so I gave up and thumbed through my copy of *Romeo and Juliet* instead (Dave handed them out to everyone at the end of the lesson). He wants us all to read it at least two times this month, which shouldn't be too tough. It's only the size of a screen-play and I can get through one of them in just a few hours. Granted, Shakespeare will probably demand slightly more attention than *Star Wars*, but they're roughly the same thing, right?

I am now shut away in my bedroom with the curtains drawn and the door locked (we live in a really old house with big old locks on every door, except my bedroom is the only room we still have the key for). The lamp in the corner of the room is giving the pages a warm amber glow, and to make sure I don't fall asleep I've got a lively playlist that I compiled a few months ago blaring out of some cheap tinny

speakers I got from a car boot sale last year. Five minutes ago
Mum brought my dinner up (jacket potato with beans) and
three minutes ago I finished it. I'll get some more in a
second. I know that these minor details are all a bit dull, but
I can't write a project about myself without including at
least a few lines of how boring home life is. The fact is, it's
so boring that I'm struggling to find anything to write about
that won't put a serious downer on this story.

I'll be brief . . . I live and always have lived in a sleepy
little village somewhere in the middle of nowhere. The
village consists mainly of the following types of people – 1.
Old people, 2. Rich people, 3. Strange people, 4. People who
have joined the army. And somewhere nestled between
those categories sits my family (and maybe a couple of
others). The village has a primary school (for about forty children, mostly from neighbouring villages), a pub (that stinks),
a church (strictly for the old and rich) and a corner shop
(over-priced, out of date and closing down). All my friends
live at least twenty miles away and they always come into
school with fun stories about what they got up to at each
other's houses the previous evening/weekend. They all live
within a stone's throw of each other or at least a short bus
journey away, which for some reason makes me feel slightly
cut-off, out-of-the-loop and extremely jealous.

On an average evening I would be watching a DVD by
now, but I'm too busy writing this stuff – I can't believe how
hard I'm working on this, it's kind of a novelty for me, but
sort of fun. The joint in my right index finger is starting to
get sore because I've been writing for nearly two days solid
now. In fact I don't think I've ever put so much effort into a

piece of homework before in my entire life. It's not going to last for long though – Friday, that's my cut-off point. I don't have to hand this in until Monday but I've got to give myself time to type it up and everything, which at this rate is going to take for ever. I know it's only homework but I might even miss it when I've finished. Stupid huh? But then again, if everything goes to plan (unlikely), by next week I'll have a beautiful girl-of-my-dreams to keep me occupied. However, it's Wednesday tomorrow, that gives me three days in which to woo Eleanor and I've barely said two words to her this week. Nice start.

This whole thing would be a lot easier if, like in the films, I had a better deadline than just Friday – a school dance would be perfect, an end-of-year ball. Unfortunately my school doesn't have anything that flash. We get the Christmas disco and I am unable to describe in detail how bad it is because I've never sunk so low as to ever go to it. I can take a wild stab in the dark and assume that it will consist of loud shit music, terrible dancing, all the skanks and wankers getting together for a game of feel-me-up tonsil tennis and all the nice girls dancing with any guy other than me – I just don't think I can handle that kind of rejection. We will get our leavers' ball a little later in the year, but that seems kind of pointless – why wait to start a relationship with Eleanor just days before we both leave school and head in separate directions? It's now or never. If only I had a decent plan . . .

WEDNESDAY

1st Period
I.T.

Last night I put 'Myself' down at around ten-thirty, said good night to my mum (hugging her slightly tighter than usual to ease my guilt about being a grumpy shit lately), went to bed and stared at the ceiling whilst I racked my brains for a way to get my foot in the door of Eleanor's mind. (I know, it's a terrible mixed metaphor. I tried to find some clever alternative word for 'mind' that might relate to 'door' – closet, room, china shop. No luck, they all just sounded a little bit pervy, so I just settled for 'mind'. Sorry.)

I was really beginning to feel the pressure, not only because I'd set myself the ridiculous deadline of Friday to win Eleanor's affections, but also because the success of this entire story is hanging on my every decision and the final outcome of this week. Maybe this wasn't such a good idea. A failure with Eleanor will mean a failure with this project, a failure with this project will mean a failure with exam grades, which could mean failure in getting into the right college/film school/career. It's not just this project on the line here – it's my entire life. Holy crap, that's deep! When you actually stop and think about it, this isn't an isolated case – everyone's future is determined by every single decision they make in their entire lives! A decision to go into Burger King instead of McDonald's could mean getting caught up in an armed robbery and shot in the head; a decision to have fish and chips for lunch instead of beans on toast could lead to an emergency toilet visit, which could lead to missing the bus, on which you might have met the woman of your dreams with whom you would raise a beautiful happy family, live a long and happy life writing music for movies in a big house in the country. What if I did a fart then two seconds later Eleanor comes round the corner with the intention of telling me how in love with me she is, but she smells the fart and changes her mind for ever? The rest of my life ruined by the decision to fart two seconds too soon!

OK, I get the impression that from now on I will be thinking long and hard over any future decisions – this story has to end happily, I'll be damned if this is going to end as a tragedy. Apart from anything else it'd never get adapted into a film.

As far as lessons go, Wednesday is probably the best day of the week. It's all plain sailing except for Physics this afternoon and even that's not too bad.

First lesson of the day is I.T. It's not an exam subject so there's no pressure to be any good at it and there's also never any homework. In fact there's barely even any work whatsoever as we don't even have a teacher most of the time. Our teacher was supposed to be, of all people, Dave Kross, but he has to take over someone else's English class on Wednesday mornings. We were meant to get a replacement teacher but we usually just get the occasional Part-Timer or maybe a P.E. teacher whose football has been rained off – neither of whom have the first idea about what they're supposed to be teaching us. Dave sometimes appears at the beginning of the lesson to set us some work and then again at the end to look at what we've done. Maybe he has to do this all the time and that's why he's always late for our English/Lit lessons?

Today is a no-teacher day. Dave came in to take register, handed out some worksheets then disappeared. I can't ever work out if this is a good situation because I don't have to do any work, or a bad thing because I'm not actually learning anything (which was kind of the whole point in taking the subject). The rest of the class seem unanimous in their decision that it's definitely a good thing and have vanished up the playing field to soak up the sun. I was tempted to join them but, seeing as my next lesson is a 'Homework Period' (basically a gap in my timetable in which I am supposed to go to the library and catch up on homework), I think I'll make the most of the rare sunshine then. I could go up now and spend all morning outside, but that would increase my chances of getting caught and given detention or even worse I could soak up a bit too much sun and end up getting the squits (is that normal or is it just me?).

There's only five of us left in the computer room now – me, a comic book geek called James, who I've never really spoken to, and a couple of computer nerds who will proba-bly stay here all through break time then come back at lunch. For some unknown reason we've all actually done the work that has been set for us. OK, I know it sounds extremely sad but it was kind of fun. We've had to create advertising campaigns for made-up products – I've done a shit animation for a soda pop and James has done a poster campaign for mental disabilities. It's a shame we're not being marked on this stuff because it's really not bad! I've invented a new drink called 'Mango Pop' – *It's so fruity…* (guy takes a sip of his drink… BOOM! His head explodes!)… *ManGo Pop!* James and I have watched it back about twenty times now and it still makes us laugh. I was thinking that maybe I should do this for a job, but then I saw James's idea, which is probably the most mind-blowing charity campaign I have ever seen in my life. His idea is about ten times better than mine but in all the wrong ways.

'I love the way you've played with the words!' he declared in genuine admiration. 'I've got to try something like that!'

Ten minutes later he had a piece of work that was verging on Genius/Insane. At first he couldn't find any pictures of people with mental disabilities, so he ended up scanning his head, whilst pulling a face like a Down's Syndrome person (trust me, it gets worse) . . . The caption reads: *This boy's family can't afford to support him on their own. Donate just £5 a week and you can help Fundamental.* Fundamental! I nearly pissed my pants! It's the most wrong thing I've ever seen in my life.

'You're going to get expelled!' I yelled with laughter.

'No, look, you don't get it – the charity is called 'Fundamental' and if you give them money you help *fund a mental.*'

Somehow, in this guy's strange little warped yet innocent

mind, this is actually a serious idea. I'm not sure he even knows what we're laughing at, but the look of sincere pride on his face gives me the impression this is the cleverest thing he has ever done in his life.

First Break

When the bell rang ten minutes later my stomach was so cramped from laughing that I thought I was going to be sick. That didn't stop me from racing through the school in an attempt to get to the front of the ice lolly queue though. Despite my Olympic efforts I came in at eleventh place and spent five minutes cursing myself for not leaving the lesson early (why wait for the bell when there's not even a teacher monitoring us?!). James had to go and meet some friends, but Tim was in the queue ahead of me and he waited for me to get my 'icy' (that's what Tim calls them, so that he doesn't have to use the word 'lolly', which is his failed attempt at sounding less like a child), then we took them outside and sat with our backs against the mesh fence of the tennis courts whilst a couple of almost-pretty Year 9 girls played a lazy game of tennis. This is where I'm recapping everything that has happened, in between sporadic conversations. Tim and I always struggle to find anything to talk about when Cole's not with us, we're only really friends through him, but our conversational skills are definitely improving.

'Make the most of it,' Tim said.

'Of what?'

'In two weeks' time you won't be able to do this any more,' he explained, managing to not actually explain anything at all.

'Do what?'

'Watch Year 9s play tennis,' he said with genuine grief.

'Why not?'

'Because you'll be the same age as me.'

'Huh? You maketh no senseth.'

'I can't watch 'em,' he said, gazing at their bare legs and short skirts.

'What the fudge are you fudging well fudging on about?!'

'It's your birthday in two weeks, right?'

'Almost,' I agreed.

'And you're gonna be sixteen.'

'Ye-essss . . .'

'Then you can't drool over fourteen-year-old girls any more – it's like rape.'

It took a few moments of staring blankly at Tim's thick face before I managed to make any sense out of what he was blathering on about. He was right. How had this never occurred to me before? In about two weeks' time I will be sixteen – the age of consent – which means that if I have sexual relations with anyone younger than me, then it will officially count as statutory rape! Even if I look at them or think about them in an unholy manner then it will count as paedophilic tendencies or something!

'Holy shit, you're right,' I said in horrified realisation. 'That's bullshit!'

'It's the law.'

'What if you're fifteen and your girlfriend's fifteen, but

you're two months older than her and you turn sixteen, what then?'

'Then you're a sick, messed-up paedophile and you're going to jail.'

'Crap!'

'Good job we don't have girlfriends really.'

'Yeah, good job,' I said, unsure of whether I was being sarcastic or not.

We both laughed anyway. Not sure exactly what Tim was laughing at but I found the whole thing so messed up that it was funny. Or maybe I was just laughing because Tim was laughing. He has that effect. He's one of those people who's funny without meaning to be and he has this kind of oblivious innocence about him that makes you feel like you're still a little kid. (Or am I still a little kid? Does fifteen count as being a kid? It's a stupid age to be. Half the world treats you like an incompetent baby, which is crap unless they're selling you child-priced tickets or buying you sweets, and the other half treats you like you're an independent adult, which is good until they charge you for adult-priced tickets or make you pay for your own sweets.) Tim is exactly half adult and half child and he's one of those people who seems to look up to everyone else. I like that, it makes me feel good about myself (as long as I ignore the fact that he looks up to *anyone*, no matter how much of a twat they are).

As Tim finished off his ice lolly he got a serious case of the hiccups, which made him giggle after every 'hic!' Now it just so happens that I know a 100%-guaranteed cure for hiccups. None of these stupid old wives' tales like *putting a cold key down the back of your clothes*, or *drinking water upside down* – these are not cures. These are bullshit. I spent a moment or two contemplating whether or not I should share my personally-formulated cure with anyone, and I came to the decision that, hey, this is Tim, if the hiccups get real bad (if he hiccupped more than ten times before I finished my lolly), then I would unleash my miracle upon the world and tell him how to stop them. Tim was currently on his seventh hiccup.

The last bit of Twister was about to slide off my lollipop stick and (eighth hiccup), as I carefully positioned it over my mouth, something hard slammed into the side of my face.

'Shit!'

First Break
The Beginning of the End

The lollipop stick went flying, Tim's 'The Killers' T-shirt got sprayed with slush and my hand was clutched at my stinging temple. As the tennis ball bounced away I tried hard to not show the pain. I didn't want the Year 9 girls to think I was a big wuss. But the laughter coming from the other side of the tennis courts was not the Year 9 girls and I realised that this was no accident.

'Shit, sorry!' laughed Cole hysterically, as he approached us, accompanied by his annoying little friend 'Tampon' (don't know his real name or why he calls himself that), who was laughing even harder.

'I wasn't aiming for you, I promise!' continued Cole, still laughing.

'You stupid twat,' I grumbled unenthusiastically.

Normally I would have completely lost it, thrown the ball back at Cole in a huge tantrum and called him much worse than a twat, but there were too many other people around and I didn't want to lose my cool. I could already feel my cheeks burning red.

'It was an accident! Jesus! Sorry!' he said, as if it was unreasonable of me to call him a twat.

The fact that he was still laughing made me all the more angry and the fact that Tampon seemed to be laughing loud on purpose made me want to rip all the piercings out of his face. Cole is a good friend but he's a complete prick when he hangs out with his skater friends. It's not that I don't like skaters, I used to be one myself until I retired due to continuous damage to personal flesh and an acute case of the chicken-shits, but the guys he hangs out with are just arseholes, skaters or not. It's times like these that I look back and wonder why I ever became friends with Cole in the first place. It's like he's slowly morphing from one of my best friends into one of my worst enemies. If I met him for the first time today I would absolutely hate his guts and would assume that anyone who was friends with a dick like him must be a dick himself. Maybe I am a dick. I must be to still hang round with someone like him.

'Chill out, man,' said Tampon, with a menacing grin, 'it's not like it was a rock, it was just a tennis ball. Stop being such a pussy!'

Just having to look at Tampon's twisted grin, lined with his stupid baby-fluff goatee, was enough to make my blood boil, which is why I said what I said next.

'Go fetch that ball and I'll show you if it hurts or not.'

'What?' he said, cocking an ear. 'What did you say, you needle-dick prick?'

'Go screw yourself,' I muttered, breaking eye contact.

'You challenging me to a punch-a-tit-wit-in-the-face match? Cos yours is the only tit-wit face I see around here.'

'Leave it,' said Cole half-heartedly to Tampon, still gig-gling. Their non-stop giggling made me wonder what they were on. They reminded me of the freaky glue-sniffing guy that hangs out down the canal, the way he gets lairy and chases kids down the path, laughing and wailing like some Cro-Magnon man until he runs out of breath or falls in the canal. (Cro-Magnon man is a stupid caveman, right? I can't really remember.)

Maybe I shouldn't have pushed my luck. The short little twat looked ready to snap.

'You wanna feel pain? You wanna get smashed in the face by Reaper, then you'll know what pain means! Know what I mean? Do ya? Do ya? Do ya? Do ya?'

He was doing his best to wind me up and it was working. I don't know who Reaper is, he doesn't go to our school, but I've heard stories about the fights he starts and I've seen one of Tampon's home videos of skate accidents, which con-sisted mainly of Reaper punching people in the face. He's a first-class wanker. Everyone seems to fear and respect him just because he likes to fight people. I haven't even met him but I hate him for all those same reasons.

'I'm sure everything hurts to a pussy like you.'

Why did I say that?!

'You calling Reaper a pussy?' said Tampon, not laughing any more.

'No, I called *you* a pussy.'

'Oooooooooooh!' he said, sucking air in through his pursed lips as if he was already watching my head being beaten to a pulp. 'Can't change your tune now. *Reaper's a big wet pussy*; we all heard you say it. He's not going to like that when he finds out.' He was laughing again now, clapping his hands with over-dramatic excitement.

This didn't really scare me. I've had plenty of 'My mate's gonna beat you up' threats over the years and so far no one's mate has ever bothered to come and get me. At least I wasn't scared until I saw the grey look of fear wash over Cole's face as he took in what Tampon was saying.

'Don't be a dick,' he said to Tampon, with little conviction.

'He used Reaper's name in vain,' said Tampon, mimicking some church-going old lady. 'No one uses The Reaper's name in vain.'

This dick's going to make sure I get my head well and truly kicked in.

CRAP!

Why did I say anything?

I didn't just use that phrase lightly – *head kicked in.* That's exactly what Reaper does. He doesn't just punch people or beat people up, he actually enjoys what he does, he makes sure he gets people on the floor and he stamps on their heads. He literally kicks people's heads in.

Red-hot panic began to surge through my veins.

Calm down! I told myself. *Cole won't let Tampon tell Reaper anything and even if he does he'll explain it all to Reaper and nothing will happen. Nothing is going to happen. Besides, Reaper's about twenty years old, why would he bother coming to our school to beat up some fifteen-year-old kid he's never even met before?* And then I remembered – he's done it before. Last year he waited outside the doors that lead from the Art rooms to the car park. I don't know exactly what this kid had done or what exactly Reaper did to him, but this kid had to stay off school for two weeks. I think a glass bottle was involved. Jesus, a GLASS BOTTLE! This arsehole doesn't even have the common decency to not stab people!

The panic began to take hold once more. This was bad news.

Tampon began shaking his head, still sucking air in through his fuzzy butthole of a mouth, then started to walk away as if he were on his way to find Reaper right now.

Shit, he might just be down the cycle path! He could be here in a matter of minutes!

The panic began to get to work on my stomach and a wave of nausea washed over me. Cole looked at Tampon, then to me, then back to Tampon. He looked very worried.

'Wait up!' he called before jogging after Tampon.

In the matter of a few seconds I had gone from a normal person to a normal person who had the very real threat of having blood gushing from his head sometime in the near future.

The bell rang for next lesson.

'What you got now?' asked Tim, seeming to have already forgotten everything that had just happened.

'Free period,' I managed to say without even speaking.

'Bastard. I've got History,' he said, getting to his feet.

'Skive,' I suggested, almost pleadingly, as I suddenly snapped out of my trance. I could have done with the company — someone to talk to, to take my mind off my imminent head-kicking-in.

'Yeah, right,' he laughed, as if skiving off History was the most ridiculous thing he had ever heard of.

Tim picked up his bag and walked away, leaving me sat in the empty tennis courts with just my notebook and pen for company. 'See you later, you lucky bastard,' he called back.

Somehow I think he may have missed the relevance of what had just happened. I decided there and then to not share my cure for hiccups with Tim.

It's times like these when you realise who your friends are – they're the ones that stick by you no matter what. (I'm not sure I have any.)

2nd Period
No Lesson!

Free periods mean you go up the field.

Sunshine means you go up the field.

Having someone out to kill you means you definitely go up the field.

Right now I am up the field. And I am reassuring myself by singing my own soundtrack under my breath (*Don't worry . . . about a thing . . .*).

The first point here is debatable – of course if you have a free period and you are smart then you go to the library (this happens very rarely in my school). If you are an idiot you walk into town via the cycle track (but more often than not the school exits are being watched by a member of staff, waiting in ambush to deal out a deathly blow of detention). If you are somewhere in between stupid and smart then you go up the field (completely out of view of the school buildings and very rarely checked on by any staff – I'm sure they're aware that people go up there, they just can't be bothered taking the five-minute hike to go catch them).

The second point here is a no-brainer (sunshine = go outdoors). But it's the third point that is most important. It is a plan unique to just a select group of people in our school. On one hand it feels like a very risky move, to get out of sight of the school and the teachers when you're in danger of being murdered. Your instinct is to stay as close to the staff room as possible, but the outcome of that situation is always the same – at some point you have to leave the safety of the teachers and your enemies will be waiting. The field offers a form of protection far more untouchable than just staff members, a protection that walks down to the bus bay at the end of school, a protection that threatens '*Mess with us and we'll mess with you!*', a protection that goes under the collective name of 'The Metallers'.

The Metallers are a loyal group of long-haired, leather-clad, stud-adorned, headbanging animals who will tear you apart if you so much as look at them funny. At least this is the opinion of the entire rest of the school and, more importantly, the opinion of 'The Bezzers' – the natural-born enemies of anything that dares to look or dress anywhere left of the middle (unless, of course, you are a Bezzer, in which case you are allowed to wear baggy trousers with white stripes running down the outside leg seam, some form of hooded top and a Burberry-style tartan baseball cap perched at a stupid and uncomfortable angle on top of an extremely short haircut). I don't know where the mutual hatred between The Metallers and The Bezzers began, but it really seems to be based on The Bezzers' hatred for men with long/unusual hair and The Metallers' hatred of being persecuted for having long/unusual hair. (Whoever said that religion is the cause of 99% of all wars was clearly mistaken, as hairstyle is quite obviously the predominant aggravator – WWII was all about blond hair and blue eyes, the English Civil War was all about the Cavaliers picking on the poor bowl-cutted Roundheads, and there was some war in America where a bunch of Mohawks went around scalping people! (At least that's what happened in the film with Daniel Day Lewis – are you allowed to bracket a sentence that is already part of a bracketed paragraph? Pah – who cares!))

Hairstyles aside, when it comes to causing trouble with The Metallers, The Bezzers have a very strict game plan:

1. **Only the youngsters of the gang are allowed to cause day-to-day trouble and only with minor members of the opposing gang. If a leading member of any gang causes trouble or is the target of abuse, this means war. (The leaders of each gang pretend to be on amicable terms, like the dons of two rival mafia families, and the leader of The Bezzers always seems to get his followers to start trouble so that when the leader of the opposition comes to 'talk about this' then all support of these actions can be denied and a promise will be made that 'It didn't 'ave nuffin to do wiv me, mate'.)**

2. **Day-to-day trouble will only be initiated if the target is both a weakling and on his own, and if The Bezzers outnumber him at least three to one.**

3. **All conflicts must begin with name-calling
    (usually 'Metaller Freak!') and must end with at
    least a hint of bloodshed.**

The Bezzers far outnumber The Metallers (about twenty-two Metallers vs. sixty-plus Bezzers), and if they ever got the balls to start an all-out war they would win hands down. Luckily for The Metallers, their reputation of being headbanging animals is enough to keep The Bezzers at bay, but I wouldn't like to be around if The Bezzers ever realise what The Metallers really are: nothing but a ragtag collection of hardcore goths, emos, indie rockers, metallers (only about eight though!) and hippies, most of whom are pacifists who merely keep up the pretence of being on the edge of sanity simply as a method of self-preservation. But the weird thing is, they've lived with this label for so long that it's actually beginning to rub off on them – sometimes they really seem to believe their own hype, kind of like if you tell someone they're pretty eight times a day, then eventually they start to believe it, even if they have a face like a cow's anus.

Know Your Metaller From Your Bezzer

- **The Metallers were named by The Bezzers who
  have a misguided belief that anyone who wears
  alternative clothing or has hair longer than two
  inches must be a follower of heavy metal music**
- **The Bezzers were named by everyone (including
  themselves) due to the fact that it is their
  favourite word and has multiple applications:**

- *I'm bezzin, man* (I'm feeling good)
- *We bezzed it!* (We went very fast)
- *We're just bezzin* (We are merely hanging around)
- *That's bezzin!* (That is cool)
- *He's me bezzer* (He is my best friend)

It is my understanding that The Bezzers take their title to mean 'The Coolest and the Best', whereas everyone else takes it to mean 'Bunch of Chavvy Wankers'

- The Metallers try to use very adult words and enjoy debating politics, even though the majority of their conversations end up very similar to those of eight-year-olds (i.e. *'How far can you stand from the toilet before you piss on the floor?'*)
- The Bezzers try to use as few real words as possible and spend so much time on their phones that they even *talk* in text-speak

N.B. Skaters: not to be confused with either of the above. Called Skaters because . . . they skate. No natural enemies (no natural friends either).

I am neither a Metaller nor a Bezzer (not a skater either). Although I'm friends with most of The Metallers and find myself hanging out with them more often than not, I'm also fairly good friends with one of the leading Bezzers. He sits on the back row of my Physics class, directly behind me, and although he spends most of the lesson whispering to Hannah Voce and chuckling in a dumb kind of way, he doesn't actually seem like a bad guy. He never seemed to have a problem with me yet he never seemed to like me either, but he did begin to gain some respect for me when he discovered that I have a huge DVD collection and we began lending each other films.

The first time I lent him something I didn't actually expect to get it back, but sure enough it was returned to me the next week in perfect condition. I must have lent him about twenty films by now, and although he does borrow the occasional Scorsese or an old 'video nasty', he mostly watches family comedies — strange. His appreciation for me grew even larger when he discovered that I actually understood what was going on in our lessons and could offer him help when he got stuck (which was usually 99% of the time). Of course, I'm no Physics whizz, but I understand some of the more complicated words, which, to him, makes me seem like a genius. And my respect for him grew when I realised that he was really *doing* the work! I actually felt proud, like I'd taught a puppy to roll over or something. In fact Jane (Monroe, our Physics teacher) saw me talking to Ed during the lesson once and asked me to stay behind 'for a chat'. Obviously I was expecting a stern bollocking about how we do not talk during her lesson, but instead she *thanked me*! Apparently there had been a 'marked improvement in Edward's work' and she thought I was responsible. That's nice. I think she did genuinely appreciate it too. She's quite young and fairly timid so I think she was grateful that I had managed to get the cockiest, laziest student in her class to actually do some work. I'm guessing that the 'marked improvement' was that his output had increased to something more than zero. Ed started getting better grades and strangely so did I. I'm not sure if this was because in the process of explaining things to Ed I was actually helping explain them to myself and therefore gaining a better understanding of the work, or if it was just because Jane was unfairly rewarding me for helping out.

Due to The Bezzers' blatant hatred of The Metallers it had never occurred to me that they, The Bezzers, might actually be afraid of them – until one day Ed confessed that all The Bezzers think that The Metallers are Satan-worshippers who would be relentlessly savage if they got into a fight, to the extent where they would bite off ears and rip off scalps.

'They are freaks though, don't you reckon?' he had asked me.

He knew that I was friends with The Metallers, and I didn't really know what to say in reply so I chose to just laugh, as if laughing in agreement but without actually making any condemning statements. It was kind of an uncomfortable situation but, if I'm being completely honest, it was reassuring to know that The Bezzers didn't consider me to be part of The Metallers' gang, which left me free of any assault by association. Cowardly, I know, but true.

Having said that, I would much rather stand among The Metallers and live in fear than to be one of The Bezzers and be an absolute prick. The idea of lying on the field and discussing Jimi Hendrix and politics is far more appealing than cruising around in a souped-up Ford Fiesta with blacked-out windows and listening to banging trip-hop tunes whilst on the prowl for girls to howl at and geeks to lob things at.

Of course I'm generalising and stereotyping here. Not all Bezzers are complete dicks and not all Metallers are doped-up hippies. In fact no matter how pacifist The Metallers are they still have their pride and false image to protect, so if The Bezzers beat up one of the younger Metallers or one of their younger brothers you can guarantee there will be payback. I don't think any of The Metallers are into beating up any of The Bezzers' little brothers, but there are a few of them who would definitely make sure some of the older Bezzers got a good scare at least.

The main difference between the two rival gangs, in my opinion, is the girls. The Metaller girls are the conscientious types who would calmly urge, '*Leave it alone or you'll just make things worse*,' whereas the Bezzer girls are the types to say, '*What you looking at, you tosser?*' (I'm sure they say other things than that, I'm just not sure I've heard any of it.) These girls seem to make a big difference, seeing as every-thing boys do is done to impress girls. However, not all boys really care that much what the girls say – take, for example, Fram Calder: the closest thing The Metallers have to a head-banging, ear-biting animal. One year The Bezzers beat up a Year 8 Metaller for dyeing his hair red, so one lunchtime Fram and one of his friends waited down the cycle track on their motorbikes until The Bezzers took their daily trip to McDonald's. The story goes that they chased the two Bezzers responsible for the beating almost a whole mile down the cycle track until one fell over and Fram threw him over a wall and into someone's garden. One guy got away and the other suffered puncture wounds to the leg when he landed on a garden gnome. Nothing much has happened since then, although that particular incident almost sparked a full-scale war.

Anyway, up the field, that's where The Metallers hang out, far enough around the corner so that their smoke isn't visible from the school and in large enough numbers that a Bezzer wouldn't dare come looking for them up there. Except that does have the potential of backfiring some day, due to the fact that if The Bezzers really want to beat someone up then they make sure to bring three times more men than they expect the opposition to have, and if they're really scared of being beaten then they bring in outside help. Outside help usually consists of older brothers and all their friends who have just gotten out of the army . . . or prison . . . or both. In the aftermath of The Great Garden Gnome Incident, The Bezzers brought in about thirty friends just to beat up Fram and his friend. Luckily the congregation of fifty-plus hooligans in the staff car park sparked the attention of the police and the whole thing was broken up before it even began, but it does make you wonder how many people they would bring in if they ever really wanted to take on the dozen or so Metallers that usually populate 'Metallers' Corner'. If and when that day ever comes then the shit will really hit the fan – like I said, it's out of sight of the school, no one will be able to see the bunch of doped-up hippies getting their bowels knifed open, no police will be alerted, no ambulances will be called. It'll be carnage.

On the bright side I don't have The Bezzers after me, which is nice. I just have one person and even the hippies can protect me from one person. And even though I've painted such a dark and menacing picture of what life is like in our school, it might surprise you to know that I have never even seen a fight. Never! Everyone hears of them happening now and then, but it's not a regular occurrence and it hardly ever happens on school property. It's actually a pretty laid-back place most of the time. So for now I'll take comfort in the safety of Metallers' Corner and bathe in the legend of the ear-biting animals.

2nd Period
Still No Lesson
(Plus a Bit of History)

I consider myself extremely lucky to not be a constant target for bullies. Of course I get my fair share of it, but I would expect someone like me to get a lot more of it a lot more of the time, especially when you consider how I used to dress (mild emo goth with a hint of eighties glam metal – I have made a full recovery though, you'll be glad to hear). I suppose my luck with bullying began with the fact that I used to be the tallest in our year. I used to get the obvious name-calling and the occasional shove-and-run, but the bullies were always too cowardly to try anything overly threatening, so it rarely escalated beyond teasing. But it was when all these arseholes started getting taller that I really began to crap myself – there was no reason for them to fear me any more! Every day I waited for the shit to hit the fan, but I soon realised that one minor act of resilience I had displayed in Year 7 had been acting as my guardian angel ever since . . .

Monday
Lunch Break – Five Years Earlier

This incident took place when we all first started at this school. No one knew each other and everyone was desperate to make new friends. It seems that 50% of us found our best friends for life on that first day and the other 50% of us accidentally befriended our ultimate arch-nemesis. Needless to say I was one of 'the other 50% of us'.

For my first four weeks of Year 7 I was 'best friends' with a guy called Paul Eastwood. On our fourth week of friendship Paul had 'gant' my wallet ('gant' was his word for stealing) and I ended up chasing him around the classroom. The whole thing was done half-jokingly, but even so it was pissing me off, especially when his friend Michael Stokely joined in and they began throwing it to each other, piggy-in-the-middle-style. I tried all the 'Don't be a dick's and 'Come on, give it back's but clearly the Force was not strong with me back then, because it only spurred them on to throw it about even rougher. I was gradually beginning to lose my patience.

'Give it back, Paul, I'm serious, it used to be my grandad's,' I told him. But Paul didn't bat an eyelid, even though he knew my grandad had died three weeks before. It was a complete lie, of course. Why would my grandad have ever owned a desert-camouflage Quicksilver wallet? But Paul wasn't smart enough to consider this. As far as he was concerned I was telling the truth. That's what made me really mad. As Paul opened the door and reached out to dangle my wallet over a bin in the hallway, I kind of lost it in a small way. I was there in a heartbeat. Face to face. One hand on my wallet, one hand on the door.

'Let go,' I growled.

He kept a firm hold on it, staring me out.

'I mean it, Paul,' I told him with a hint of warning.

But still he didn't budge.

What had started out as a stupid game had soon become a game of chicken. A stand-off. I'd seen it on the wildlife documentaries – the lion that doesn't back down becomes king.

I am no king.

Both me and Paul knew it, but there was no way I was going to back down. (OK, that's a lie, there were many ways in which I would have backed down, especially if the tiniest threat of violence was hinted at.) That was *my* wallet, with *my* £2.85 in it, and I wasn't going to let someone like Paul Eastwood make me beg for it. I took a deep breath, stepped forward, stared him straight in the eyes and . . .

'You better let go right now, Eastwood, or I swear to god I'll make sure you regret it,' I warned him menacingly (or as menacingly as an eleven-year-old with a bright red face and trembling hands can get).

Of course the only plan I had in mind was to go running

to a teacher and make sure he got a good telling-off, but it seemed to do the job. Paul let go.

'All right, chill, it's only a game!' he protested.

I snatched my wallet back and barged past him into the corridor (this would have been a lot cooler if I hadn't tripped on a chair leg and got my bag caught in the door on my way out). Neither Paul nor any of his idiot friends (most of whom grew to become high-ranking Bezzers) ever messed with me again. It must have been the way I said it, because I can't imagine 'Give it back else I'm telling on you!' would have yielded the same results. Proof that actions do not always speak louder than words. Or so I thought. I learned the truth just two weeks ago (five years later!), when I was sat with Ed in our Physics class.

Wednesday, 3rd Period, Physics – Two Weeks Ago

'How long you been doing karate for?' he asked, as I gave him back his copy of *Kung Fu Hustle*.

'Who said I do karate?' I asked, somewhat confused.

'Everyone,' he replied with a shrug. 'You beat the shit out of Paul Eastwood!'

Huh?

'I did what?'

'Well, you knocked him out, didn't ya?' he said rhetorically.

'When?!' I asked, sure that he must be joking.

'Year 7! Mike Stokely said you went all Jackie Chan on his ass and clean-sweeped Eastwood into a table.' He laughed maliciously.

Ho . . . ly . . . shit.

'I . . .'

I couldn't quite believe what I was hearing.

'I . . .'

I didn't want to deny it. This is what has kept me alive for the past five years!

My little brain slowly replayed the scene.

The chair I tripped on . . . could it have been wearing a trainer . . . and part of a pair of jeans . . . and growing out of Paul's knee??? And the door that my bag slammed into . . . I'm beginning to think that it may have been carved into the shape of Paul's head!!!

'I didn't know anyone knew about that!' I said, trying to sound casual about it.

'Only just about everyone in school,' he told me.

More like everyone in school who had ever discussed the idea of beating me up.

'I didn't know I knocked him out!'

No, don't say that!

'I only wanted to teach him a lesson!'

Nice recovery.

'He took, like, two days off school or something!' Ed laughed again.

I knocked someone out!

I knocked Paul Eastwood out!

In the HEAD!

BY ACCIDENT!

And I didn't even know it!

I felt terrible. (Terrible but good at the same time.)

I actually genuinely stood up for myself and . . . A horrible echo of a conversation I had with Katie 'Cow' Harrigan, the day after the Eastwood incident, came dribbling back into my memory.

'That was well out of order what you did to Paul!' she whinged up in my face. I didn't like it. Katie 'Cow' Harrigan was twice as intimidating as Paul Eastwood ever was.

'No, it wasn't,' I corrected her.

'He didn't come into school today cos of you!'

What kind of nancy bad boy is he that he'll skive off school just in case I told on him?

'Good,' I told her, not as defiantly as you might think.

'You're a prick, you know that?' She gave me a little shove.

'If he's going to go around acting like a wanker then he has to live with the consequences!' I protested, properly afraid that she may well beat me up very very soon.

'What did he ever do to you?' she sneered, shoving me again.

'He's a bully, and so are you, and if you don't get out of my face then you can expect the same consequences!'

She backed off.

Who would have thought all these troublemakers would be so afraid of teachers?

'My dad is so gonna sort you out,' she snarled as she stalked off . . .

Yes. Not only did I accidentally bash Paul Eastwood's head into a desk, but I unwittingly threatened to do the same to his girlfriend. Christ, how many people know about this? People must think I'm a complete dick! No, like I said, the only people who would have paid any attention to such rumours are the kind of people who want to know the fighting skills of potential victims.

Unfortunately, like the legend of The Metallers, this could be a double-edged sword for me – if anyone ever wants to take me down they'll make sure to send in at least one real black belt to do the job. Considering a fight with a Year 8 girl would probably be enough to put me in hospital, I expect it would only take a genuine black belt to whisper the words,

'Karate chop!' to make me bleed from every available orifice. Or Reaper . . .

If Reaper . . . if he thinks I'm a badass streetfighter then he's not going to hold any punches . . . he'll hit me with everything he has! The one thing that has been keeping me safe might just end up being the one thing that keeps me dead!

Still 2nd Period
Still No Lesson
(Plus a Lesson in Survival)

As I walked around the bend in the field I was greeted by the familiar sight of a bunch of black-clad hippies lounging around in the shade of the small trees, of which I wish I knew the name/species. Even though it was scorching hot outside, most of them were still wearing their black jackets and nearly all of them were puffing away on one carcinogen or another. Someone had the Foo Fighters playing through their mobile phone at a reasonable volume (mobile phone music – maybe they're not so different from The Bezzers after all). Two or three hands lazily reached into the air as I approached – this was the most enthusiastic hello you were ever likely to receive up here. I consider myself blessed to get a 'Hello' of any kind seeing as I have been known to consort with their sworn enemies.

Although I've never taken a side with any of the gangs and I've always sat on the fence when it comes to disputes, it's widely accepted that I lean towards The Metallers and that seems good enough for them. The fact that they bother to wave 'Hello' is a good sign that they won't throw me to the wolves if Reaper should ever come looking for me. I think they consider me more a part of their gang than they do the 'New Generation' of Metallers, who are more indie-popster punks than 'true' Metallers and spend most of their time sat over by the fence, so that if a teacher should ever appear up here they have a quick escape route into the neighbouring field. We call these guys 'Fencers' and their lack of balls means they'll never truly be welcomed into the Metaller community.

The real Metallers were in deep conversation about something or other so, not wanting to interrupt, I dropped myself down on to the dry grass on the periphery of their huddle, got my notebook out and listened in with amusement at their heated debate about bathroom habits.

'How can you do it sitting down, man? The toilet seat is in the way!'

'Not at all – well, maybe if you've got a huge fat arse, but that's what it's designed for—'

'Bullshit! It's designed for sitting and shitting. If you wanna wipe your arse properly you've got to stand up!'

I tried my hardest not to get caught up in it but I couldn't help myself.

'What the hell are you guys talking about?' I asked in disgusted amusement.

'Right, Jack, put this straight,' said a sixth-former named Dwight Rimple (surely not his real name but I've never asked), 'when you wipe your arse, do you stand up or sit down?'

'You stand up, right?'

'You sit down, yeah?'

Everyone began shouting the answer at me before I'd even had time to process the question. It was like being on some messed-up episode of *Strike It Rich* where the audience had forgotten how to say 'Take the money' or 'Gamble'. It seemed that everyone there (about eight people) were completely split down the middle – half of them were sitters, half were standers.

'Shhhh! Let him answer for himself. You stand up, right?' urged Dwight.

Everyone was watching me, waiting on tenterhooks for me to answer their six-million-dollar question. I was very uncomfortable with this. There were girls present. Pretty ones! I wasn't entirely sure I wanted to get dragged into an argument that was clearly so important to them and I certainly wasn't sure I was ready to discuss my bum-wiping activities with these people.

'Come on! Don't pussy out on us, man!'

'Honestly?' I asked, as if daring them to hear my answer.

'Yeah, honestly. You stand up, right?'

'If I'm being completely honest . . .' I wasn't looking forward to the aftermath of what I was about to say, '. . . until right now, I didn't know there was even an alternative to sitting down.'

I cringed as they tossed my answer around amongst them like a pack of hyenas with a chunk of flesh. There was complete uproar! Half looked ready to kiss me, the others looked as if they could have killed me.

'I never even knew standing was an option!' I laughed.

'Exactly!'

Someone gave me a congratulatory slap on the thigh.

'Good answer, man!'

'Bullshit!' yelled a crestfallen Year 9 kid.

'You don't know what you're talking about, man!' one guy yelled at me.

I didn't want to say it, but I was pretty sure I did know what I was talking about. After all, as far as I could remember, I've been present at far more of my own bum wipings than him. I never realised my opinion could mean so much. It made me feel kind of important.

Content with the anarchy I had created, I rolled on to my back and grinned happily, whilst a fluffy summer cloud drifted by and Louis Armstrong crooned inside my head: *And I think to myself, what a wonderful world . . .*

'Here, these guys will settle the argument,' said Dwight.

I turned to see who else was going to be dragged into the political debate . . .

My internal soundtrack came to a grinding halt.

Ohhhhhh CRAP!

Free Period
Free Speech

I could barely believe my eyes.

There, walking around the corner, were two people I never expected to see up the field, two people I never even expected to ever see walking *anywhere* together – Em and Eleanor.

Seeing them together, here, now, felt as alien as seeing the Queen and Lindsay Lohan sat on the table next to you in McDonald's on a weekend break to Bournemouth (except this was more appealing). What was Eleanor doing hanging round with Em? I know they're friendly with each other but they've never actually been friends. And Eleanor has definitely never been up to Metallers' Corner before. What's she doing up here? She must be scared shitless. She's too nice for this place. She's WAY too nice for this bum-wiping conversation. What is she going to think of these guys? What will she think of *me*? She'll think I'm some kind of bum-wiping enthusiast! I quickly tried to disassociate myself from the bum-wipers. I shuffled almost a whole foot away from them and focused such a studious look upon the clouds that it made my head hurt.

'Who's the fit one?' someone muttered.

If only I was a brave person I would have stood up and pulled his face off.

'How do you think she wipes her bum?' he added.

NO! NO! NO! That is private! Her bottom is nobody's business but my own! *Please* don't ask her. What kind of a welcome is that? Imagine if the rest of society caught whatever it is that these guys are suffering from – *How do you do, lovely to meet you, how do you wipe your bottom?* Then I heard someone lighting a cigarette, except the smell that was wafting my way was certainly not standard tobacco.

Please keep walking. PLEASE keep walking, I urged them in my head, hoping that I had finally mastered the Force. And then something amazing happened . . . they changed course! It was only a slight angle but it was a definite drift away from us. They might go right by us! It worked. It bloody worked!

'Oy, girlies! Can we ask you a question?' called Dwight.

No!

'What?' replied Em, actually asking what he had said, not what the question was.

'Do you wipe sitting or standing?'

Bugger . . . bugger . . . bugger.

'Piss or shit?' replied Em, who was familiar with these heathens.

'Shit.'

'Stand,' said Em casually.

There was another explosion of cheers and leers and I have to admit, inside my head I was joining in. I actually cared! How could someone I thought I knew so well after all these years actually be someone who would stand up to wipe her own bum? The cheering mutated into another full-blown argument. Good. That'll do. They got an answer, now they don't need to ask Eleanor.

'What about you?' someone called to her.

Oh god no.

Don't answer. Tell them to piss off. You do not have to answer.

'Erm . . .' She began to blush.

Oh no, she *is* going to answer!

Please say sit. PLEASE say sit! I don't know if I could love someone who stands . . .

'Stand,' she replied, somewhat perplexed.

This time there were two explosions: one from The Metallers, and one inside my head. Surely it could get no worse than this.

Em and Eleanor were now approaching us.

'Wanna toke?' asked Dwight, offering her the crinkled and soggy-looking mash of smouldering paper.

Please say no! I'm not sure I could love a standy-wipey fag hag!

'Sure,' said Eleanor, as she took the joint and sat down with them.

My entire life was falling around my feet like a pair of piss-soaked pants. How could this be happening? This is Eleanor! Eleanor the pure! The sweet, innocent, beautiful girl of my dreams. From now on, whenever I picture her going for a poo she's going to be standing up and surrounded by a cloud of dope smoke! How can I live like this? I'm not joking! I was actually *shaking*. The whole thing messed me

up more than the news that someone was coming to school
to kick my head in.

'So how's your project going, Jack?'

She noticed me! Out of all the weird people that were sat
around, she chose me to speak to! I love her!

*OK, calm down and be cool. Answer her question . . .
what the hell did she say?!! Shit! I can't remember what she
asked me! What do I say? Do I smile and nod? No, that's
stupid. Say something intelligent, it doesn't even matter if I
change the subject, as long as it's smart enough to dazzle her
with my intellect . . .*

'Huh?' I said.

The single eloquent word fell from my lips like a soggy
dead hamster.

'How's your project going?' she repeated with a smile.

*How the hell does she know about my project? I haven't
told anyone about it! My book is laying open by my side,
please don't tell me she's been reading it from over there! Is
it open on a page about her? Shit!*

'Aren't you doing a mime in a lift or something?' she
prompted.

Ohhhhh, THAT project.

'Ohhhh, *that* project!' I said.

'What did you think I was talking about?'

*My undying fascination and lust for every little thing
about you.*

'I didn't have a clue,' I answered.

She laughed like someone had set off a giggle-bomb in her
throat. It was amazing. *I* made her laugh – ME! I've made her
laugh in the past but that was different, it was always a

character I was playing on stage that made her laugh. This time it was actually me. All me. Well, it was either me or the lungful of mind-altering narcotics she had just inhaled (I like to think it was me).

She reached her arm out and offered me the mashed-up joint that sat between her fingers and had been sucked on by at least five other people already.

Two things almost made me reach for it –

1. **The fact that it had just been between her lips and could soon after be between mine made me feel warm inside (it would almost be like kissing her, right?)**
2. **I was afraid of looking like a wimp**

'No, thanks.' I resisted with a small wave of the hand.

'How come?' she asked, surprised.

'I don't really do that stuff,' I shrugged uncomfortably.

Normally I would have used some self-deprecating humour to lighton that situation, liko, *I'm too wussy for that stuff* or *It makes me wee in my pants and cry like a baby*, but, face to face, Eleanor made me way too nervous to think straight. I was lucky to be speaking at all. It did cross my mind to make up an excuse. When you don't partake in a ritual mind-numbing like this it kind of makes everyone a bit edgy. Half of them glare at you as if you've just insulted their mothers, and the rest keep glancing shiftily as if I might pull out a gun and a walkie-talkie and call in the SWAT team to flush them out. The pressure to join in, just to be one of the gang, is immense, but making up an excuse is not the right move – I learned this when I was up here one day a couple of years ago and some kid, who obviously didn't want to smoke, told them that he was allergic. The response was as relentless as if he had just told a bunch of Jehovah's Witnesses that he was allergic to Jesus. They were having none of it. In fact I think they saw it as an ultimate conversion challenge. They quizzed him and drilled him on the specific facts of his supposed allergy, like hardened cops in a brutal interrogation, until finally the kid tripped up and contradicted himself with his asthma 'facts' (something to do with him not having his inhaler on him even though he'd just played a game of football). It soon became very apparent that he was just making up stories to get out of smoking dope. Dwight called him a 'cock-sucking pussy' and told him to piss off and never come back up to Metallers' Corner. The kid finally snapped and was practically begging for a toke as his mates escorted him off the field before he got punched.

Man, was I glad not to be him. And then . . .

'Wanna puff?' Dwight had asked.

He was talking to me.

He was offering me his spliff!

Everyone was awaiting my acceptance.

The thought of smoking drugs scared the hell out of me.

The thought of smoking *anything* scared the hell out of me!

There was no way they were going to accept 'No' as an answer.

What the hell was I going to do?

Here's What Happened . . .

I felt my face burn red. I was *this* close to buckling under the pressure and taking a pretend puff when someone brave and bold possessed my body and said,

'No, thanks.'

The thing that had control of my body went on to tell them that it wasn't something I was interested in trying, and I hope they weren't offended, but I just wasn't into it. Of course Dwight went mental, told me it was better for my health to smoke weed than it was to drink milk, said that everyone should experience new things and accused me of being narrow-minded. Clearly Dwight gets a bit paranoid (a side effect) and likes to know that everyone's in the same boat when it comes to breaking the law, so I pretended to be calm and told him that I didn't have anything against marijuana or people who smoke it (a lie, in that I have a big problem with the doped-up pricks on the cycle path with knives who try to sell pot to the Year 7s) and also informed him that, 'I've eaten live grubs (a lie), I've been hang-gliding over Ireland (a lie), I've abseiled the Rocky Mountains (a lie) and I volunteer at the homeless shelter, but if you say that I'm narrow-minded because I don't want to smoke pot then

I suppose you must be right.' Everyone seemed pretty impressed by my honesty, except for Dwight, who was obviously hiding his admiration behind his scowl.

'If you're so open-minded then how come you won't even take one little toke of weed?' he pushed.

'If you're so open-minded why can't you accept that there are decent people who smoke and decent people who don't?' I retaliated.

Did I push it too far? Was that it, had I burned all my bridges? Well, you already know the answer is no because otherwise I wouldn't have gone back up the field today. Dwight shook his head and laughed quietly.

'He's a cocky little shit, isn't he?' he said, admiringly.

I think that was Dwight's way of saying he liked me, or that at least he was going to pretend to like me because he lost the argument. I smiled smugly, which was my way of pretending to like Dwight because he scared me.

'Do you drink?' he asked kindly.

Was he ever going to let this go?

'Yeah,' I said with a smile, knowing exactly where he was going.

'You know alcohol's far more dangerous than cannabis, right? If you're gonna drink then you may as well toke, man.'

My brain desperately scrambled for a winning reply.

'That's kind of like saying, "You've broken your left foot, so you may as well break your right one, too."'

'No, not at all, mate, not at all,' he said with a smile that made me want to poke his eyes out. 'You'll understand one day.'

And that was it. That was his way of winning the argument – by ignoring my logic and pretending it made no
sense, then pulling the 'superior by age' card on me. What
a cock.

Dwight and I have gotten on like a house on fire ever
since then.

Free Period
Back to the Present

Since everyone knows that I don't smoke it seemed point-less to lie to Eleanor about it. I awaited her reply to my decline of her pot-offer and hoped to Jehosifer that she wasn't going to be a bad sport about it like Dwight. That would be the clincher. If she couldn't accept my wussiness then she was not a very nice person and I had clearly been wasting my time. And I suppose that if I can't overlook the fact that she *does* smoke and stands up to wipe her bum then I am not a nice person.

Eleanor passed the joint to someone else then turned back to me.

'That's cool,' she said, politely blowing smoke out of the corner of her mouth with a squint in her eye, as if trying to suss me out with one almighty piercing stare. That look seemed to say that either she thought I was full of shit, or that I was an all-right-kinda-guy. I couldn't tell which though.

Twenty minutes later the bum-wiping debate finally gave way to the silent pondering of pointless shit, the way all smoking sessions seem to do. One minute everyone's having fun, the next minute they're all spaced out and incapable of stringing a sentence together (except for the occasional pair who can't seem to stop giggling at absolutely nothing). Why do they call it a 'social drug' when it's the quickest way to put an end to a good time? There were, however, two people up the field who were still talking – me and Eleanor!

'Have you seen the one where Ernie can't sleep so he wakes Bert up?'

'Bert . . . Bert . . . Bert . . . I can't sleep, Bert,' I said in my best Ernie impression.

'Yes!' confirmed Eleanor, clapping her hands in excitement. 'That was amazing! Can you do Bert, too?'

'No, not really,' I admitted sadly.

'Go on, I bet you can.'

'No really, it'll ruin it.'

'Do it!'

'OK, Ernie!' I said in my best Bert voice, sounding exactly like Stephen Hawking.

Eleanor laughed charitably. 'You should just stick with Ernie.'

'I know I should! I did say!'

'You ruined it,' she giggled. 'I'm ashamed of you.'

'Piss off,' I sparred playfully.

'Anyway,' said Eleanor, picking up her bag, 'lunchtime in a few minutes. You coming?'

'Yup!' I said a little over-enthusiastically as I jumped to my feet. Eleanor ruined the moment by asking if anyone else wanted to join us, but luckily they all declined, somewhat ill-temperedly (I think our chatting interfered with their high).

OK, now let me just underline this moment for you. Damn! If I were Shakespeare I could have made that entire paragraph rhyme or something. Oh well, the important thing is that I had just spent over half an hour *talking to Eleanor*! Do you understand that? Can you comprehend the mind-blowing amazingness of what just happened? No plan, no pre-written dialogue, it was all genuine. I had just spent <u>HALF AN HOUR TALKING TO ELEANOR WADE!</u> And I was actually talking! It wasn't the usual bumbling, gibbering bollocks that normally dribbles out of my mouth when a pretty girl speaks to me – it was real English! OK, so at first it was a bit awkward and my sentences were somewhat monosyllabic, but then it evolved into a proper conversation. She didn't yawn or look around to see if there was anyone more interesting to talk to; she didn't make up any excuse to leave and 'meet someone'; she didn't get an 'emergency' phone call from someone minutes after sending a suspicious text. She stayed. With me! And she laughed! She actually enjoyed my company! It's cheesy and clichéd but as we walked down the field together I really did feel like I was walking on air (of course that could have had something to do with the second-hand smoke I'd been inhaling). Fate/luck was surely on my side. Of all the days, of all the months, of all the years I've been at this school it was today, just now, that Eleanor decided to talk to me. It had nothing to do with my deadline, nothing to do with my plan, it was just pure coincidence. I imagined Reaper waiting at the bottom of the field for me and it didn't scare me in the slightest. I felt invigorated. I felt invincible.

Bring it on, you piss-bag. Me and my pot-head army will

*tear you limb from limb! Even if we don't and for some
reason my pot-head army are sleeping, I'm going to unleash
seven shades of hell upon your arse. Kick me in the head,
see if I care, you big twat. Bring it on!*

'They're all kind of quiet up there, aren't they?' Eleanor
nodded towards Metallers' Corner.

'Yes and no,' I replied. 'They can be rowdy as hell sometimes, like if they're debating whether you fart kneeling
down or hopping on one leg . . .'

There was that laugh – if I were a better writer I'd probably be able to describe it to you with phrases like, 'It seeped
through my skin like warm butter and bounced around my
body like a dozen pinballs. It was soft and warm and made
my heart feel like snuggling up in a cosy blanket,' but you'll
just have to settle for this – it was the best laugh I have ever
heard.

'But as soon as they get the ganja out they turn into a
bunch of mongs,' I continued, trying to ignore the big shiver
she had just sent down my spine.

'I guess that's why they call it dope.'

Her voice sounded suddenly serious and I worried that,
as a dope-smoker herself, I may have insulted her.

At that moment Eleanor slowed down, and with a wry
smile she looked me in the eyes and asked, 'Do you want to
know a secret?'

Free Period
The Secret

A secret? Did I want to know a secret? She wanted to share a secret with me! In the space of an hour I had risen in ranks from 'The guy from Theatre class' to 'Confidant No.1'!

Hang on . . . What kind of secret was this? Did I want to know what it was? If it was that sometimes she likes to watch other girls washing themselves in the shower after a game of netball and sometimes they find themselves washing each other and getting all slippery and soapy, then I think I could handle it. Fire away. But if this was a 'you can't tell anyone, but I fancy one of your friends' secrets then I wasn't sure I wanted to hear it.

'It… depends,' I said cautiously, 'does it involve showers?' But she had already begun.

'I think it's really cool that you don't smoke.'

Oh! I feel she may have over-exaggerated the whole 'secret' part, but this was definitely not bad news. I wasn't sure exactly what to say to this. She used the word 'cool' in reference to me. Me! Cool.

'Me too,' I said. Then, 'You don't think it's a bit weird

though? I'm, like, the only person I know who's never even tried it.'

'Meh,' she shrugged, 'just makes you unique then, doesn't it?'

She's still complimenting me!

'Do you want to know another secret?' she asked.

Slippery soap?

'I didn't inhale. I just held it in my mouth,' she admitted, looking half ashamed and half proud.

She is so nearly perfect. Now all I need to do is teach her how to wipe sitting down.

Lunch Break

We got to the canteen about two seconds before the lunch bell rang, so there were only about eight or nine people ahead of us in the queue. Two of those people happened to be Zack and Helena from our Theatre and Lit class.

Please don't let them sit with us! I pleaded to myself.

Of course, if Eleanor had found the note in her bag then there was no way she would sit with 'Zed'. It didn't matter anyway, it turned out I only had 65p in my pocket – just enough to buy another cheapo ice cream.

'Is that enough?' asked Eleanor, looking at my pitiful lunch as we approached the checkout. 'Do you want me to get you something else?'

She's so kind!

'No no, I'm fine, thank you. I'm not very hungry really,' I lied.

In actual fact I was starving and the reason I only had 65p in my pocket was because I had a perfectly good packed lunch in my bag, screaming for me to eat it. But there was no way I was going to sacrifice my canteen time with Eleanor for a stupid thing like food (the canteen is strictly a cafeteria-food-only area, due to limited seating, which means no packed lunches allowed). Eleanor paid for her jacket potato with beans and side salad, I paid for my Mr Men ice lolly (they were all out of macho ice creams in the 65p range) then we both stood in awkward silence in the middle of the canteen. Neither of us knew what was supposed to happen next: were we going to sit together? Was I supposed to take my ice lolly out into the brilliant sunshine like a normal person? Was Eleanor supposed to sit with Helena and Zack? All of a sudden I felt extremely self-conscious, as if Eleanor was waiting for me to leave.

'Anyway,' I said uncomfortably. 'I'll see you later then.'

'Seeya later, Jack,' she smiled.

It's odd how one minute you can be so exultant that your head feels like it's filled with helium, then two seconds later it can feel like it's filled with fat men's turds.

'You . . . are a bloody . . . idiot,' I reminded myself.

I've probably never been more right in my entire life.

Lunch Break
The Library

I walked halfway round the perimeter of the school before I remembered that there was a homicidal maniac out for my blood, so I scoffed my packed lunch and quickly made my way to the library so I could write this stuff down before I forgot it all.

I just got to the end of the previous paragraph when James from my I.T. class walked in and made a beeline straight for the comic books and graphic novels. He has a strange look of perpetual bewilderment. No, not bewilderment, that makes him sound dopey, it's more like a look of surprise mixed with concern. He also has a really slow and delicate walk, like a small child that's just woken up (only not as dopey) and he glances inquisitively at anything that makes a sound. Man, I'm doing a really good job of making him sound like a mental patient, when what I'm actually trying to convey is that he seems quite a . . . someone who stops to consider things, someone who is both in tune with his surroundings, yet somewhat oblivious at the same time. Christ, I really am beginning to sound like a writer, I just managed to write all that bollocks about someone who walks softly and looks at things.

The librarian just stamped a book, which makes James look up and catch me observing him. I give him a raise-of-the-eyebrows, nod-of-the-head smile, through which I try very hard to convey the message *I'm not gay and I wasn't trying to check you out.* He's now struggling to get up from the beanbag he's sat on and . . . man, who would have thought it could be so difficult? . . . Just stand up! . . . Oh Christ, I'm beginning to feel sorry for him . . . Should I go and help him? . . . Maybe he *is* dopey.

He eventually rolls out of the beanbag (comic still in his hands) and stumbles to his feet. I assume he's on his way over to me. That's cool. 98% of people who decide to sit with me in the library, or anywhere else for that matter, are usually the exact type of people that I want *not* to sit with me, but James isn't one of those 98%. Him and his circle of friends are probably the most approachable and easy-to-get-on-with bunch of people in the entire school. They're all teetering on the precipice of geekdom, but aren't too far gone that they can't conduct a conversation without making half a dozen references to *Red Dwarf* and *Doctor Who*; they don't dress too radical but at the same time aren't neat freaks with ironed shirts and tank tops; they don't get high, don't get pissed up and they don't generally swear (at least I'm not aware of any of these things, but who knows what they get up to outside of school – they could be drug-dealing pornographers for all I know); and they don't talk constantly about who they're trying to shag next, they generally seem to talk about normal human stuff – TV, books, comics, music, that kind of thing. In short they're very . . . normal. I'm kind of jealous of them. They remind me of being nine – I like it. I've tried talking to these guys quite a few times now, but they always seem to get nervous and bottle up, as if I intimidate them. I suppose I can see how – in their eyes I could seem like a bit of a rebel, which is weird because I think that in The Metallers' eyes I'm as straight-laced as they come.

'Hiya,' he said politely, sitting down opposite me, 'had a bit of trouble with the beanbag.' His cheeks burning red as he glanced back to see a group of giggling girls who had obviously just witnessed his battle to stand up. He quickly buried his head in his graphic novel and didn't say anything else.

'Yeah, I do that all the time,' I lied in an attempt to make him feel less embarrassed.

He gave me a strange contemplative look.

'Yeah,' he said slowly, 'you didn't see me fall over though.'

'Oh,' I wasn't sure how I could make that any better, 'bugger.'

'Yeah,' he agreed and returned sheepishly to his comic.

I don't think I've ever spoken to James outside of a lesson, and, to be honest, I can kind of see why. He's one of the shyest people I've ever met. This morning was different, he was in comfortable surroundings – computers, geeks, 'Fund a mental' campaigns – but out in the open he makes my neuroses seem minuscule. Someone who's more messed up in the head than me – I find that strangely comforting.

Every now and then James's head pops up over the brow of his book and I guess he's trying to see what I'm writing, probably wondering what Jack-the-rebel could possibly be working so hard on in the library. He seems to be paying more attention to my book than to his own and I know that he's itching to begin a conversation but either can't pluck up the courage or doesn't want to disturb me while I'm writing at the speed of light. There's something strangely endearing about someone that wants to talk to you but is too scared, it almost feels like they . . . respect you? Little does James know there is a very simple conversation starter sat right between his hands – Batman. He's reading a *Dark Knight* graphic novel, which, if I'm going to be honest, I've only ever flicked through. I was more of a Spider-Man/Superman fan as a kid, but read a few *Dark Knight* comics a couple of years ago (my auntie bought them for me when I was ill) and I loved them. Having said that I'm not sure I could withstand a full-blown conversation on comic books as I think I've only ever read a total of eight in my entire life. But if he likes the Batman comics then he likes the Batman films and I *do* know the films.

'Have you heard the bad news?' I ask him in a hushed voice.

'Pardon?' he replies a little too eagerly, with a nervous laugh as if I were telling him a joke that he was pretending to understand.

'*Batman 3*, have you heard the bad news?'

'No,' he said, kind of bewildered.

'Apparently Val Kilmer's taking over as Batman.'

His look of bewilderment multiplied by ten. Then . . .

'Oh! Right, yeah. Bloody hell, that sounds dreadful!' He played along. 'The mole!' he added in disgust, pointing to his cheek and making me laugh.

'I know.'

'It'll probably only be mildly awful, whereas the fourth film is starring Clooney, Uma and Schwarzenegger and is allegedly going to be one of the worst films ever made.'

'Do you think that's how they'll pitch it? It's a wonder how they'll ever get it funded.'

'What do you think of the new ones?' James asked seriously.

'I like 'em!'

'Me too!'

'Not very comic-booky, though.'

'No.'

'Preferred the Tim Burton ones.'

'Me too.'

'Christian Bale's voice gets on my tits.'

'Me too.'

Before long, Shirley the librarian finally asked us to stop talking or leave, so we continued our conversation whilst we walked aimlessly around the school. And it was only a matter of minutes before our convorsation naturally turned to a subject that all fifteen-year-old conversations inevitably end up on.

'Who do you fancy?'

Lunch Break
Out of the Library

It would be unprofessional and almost impossible for me to recite the twenty or more girls that James named in his list of fanciable females. Although there was no one on his list as trampy as Sarah Carmichael (does that make it sound like she was on his list? – she wasn't), some of them were disappointingly popular slags who would probably rather spit on James than even look at him. But the majority of them were nice, sweet girls (if a little plain), and they got my seal of approval (especially the ones with flawed features; there's just something about an unusual face that I can't resist). I was pleased to see that Eleanor was not on his list (even though it did make me doubt his taste) and I got the impression that even if she were, then James would promptly remove her, purely as a courtesy to me. Much to my surprise James's No. 1 girl is Helena, Zack's friend. Needless to say he was extremely jealous when he found out that I have four lessons a week with her, compared to his measly two (History double), which gives him little chance to get to know her. But far surpassing that jealousy was the bitterness he harboured towards Zack when I mentioned that he was also in those four lessons with her. To my great surprise (and amusement) it appears that James holds a very firm, and somewhat unjustified hatred, of Zack. I would have found it hard to believe that James could hate *anyone* if I hadn't heard his rant on the subject first-hand.

'He's a bloody twat who should have his twatting eyeballs gouged out with . . . a stick of shitty celery!'

James in angry mode is one of the funniest things I have ever witnessed: his neck cranes forward almost a whole foot; his voice goes all high-pitched and squeaky, like his balls are only half-dropped; and best of all he *swears*! But James's swearing isn't like that of other people – the words are very carefully pronounced yet almost stumble out of his mouth, clumsily, like a baby's first steps. It was very clear that he had not had much practice in the swearing arena. As if this wasn't funny enough, I also had the image of James, who's as skinny as a rake and a good foot shorter than Zack, chasing after the guy with a stick of poo-covered celery in his hand.

'Stop laughing. I'm being angry here!'

'Sorry,' I said, trying to squish my cheeks back into their normal position. 'Why do you hate him so much?'

'Because he's a complete twat!'

Surely there was more.

'And he's annoying and he loves himself and . . . grrrr!' He stopped, frustrating himself at his inability to clearly express his anger.

It's as if he only has the ability to get a *liiitle* bit angry and has to top it up with pretend anger that he learned from a bad soap opera. All the same, I could see where James was coming from – not that I hate Zack, I don't even dislike him, to be honest, but he *is* annoying and self-righteous and . . . grrrr! Yet even though I don't hate Zack, I *love* that James loathes him so much. I don't know this for sure, it's just a guess, but I'm pretty certain that the majority of James's hatred for Zack stems from the fact that Zack has been out with at least five of the girls on James's list and now looks set to steal his No.1, too. If I'd had to watch a guy work his way through all of my favourite girls before tossing them aside like unwanted hamburgers then I, too, would probably want to gouge out his eyes with a stick of shitty celery.

James and I were talking for less than an hour, but it felt as if we'd been friends since playschool. Not wanting to sound gushy or anything, but I don't think I've met anyone else who I have gotten on with so well in such a short amount of time in my entire life. I felt like I could tell him anything.

'Not wanting to sound gushy or anything, but I don't think I've met anyone else who I have gotten on with so well in such a short amount of time in my entire life!' I told him gushingly.

'Seriously? That's really nice! I know what you mean, this is brilliant!'

I just have to add here – no, we're not gay and we're not going to be gay, we are just both nice guys, OK?

'Why have we never done this before?' I asked.

'I know! Probably because you're too cool to hang around with a nipple like me,' he added.

Brilliant, he is self-deprecating *and* worshipful of me –

everything you ever wanted in a friend. I wasn't sure whether to soak in his admiration or explain to him that I'm not quite as respected or as cool as he thinks I am . . . hell, why shatter the kid's illusions? He seemed quite proud to have a cool friend, so a cool friend was what he was going to get. First things first, I made sure to say 'Hi' to everyone I knew as they walked past us (even if I didn't really know them that well) – surely he'd think that was cool.

'You know *everyone*, that's so cool!'

Cool.

Now that I'm friends with James it kind of makes me feel that the past four years of school were sort of wasted by not being friends with him. He makes all my other so-called friends seem pointless and selfish, and the nice thing is he seems to feel the same way.

'You're like Nemesis,' he said (referencing the super-fast, super-scary rollercoaster at Alton Towers).

I didn't have a clue what James was talking about.

'I don't have a clue what you're talking about.'

'Nemesis! The rollercoaster!' he explained.

'Oh, of course, Nemesis! I haven't got a clue what you're talking about.'

'That's because I haven't explained.'

'I know you haven't explained.'

'Well, I'm going to.'

'Go on then.'

'You're a twat.'

'I thought I was a rollercoaster!'

'You were.'

'Then how come I'm a twat now?'

'Because you won't let me explain!'

'What?! Erm, hang on, I do believe the last words I said before you flagrantly slurred my name and reputation by labelling me a twat were, "Explain then".'

'No, they weren't, you said, "Go on then".'

'Same thing.'

'Not really.'

'In what way?'

'Well . . . if I was about to jump off the roof of the school and I said, "I'm gonna do it!" and you said, "explain then", I probably wouldn't jump there and then. But imagine if you said, "Go on then"! Blood and guts and . . . spleen!'

'Spleen?' I asked, laughing.

'I've got a spleen.'

'I'm not saying you don't, it was just a strange organ to pick. I think "entrails" would have been more appropriate.'

'Not very original though.'

'True. So why am I like Nemesis?'

'It's too late. You've ruined it.'

'No, I haven't. You can't just leave it at that. Explain!'

'The moment's passed.'

'No, it hasn't. You were being gushy. Continue. Please.'

'You were the one being gushy,' he stropped.

'Yes, I was, like a great big lovely homosexual. Now please explain why I am like a large, vomit-inducing roller-coaster.'

'Because . . .' He sighed reluctantly. 'For years I was too afraid to go on it, then a couple of months ago I did and then I wished that I'd been going on it all my life,' he explained in a flat, expressionless manner. 'There. Happy?'

'So I excite you and you want to ride me?'

'Oh, piss off,' he laughed.

We even have the same dry wit. This is fantastic! I feel like our friendship is like Nemesis (I too had been afraid to ride any rollercoaster until about two years ago, and I too had that same feeling of 'Why didn't I try this earlier?').

'Maybe *you're* a big lovely homosexual.'

Somehow in this amazingly short space of time we had managed to progress to the most important stage of male bonding – being able to enjoy calling each other gay.

3rd Period
Physics

This afternoon's Physics lesson wasn't bad, but it could have been much better. I had been hoping to get the occasional chance to have a few brief chats with Eleanor across our workbenches, but that did not happen. However, she did smile at me as I came into the room and she mouthed the word 'Hi' when I passed her bench (it made my stomach do a kind of somersault that almost resulted in my knees buckling beneath me). Jane five-pints-moley-face Monroe dashed all my hopes to hell when she announced that today's lesson would be a practical (usually fun) and that we had to work in pairs (*could* be OK) and that she would be choosing who worked with whom (torture). I was paired up with Simon Cleat (pissing crapping bollocks).

Simon and I have never gotten along. He's a slimy, B.O.-smelling idiot who wears the same stupid Everton T-shirt every day, which is repulsive to say the least. But what's worse, what really makes me angry, is that girls seem to find him irresistible. And I'm not just talking about the slags. Nice girls like him too! What the hell is wrong with the world? He has about as much personality as a ball of snot, he has the sense of humour of a caveman and I know for a fact that he shat his pants last year. (He told Cole in confidence, Cole told me and I told as many people as I could, but unfortunately by then the story only qualified as 'vicious rumour' rather than 'fact'.)

The story is . . . he was rushing home from school (he lives near Cole) and he was desperate for a massive dump. (How hard could it be? His house is only a ten-minute walk from school!) He managed to hold it in until he got home, rushed to the bathroom, bent over to lift the toilet lid and, as he did, a full-sized turd exploded into his pants. What a twat! Not only is he an idiot for shitting himself, but why would you tell someone about it? How could you possibly expect anyone to keep that story a secret? Especially Cole! Anyway, the vicious rumour is out there and, as far as I know, Cleat isn't aware that I am the one fanning it about in every possible direction.

However, this doesn't stop him from being a complete twat towards me at every available moment. He never really classified as a bully, but it wasn't for lack of trying. He used to *really* try hard to bully me but, firstly, he's just not very good at it and, secondly, he's a bit of a coward and none of his friends are interested in backing him up (either they don't have a problem with me, or they're scared of me, or they're just not bullying wankers). The majority of Cleat's bullying tactics ended up being little more than sarcastic passing comments like 'Nice hair' or 'Nice T-shirt' or 'Nice shoes' (not the most imaginative of bullies), to which my reply would invariably be, 'Thank you!' It enraged him that his vicious taunts never sent me running away in a fit of fearful tears and it enraged him even more that his friends would never join in. Unfortunately I have subsequently let his lack of support go to my head and I now, on occasion, try to get him back with ever-so-slightly-more-intelligent insults than he would give me.

Today we were doing tests with potato starch and heat or something. Simon was in charge of taking small quantities of starch from our piece of potato with a sewing needle and I was in charge of the Bunsen burner. Every time I needed some starch I would let Simon know by saying, 'Prick!' This amused me no end, especially as Simon didn't really seem aware that I was calling him a prick every sixty seconds. Eventually Simon had enough of the prick game and when I turned to camera and said, '*Thish ish fun!*' Simon took the opportunity to melt my pen over the Bunsen burner.

'Touché!' I congratulated him, deciding to let him find out for himself that the pen I was using had come from his own pencil case.

It was then that I noticed Eleanor glance at me with a somewhat quizzical brow and I hoped that she hadn't just witnessed me speaking to an imaginary camera.

'She must think . . . I am out . . . of my bloody tree.'

This time it was Simon who noticed the invisible camera. He gave me a look that seemed to say . . .

'Prick!' I ordered again with glee.

I then decided it may be a good idea to not talk so much for the rest of the lesson, as I was in danger of Eleanor thinking I was some kind of mental patient and of Simon setting fire to something I actually cared about. I didn't even say anything when I dropped the potato and Cleat called me a 'nob-jockey', and you know what? I feel a better person because of it. It's not that the whole 'prick' thing wasn't funny, but it kind of made me feel like a bit of a twat and, seeing as Cleat hadn't really done anything to deserve it *right then*, it made me feel like a bit of a bully too. They say that's how bullies start out – they protect themselves by doing what was once done to them. I'm a shit.

Free Period
R.E.

The last lesson of the day was another free period. I would have liked to have gone back up the field to continue writing. (I'm actually enjoying it! Though I couldn't do it for ever – I don't know how people do it full-time, or even how people keep journals and diaries: it takes up so much time that there's barely enough time to get around to doing anything worth writing about!) Unfortunately, though, my old notebook ran out of space about eighty-three words ago and I therefore had to walk into town to get this new one.

There was a man stood outside WH Smiths wearing a black suit and white shirt, with a bunch of leaflets in his hand, trying to stop passers-by for *a minute of their time.* Like any other normal person I usually mutter something about being in a hurry, or I pretend to be on my mobile, but when this guy said, 'Do you have a minute to talk about Jesus?' something in my head went wrong and for some reason I said –

'Umm . . . OK.'

'Cool! That's great. Are you a religious person?' he asked.

'Not really,' I admitted with an inexplicable pang of guilt.

He laughed as if to say, 'I hear ya buddy!'

'And may I ask, do you believe there is a god?' he continued.

Do I believe in god? Now here's a subject I can sink my teeth into!

'Well . . .' I began.

The truth of the matter is that once upon a time I did believe in god. I believed in god like I believed in the alphabet, because god was a simple fact of life, taught to me the second I started primary school.

'I wouldn't like to guess either way,' I told the polite and smiley man.

'I can appreciate that,' he nodded, still smiling.

It was weird, a grown-up was treating me like a grown-up!

'But,' he continued, 'what if there *is* a god? Wouldn't you like to be prepared for when you meet him? Don't you think he would be more welcoming?'

'Ummm . . .'

Bollocks! I had no answer for this question!

'Maybe . . . but isn't that kind of like saying, "Shouldn't you wear padded clothing and a crash helmet all your life *just in case* you get hit by a bus"?'

Phew!

'Well, that sounds uncomfortable and restrictive, whereas joining our faith is completely the opposite to that, it's liberating and life-affirming, it makes you feel like you're being the best person you can possibly be.' He was getting kind of excited about the whole thing.

'I'm already there,' I explained. 'I'm a happy person, and

as far as I can tell I'm already a good person. I'm kind of grown up now so I don't really need anyone to teach me right from wrong any more.'

It suddenly occurred to me that what I had just said may have come across as a teensy bit insulting.

'That's a good point,' he agreed, still smiling but not looking as if he meant it as much any more (can't blame him really), 'but don't you think that if there is a god he would only recognise his own church?'

Huh? How did that relate to what I just said? What did he mean?

'What do you mean?'

Ooh confusion! He liked that! A sudden look of wisdom spread across his face and he finally spoke to me like I was a child.

'I mean, if there is a god, it would make sense that he only has one church, and god is surely only going to reward the people of his church, wouldn't you think?'

Is he trying to sell me a membership?

'And that's your church?' I asked, eager to learn.

'That is our belief, yes,' he said, with a small look of triumph, as if he had now made a believer out of me.

'But . . . what about the millions of people practising other religions? They've, like, spent their entire lives worshipping god too, so . . . is god going to turn them away from heaven because they were reading the wrong book?' I asked. 'That sounds kind of . . . evil.'

That may have been the wrong word!

The smile slowly dried up and the guy simply handed me a leaflet and said, 'Read through this, it'll answer some of your questions.' Then he forced his mouth to turn up at the edges and, before he walked away, said, 'Thanks for talking.'

A cocktail of potent emotions bubbled up inside me – on one hand I was elated to have just made an intelligent argument *whilst the argument was still in progress* (rather than ten minutes later, which is how it usually is); on the other hand I felt like an absolute arsehole! There was this guy, who was happy and passionate about something, and I managed to stop him from smiling. He was so determined, I didn't think he would *ever* back down. But he did, quite easily. I feel like a bully. That's twice in one afternoon! I'd like to think I'm not, but . . . do any bullies actually consider themselves to be a bully?

I don't even have a problem with religion! But, like with the dope-heads, I get a bit uncomfortable when they try to push their beliefs on me. I think I may have unjustly projected my anger for drug-pusher Dwight on to this guy. I'm not supposed to make people feel bad. That's not who I am. It's not that I didn't mean what I said, it's that I didn't need to say it. I went back to find him, to apologise, but he was nowhere to be seen. I did stand in dog poo though, which surely makes up for it. Maybe there is a god and I am now on his naughty list.

This would not bode well for my upcoming appointment with Reaper.

The Long Ride Home

I've now spent the entire bus journey writing all this crap down and not only do I still feel that little twinge of guilt, but I also stink of shit. When I get in I'm going to my bedroom to lift some weights in preparation for my head-kicking-in. I don't expect that half an hour of knackering myself out with my mum's pink plastic dumb-bells is going to turn me into Jackie Chan overnight, but it's better than sitting around and worrying about it.

(Five hours later . . .) When my arms got too weak and shaky to pick up even a glass of water I moved on to my shadow-boxing routine. After forty-five minutes of getting beaten up by a figment of my imagination I decided to call it a day on the practical workout and studied some theory by watching an old copy of *Police Story 2* that I borrowed off Ed (I had to turn the disc over halfway through!).

THURSDAY

Back to School

Not a wink of sleep. Complete insomnia and total paralysis due to insurmountable fear of what might happen to my head today – that was what I was expecting of last night.

As it happens I slept like an extremely lethargic log. I had a few minutes to wallow cosily into my pillow whilst thinking pure and fluffy thoughts about Eleanor, before I slipped into a solid night of warm and fuzzy dreams. (Please do not judge me too harshly on the fact that I just used the words 'pure', 'fluffy', 'warm' and 'fuzzy' all in one sentence.)

I woke up feeling alert and sharp and, to be honest, not very scared at all. Not sure why. I did get the occasional burst of panic coursing through my veins as I broke into a cold sweat and imagined my brains being beaten to a pink and bloody pulp, but mostly I was OK. I was so awake and on the ball that I felt I had a pretty good chance of dodging any punches that might come my way. Even now, on the bus, I'm not feeling the all-consuming drowsiness that usually envelops me like a big warm blanket most mornings. And I actually think I'm going to put my notebook down and relax for the rest of the journey!

*

The state of fearlessness was short-lived. Panic kicked in with a vengeance when the bus pulled in to school (I didn't want to waste energy or risk my luck by walking in along the cycle path) and I saw a group of people gathered just beyond the bus stop. I couldn't make out who everyone was or how many people were there but I thought I saw Tim, Cole, Tampon and another Skater/Bezzer hybrid called Marey (Mike Mare). But there was definitely someone else with them, someone I had never met before.

Shit.

All of a sudden I was in desperate need of a rather large crap and something in my belly told me it would be the consistency of mincemeat.

He was a ginger guy wearing a sleeveless T-shirt and had large tattoos running up both arms. As I stepped off the bus my instincts were to slip into school and hope to not be seen. I had hoped that today could be spent in the safety of large groups of people, where a stranger might not even be able to see me, let alone bother to come and start a fight with me. As I stepped off the bus with the two Year 8s and a Year 9 girl, it dawned upon me that perhaps my plan had been foiled.

'That's the one!' I heard Tampon shout as I stepped off the bus. The little shit. Unfortunately it is not in my nature to run – if it were I wouldn't have come into school today. This left me with only one option. I had to face this head-on, with both confidence and nonchalance. I raised my hand and, with a smile, waved a big arc of over-exaggerated glee towards the group.

'Yoohoo!' I cooed confidently.

Yoohoo? *Yoohoo?* What the hell was I doing? I was hoping that if I walked straight towards this guy (who I assume is Reaper), and didn't show any fear, he might feel intimidated and merely mock me a bit, rather than slaughter me. After all, a cat won't chase a piece of string purely because it is string, it will chase it because it *moves.* Perhaps if I waltzed over there as if nothing was wrong then Reaper might feel a bit silly if he started a fight over practically nothing. Perhaps the fact that I'm not running scared and I'm doing this face to face might convince Reaper that I may not be the best person to mess with, or maybe he'll respect my bravery and let me off with a few gut-punches and a head-butt. All I know is if you run they'll chase you. If you feel like you're a piece of string, then you better make sure you do a damn good job of pretending to be a brick. All very wise and philosophical, I'm just not sure what I thought I would achieve by calling 'Yoohoo'. It had been an attempt at being confidently casual and cool, but I fear it may have come across as dramatically camp and absurdly homosexual.

Everyone turned to look at me as I approached and I tried my best to look calm.

'I do not believe . . . I wanted to do that.'

Maybe if Reaper sees me talking to myself he'll think I'm more messed up in the head than him.

The twenty seconds it took to walk from the bus to those guys seemed to last twenty minutes. My joints were stiffening with fear, which made it hard to look as if I were casually ambling, and that 'Dah-Dah Dah Dah-Dah-Dah!' rhythm from *The Terminator* bashed through my brain as loud as if the cast of *Stomp* were using my skull as a new kind of percussive paraphernalia. I shoved my hands in my pockets and casually mingled in amongst the rest of the gang.

'All right,' I said in a businesslike manner, looking around at everyone, giving the occasional nod. (Please note: this is a highly masculine, slightly wanky way of saying hello and is not my usual style of greeting people, it is merely a loser's survival tactic – if they intimidate you, pretend to be one of them.)

'All right, Jack,' said Cole mournfully.

'Jack', replied Tim with a nod.

'Hey, Jack, I brought in that CD you wanted to borrow,' said Marey in his Mick Jagger/Ozzy Osbourne-hybrid voice.

I didn't have a clue what he was talking about. I can't stand Marey's taste in music and I don't even own a CD player any more. His drug-addled brain has obviously confused me with someone else.

'Oh, nice one, cheers, Marey, I'll grab it off you later.'

'Yeah, man.'

I could have told him that he had the wrong person but, in truth, I was glad that someone had actually bothered to acknowledge me as a normal person, rather than some cursed leper who was dying from a highly contagious strain of gonnagetyaheadkickedinitis.

'All right?' I asked the tattooed stranger.

'Yoohoo,' he said in a mockingly camp voice and waved at me.

'This is Thieko,' said Cole, introducing me to the guy that turned out not to be Reaper after all.

Phew!

'You the one that called Reaper a pussy?' Thieko asked.

I tried to gauge his tone but it was impossible. His face was totally blank. As far as I could tell he could either be a goon sent by Reaper to smash my face in or he could merely be another guy, feeling pity for me.

'Yeah, well . . .' (Was I? Did I call him a pussy? I'm pretty sure I didn't. I don't even remember!) I gave a small laugh, which I hoped would emphasise what a silly mistake this whole thing was. 'So, everyone's taking that seriously then?' I asked in mock surprise, as if the subject hadn't crossed my mind once since yesterday's interlude with Tampon.

'He's pretty pissed,' Cole said gravely.

'Even though it was a joke?' I said, with an expression which in retrospect probably looked like, *What a big baby!*

'He said, "No one takes the Reaper's name in vain!"' announced Tampon, stepping up to me in an annoyingly over-the-top imitation of menace.

Everyone laughed uncomfortably, as if Tampon had made a joke about my dead dad. (My dad isn't dead, by the way.) *What kind of friends are these?*

'Yeah, er, you might want to make yourself scarce, mate,' said Thieko with friendly sincerity.

The fact that this extremely tough-looking guy was scared for my safety suddenly made my shit boil and I could feel the shakes trying to take hold of me.

'He's comin' for ya, man!' growled Tampon with wild eyes.

I couldn't look the little twat in the face.

'If that's what he feels he's got to do.' I shrugged nonchalantly.

As long as my shakes weren't visible and my cheeks weren't red then I'm pretty sure I pulled off an Oscar-worthy performance.

The bell rang. Everyone said goodbye to Thieko (he, like Reaper, doesn't go to our school) and he went on his way. I hoped that he was on his way to see Reaper to tell him that I seemed like a decent guy and not to bother beating me up, or maybe even to tell him that I seemed pretty confident and that starting a fight with me might not be such a wise idea (I might even know kung fu for all he knows!). The rest of us shuffled into school and Cole explained to me that Reaper was planning to come to school to beat up both me *and* a kid in the year below who supposedly spat on Reaper's little sister. For some reason the news that someone else was in the same boat as me came as quite a relief, especially as this other person had actually done something to deserve punishment. Perhaps by the time Reaper got to me he'd be kind of tired of kicking heads in.

'How big is he?' I asked Cole, not bothering to hide my fear so much now that Thieko and Tampon weren't around.

'A little bit shorter than you,' he replied. 'But . . .'

Uh-oh.

'. . . kind of . . . bulkier.'

I assume the pause was to think of an alternative description to 'built like a brick shithouse'. Bollocks. The short ones are always the most vicious. You ever seen a St Bernard and a Yorkshire Terrier together? The St Bernard doesn't stand a chance.

After registration I had to force all thoughts from my head otherwise I was going to collapse from panic. I'm not sure how scared I should be. Is Reaper going to take this thing 100% seriously? Is he really going to put his heart and soul into it and beat me to within an inch of my life, or is he just going to push me around a bit to make a point? Surely he must have some sense of reason, otherwise why would Cole hang out with him? Then again, judging by what I saw of him on those skating videos (oh yeah, I saw him on the videos – shaved brown hair – looks nothing like Thieko! Idiot), Reaper does look like the kind of person who considers a bit of violence to be an integral part of his daily routine. Maybe he'll hit me once to teach me a lesson, then help me to my feet and explain why he had to do it and apologise.

Would I fall over from just one hit? I have no idea. I've never been in a fight before! I have no idea how much of a pussy/hardass I am, I have no basis of reference on which to gauge my fighting abilities. It is very possible that I'm a total wimp and that a single punch would knock me out and break my neck. On the other hand, I may be a natural-born fighter and not even know it yet. I might be twice as quick, twice as sharp, twice as resilient, than this Reaper tit. If he really is this all-powerful being then why does he need to prove it by kicking people's heads in all the time? Perhaps it's all to cover up his own insecurities. Perhaps he lives in fear of getting beaten up so he has made a reputation for himself as being the No.1 badass by beating up smaller, weaker people when they're not expecting it. Does he live by my philosophy of 'If they intimidate you, pretend to be one of them'? Perhaps he has made it a daily routine to confront his own fears of fighting. Come to think of it, I don't remember seeing one single fair fight on that skating video. I must have seen him hit about ten people, all of whom were either smaller than him or were not even looking when he decided to jump into the air and slam his fist into their faces. That's it! He's nothing but a coward . . . a bully and a coward!

All of a sudden my fear of Reaper was dramatically reduced. (Temporarily.)

1st Period
Maths

The first lesson of the day is Maths and for the first time ever I am sat by the windows because, for the first time ever, I am sat with James. I intend to make it my mission to sit in this exact seat for every Maths lesson hereon. James is no idiot. Our table is situated directly above the entrance doors that lead in from the playing field, and we have just discovered that if you take your seat *before* the bell rings, you get a real eyeful when all the girls in their low-cut tops file into school. Why have I never realised this before? It's that whole Nemesis comparison thing again.

James is in an exceptionally good mood, which is rubbing off on me. Julie Quill's see-through blouse is kind of helping things too (she is easily the hottest/only attractive teacher in the school).

'Put these on,' I said, handing James my mirrored sunglasses when Julie came to do her 'Everything all right?' rounds.

'What for?' he asked, inspecting them as if they were booby-trapped.

I put them on myself to prove that they were safe and had no ink smeared around the rims or anything.

'Can you see my eyes?' I asked him.

'No.'

'OK,' I said, handing the shades back to him, 'remember that. Now put them on.'

He hesitated.

'Trust me,' I told him. 'You'll thank me for it.'

James reluctantly put them on and checked his reflection in the window in case he looked like an idiot. He did, but only a little bit. Julie was at the table next to ours, showing Amy Brackett how to work out the angles for something or other, so I quickly balled up a piece of paper and dropped it over the edge of our desk. Moments later Julie was making her way towards us.

'Very cool, James,' she said, admiring his glasses and speaking in a way that implied James was about six years old.

James blushed so brilliantly that he looked like a beetroot that had an allergy to beetroots.

'Everything all right here?' Julie asked breezily.

The sunlight was shining straight through her thin white shirt and it was extremely difficult not to stare. Then, like clockwork, she spotted the rubbish on the floor and bent down to pick it up and . . . GO GO GO! SWARM SWARM! ALL EYES ON THE TARGET, THIS IS OUR ONLY CHANCE! GOLD LEADER TO RED LEADER, WE'RE GOING TO NEED BIGGER PANTS. HOLY CRAP! TAKE A LOOK AT—

Before you can say 'C-cup bra' she was standing back up

again and all of a sudden X + Y seemed to have more of my attention than ever before.

'I'm fine, thanks,' I told her casually.

She looked to James.

'Oh-oh-oh,' he stammered. 'Fine . . . thanks,' he said woodenly.

The term 'woodenly' made me wish I had sat a little further away from him. Julie smiled and sauntered over to the next table. There she went, the highlight of my adolescence (at least I think this is my adolescence). A quick bend over, a gaping blouse and then a bra-cupped breast for nearly a whole second – does life get any better?

'That's the best thing that's ever happened to me,' gawped James. I couldn't see his eyes but it was kind of obvious he was taking full advantage of their shelter and was still gazing dreamily at Julie's boobs.

'Have you done that before?' he asked.

'Every single lesson,' I informed him. 'As long as the sun is shining.'

James was speechless for a few moments.

'I . . . all of a sudden have a newfound love for Maths.'

I was about to admit that Boobwatch (that's what I call it – very immature, I know, but for someone who's never even kissed a girl it's like food and oxygen) was never usually that successful and usually resulted in only the briefest flash of cleavage if you were very lucky, but I decided not to burst that bubble just yet. I get the impression James is in the same league as me when it comes to girlie experience, but I'm sure he thinks I've shagged half the girls in school. He went out with a semi-cute girl called Marie last year but it only lasted two weeks, so I'd be surprised if he got any further than holding hands with her. Maybe I'll ask sometime, when the moment is right.

'How far did you get with Marie?' I asked.

'What?' said James, kind of shocked.

His face was doing the beetroot thing again, which told me that either he got too far to mention or he didn't get very far at all and didn't want to admit it to a big-shot sexpert like me.

'Errr . . .' He shrugged uncomfortably. 'Not very far. Just a few snogs really.'

'Seriously?' I asked in genuine shock.

'Errr . . . yeah.' He looked at me shiftily. 'Why?'

'I just thought that you two were a lot more innocent than that, you know, holding hands and not talking much.'

He frowned. Oops.

'That's *really* condescending!'

'No, it's not!'

'Err . . . yeah, it is.'

'It's complimentary! I'm suggesting that you go for sweet girls, not the run-of-the-mill skanks that everyone else is getting pregnant round here.'

He looked dubious but I could tell it had worked.

'OK, so you're right,' he said in comical defeat. 'Holding hands and not talking pretty much sums up the other 99% of our relationship. It was all kind of . . . primary school.'

'You two . . .'

We looked up to see Julie Quill standing over us with her arms crossed sternly.

Oh crap, we've been rumbled! We weren't looking at your boobs! We weren't!

'There's far too much noise coming from this table.'

Is that all? For a moment there I thought we were going to get suspended and publicly humiliated for being filthy tit-peeking sex pests! In my elation I couldn't resist – I leant forwards, pressed my ear against the desk, listened hard and shrugged.

'Sounds fine to me. Maybe it's that one,' I said, pointing at the desk next to us and trying to listen to that too.

I could usually depend upon Julie to breathe a deep sigh and roll her eyes whenever I crack a bad joke, but not today. She stared at me for a moment as if deciding how to react, until . . .

'Outside, please, Jack,' she said with a calmness that was in danger of exploding into blind fury.

'Huh?' I replied in genuine shock. 'Seriously?'

She didn't need to repeat herself. Her progressively widening eyes said it all. She walked to the door and held it open, waiting for me to leave the room. I've never been sent out of a lesson before in my life! Why now, just for a harmless little joke?

Luckily the rest of the class were in deep conversation, just as James and I had been, so no one noticed as I bashfully exited, cheeks burning. Julie closed the door and left me out in the hallway by myself. A minute later the door opened and she stepped out in front of me, closing the door firmly behind her. She was only inches away from me as she sucked her cheeks in and glared at me. She was almost too close. Her nipples were nearly brushing against my T-shirt.

Oh dear god. If there's one thing that won't help this situation it would be poking Julie in the hip with my willy-rod. *Margaret Thatcher! Margaret Thatcher! Margaret Thatcher!*

'I do not appreciate being made fun of in my lesson, Jack,' she said in a tired sigh.

'Sorry!' I grimaced, with my 'I'm sorry' eyebrows thrown in for good measure. I couldn't believe she was telling me off. One of the most easy-going teachers in school and she was telling *me* off! 'It was only a joke,' I explained innocently. 'I thought you'd think it was funny.'

'No, Jack, surprisingly I don't. Not when I've got a classroom full of people that won't shut up and a migraine so bad it . . .' She trailed off, unable to continue.

She looked as if she might cry! I suddenly felt extremely guilty. What was wrong with me lately? Why am I accidentally bullying people? Why am I making teachers nearly cry?

It was as if she could tell what I was thinking because she forced a very small 'What am I going to do with you?' smile and shook her head. I wanted to hug her and she looked like she needed one, but I thought better of it (Margaret Thatcher was failing me and not for the first time).

'Go on,' she sighed, ushering me back into the classroom and looking completely helpless.

Feeling like a complete arsehole, I stuffed my hand into my pockets, wrangled my raging trouser-snake, and shuffled shamefully back to my desk and sat next to James, who was doing an impressive job of pretending to work.

'What did she say?' he whispered without moving his lips or taking his eyes off his work.

'Bollocked me for staring at her baps.'

'Shit!'

'Yeah, she wants to speak to you now.'

James's face turned a very grey shade of green and his pen froze in his fingers.

'Not really. Just think she's having a bad day, wanted to hug my willy.'

'You . . . absolute . . . wanker,' he mumbled with weak sincerity, as though he was going to be sick.

I think I just discovered a new favourite game.

2nd Period
History

Absolutely nothing remotely interesting happened the entire lesson.

Lunch Break

I am the only person from our Theatre class who is allowed to know where the key for the lighting box is kept. Frank, the theatre technician, keeps it under lock and key at all times, allowing only a handful of people to know its secret whereabouts. One of those select few is me. This is because my genuine interest in lighting (which is actually more for my film education than Theatre) has somehow translated as meaning that I am a serious, reliable and mature student. (How little they know. Mwahaahaa!!!)

I am therefore trusted and treated like Frank's geeky little pet. And strangely enough, because I am trusted with the responsibilities of a co-worker, I actually *am* responsible when I'm here. Not sure I like it though. But not once have I let anyone else know where the key is kept (weirdly some people, mostly school bands, are actually desperate for that key), nor have I allowed anyone into the lighting box who is not supposed to be there. Ordinarily I wouldn't give a crap, but I guess the way people treat you rubs off in the end: if people keep laughing at your jokes, you end up believing that you are genuinely funny; if people expect you to be confident, you trick yourself into feeling confident; if people treat you like you're worthless, that's exactly how you feel. Frank treats me as if I'm competent and responsible, so when I'm in the lighting box that's exactly what I am. Strange. Even though I like being treated as an equal, I sincerely hope it doesn't result in me being like this all the time. I'm pretty sure my personality hasn't changed at all since I was twelve so I think I'm safe . . . for now.

The theatre is completely dark except for the small flexi-lamp in the lighting box that is lighting up the mixing desk so I can see my notebook. I've arranged to meet the rest of my group here to rehearse our 'play' before our Theatre lesson, but they are yet to arrive. I guess they're still queuing for lunch (I brought my own again) so that probably means . . .

Hang on . . .

Back in a minute . . .

The theatre doors just opened and someone flicked all the lights on.

I was about to call down to my group to ask them to turn the lights back off, but as I looked out of the window I didn't see Zack or Em or anyone from my group at all . . . It was Eleanor.

Is she looking for me?

Of course not. She wasn't alone. Helena and Carla were with her.

'Lock the door! Lock the door!' I heard one of them giggle excitedly.

It is an unwritten rule that if you want to use the theatre for rehearsals then it's a first-come first-served basis. It's very rare that the theatre is just sitting waiting for you with the doors unlocked, though – you usually have to get a key from Connie or Frank. If it *is* open, the chances are that someone else is using it. I heard the locks click shut as they bolted the doors.

Cheeky cows!

I was about to call down to them that 'I was here first!', but I didn't want to be the arsehole that tells them to piss off – not to Eleanor at least.

'Quickly, before Alex gets here!' one of them whispered with giddy urgency.

Quickly what? What were they up to? I assumed they meant Alex-the-boy, the fourth member of their group. I leaned closer to the window to see what it was they were doing that had them sounding so suspicious. I had a feeling I was going to catch them in the act of *something*, only I didn't expect that 'something' to be the something that it was. The three of them rushed across the centre of the stage and proceeded to pull a load of fancy costumes from a large bag.

They must be having a dress rehearsal, which probably means that . . . no . . .

They weren't . . .

. . . They were!

They were getting undressed!

Before I even had time to register what was going on, Helena slipped her T-shirt off, revealing a pink bra and a chest so perfect I began to understand why she was No.1 on James's list. Down came Eleanor's jeans . . . *Sesame Street* knickers! She was wearing *Sesame Street* knickers! There was Ernie's face smiling up at me. Was this because of our talk yesterday? Did she already own these or had she gone straight out and bought them after our conversation?

The girls were undressing behind one of the flats at the side of the stage, but from up here there was little I couldn't see. I knew I shouldn't be looking but I was absolutely frozen to the spot, I didn't move a single muscle. I'm not even sure I breathed. Smooth skin and underwear was flashing before my eyes. I hadn't experienced such excitement since I discovered the guitar-shaped present underneath the Christmas tree seven years ago (which actually turned out to be a horse's head on a stick for my little sister, but something gave me the impression that this was not going to be quite so disappointing). This was the kind of thing that I would feel lucky to *dream about*, and here it was, in real life, happening right before my eyes.

Just as I was wondering what I had done to deserve such good fortune, something amazing happened . . . Eleanor began to unbutton her blouse. The opening of the first button revealed the smooth curve of her chest where I have imagined resting my face more times than I can remember. I grew extremely hot all over and my heart was beating so powerfully in my throat that I wondered if I was ever going to be able to breathe. I didn't care. The second button revealed the first glimmer of cleavage. A shock of boiling blood shot from my groin to my brain. The third button opened and . . . I can barely believe it myself . . . What happened next is one of the most abnormal moments in my entire life . . . It is a phenomenon that I will never understand . . . I imagine that I will still be pondering it when I'm ninety-six years old and clutching on to my final seconds of existence . . . Why did it happen? . . . How could I have ever done such a thing . . . ?

Lunch Break
WHHHYYYYYYY?????!!!!!

Why oh why did I CLOSE MY EYES?!?!

There I was, alone in the theatre with three beautiful half-naked girls, one of whom just so happened to be the girl of my dreams. She was about to reveal her heavenly melons that have haunted every moment of my adolescence. I was actually given what may be my first and last chance to see her beautiful boobs and I closed my stupid dumb idiot eyelids! I CLOSED MY EYES! What is wrong with me? Am I not entirely straight? Perhaps I had been infected by some inexplicable wave of chivalry. I – AM – AN – IDIOT! This is the twenty-first century, for Christ's sake, chivalry like this became extinct hundreds of years ago.

Kicking myself was put on hold when, eyes still closed, I heard the girls squeal in shock.

Oh holy crap. They've seen me, standing up here in the dark room!

Then I heard a banging on the door. I opened my eyes to see the girls, now wearing party frocks, dash around in a frenzy of hysterics. Finally Helena put on her jacket and opened the door.

'What are you doing?' I heard Zack ask, sounding surprised (can't say I blame him).

'Rehearsing,' replied Helena, casually yet firmly.

'But we're supposed to be in here.'

'Well we got here first.'

'Where's Jack?'

There was a pause.

Do they know? Are they all putting two and two together and guessing I'm up in the box?

'He was supposed to be here,' continued Zack, growing agitated.

Please don't come and check. PLEASE don't come and check!

'Sorry!' chirped Helena, and she began to close the door.

'What are you doing anyway?'

I couldn't see him but I imagined he was craning his neck to get a peek at what was going on.

Keep your eyes to yourself, you filthy pervert!

'We're *trying* to rehearse!'

Where are we going to rehearse?

The door clicked shut and the lock slid into place.

And how the hell am I going to get out of here? I'm locked in with them!

I could hear the muffled grumbles of my group on the other side of the theatre door. '*Aaaarghh!*' was the clearest word I could decipher before Eleanor pressed play on a stereo and something girly that sounded like it was from *Glee* or *High School Musical* came blaring out.

The reality of the situation started to sink in and a slight sense of claustrophobia began to wrap itself around me as I realised that I was going to be stuck in the dark box for at least an hour, unable to move around, speak, or do anything at all. After ten minutes of frozen panic I decided to use my time constructively . . .

. . . writing. It is so dark I can barely even see to scribble this stuff down. There is no way I am going to be able to silently creep down the creaky ladder, scuttle along the back of the auditorium, unlock the door and then *open* the door, letting light flood into the darkened theatre, without being seen by any of the girls. But I can't stay up here! The girls will stay here until our entire class arrives for our lesson straight after lunch, and I will either have to come down and reveal myself or someone will end up coming up here and exposing me as the sicko that I am. Word of me being a creepy peeping perv will spread around the school like Sarah Carmichael's chlamydia.

Shit shit shit shit shit!

I have to go and rehearse. I should be rehearsing now! In here! They're all waiting for me. They've probably started without me and I'm not going to get a say in any of what we do. I might not even have a part! Christ knows what crap they're coming up with. What have I gotten myself into?

Oh no . . .

As if things aren't bad enough already I have now started sweating like a pig. Calm down. Oh crap, oh crap. Stop sweating! What are they going to think if they catch me up here dripping with sweat?! That's even worse than just *watching* them! And I didn't even do that! Christ, if I'm going to get caught for doing something I may as well have actually done it in the first place!

STOP SWEATING!

Plan. I need a plan. Think . . .

OK, I could put some headphones on, go downstairs, then act all surprised to see other people in the theatre. Bollocks. How do I explain why, for ten minutes, I hadn't noticed the lights turn on and three beautiful girls running around in their undies? Plus, I don't have any headphones.

Think!

I could bash my head until blood gushes from it then stagger downstairs and say that I hit my head on the trap-door on my way up then fell unconscious. It's totally unbelievable but there would be blood! Who in their right mind questions blood? All I need now is something to hit myself with . . .

OK, here goes . . .

CRAP! CRAP! CRAP!!!!

Here's a handy tip for anyone trapped in a lighting box and needing to make their head bleed − CD cases really really hurt, but do not, I repeat DO NOT draw blood. You need something far bigger, far heavier, far pointier, like . . .

FUUUUUUUCK!

Tip No.2: Corners of tables aren't any better. They just hurt more.

This is cocking-well stupid. Time for plan B . . . no, that *was* plan B, time for plan C . . .

Maybe if I could create a distraction I might be able to slip out of the door before they spot me. Maybe if I could make a big noise from somewhere . . . but what? Throw something?

That won't work, over the noise of the music they're more likely to see me at the window than to hear anything I might be able to throw. If only there was . . .

Wait . . . I think I've done it!

I wasn't certain until I turned round and saw that the lumpy plastic box that had been jabbing into my back as I sat against the wall was, in fact, the fuse box for the whole theatre. There were some sticker-labels above the individual switches but they were all written in acronyms and I couldn't find any marked 'HL' (house lights).

Please let them be controlled from here!

It then occurred to me that I could just trip the main power switch and turn *everything* off. I placed my finger on the switch and, with bated breath, I flipped the switch.

The cheesy music suddenly stopped and gave way to a chorus of squealing girls.

'Hello? Who did that? Who's there?'

'Don't, you're scaring me!' shrieked Carla.

'Calm down, no one else is here – we locked the door, you idiot,' I heard Eleanor say. 'It's just a power cut.'

'Ouch!'

'Sorry.'

'Hang on . . .'

I heard the light switch flick a few times and then . . .

'Shall we get Frank?'

'No, he'll blame it on us!'

'Let's just go somewhere else. Open the door.'

'I . . . can't!'

After a few moments of struggling I heard the lock flip open and light gushed in. I breathed a sigh of relief. They were gone. I quickly slipped through the trapdoor, locked it behind me, put the key in my pocket and dashed down the ladder.

Bollocks. I forgot to turn the power back on!

I was just about to ascend the ladder once more when the door suddenly swung open. I flattened myself against the wall and froze. Helena's head peered in not ten feet away from me.

'Oh shit, this is *so* creepy,' she exclaimed with a shudder. 'Come with me!' She reached for someone's hand and a moment later she and Eleanor were shuffling into the theatre again.

Oh dear . . .

Carla held the door open so that the other two had light to see by as they scurried across the stage in excited fear and gathered up all their clothes.

I was in serious trouble. They hadn't seen me on their way in because a) I was behind them, and b) their eyes were not adjusted to the dark. But on their way back neither of those factors would be valid. There was no possible way that they wouldn't see me. Just two feet to my left was the curtain that hid the ladder from the auditorium. Just one large step to the side would have hidden me completely, but I was afraid that even the slightest movement would be enough to catch Carla's eye, who's head was literally just a few feet away from my own. I was even beginning to fear she might be able to hear my heart beating. I had to do something! But what? There was nothing I *could* do! Helena and Eleanor were on their way back to the door. This was it. I was done for. I did the only thing possible – closed my eyes and awaited the inevitable . . .

BAM!

The door swung shut and once again they were gone. No screams. No running. No sprinting down the hallways, yelling, 'Jack Samsonite is a depraved and twisted pervert rapist paedophile peeping Tom!' No anything.

My life was officially saved.

By some miracle they hadn't seen me!

I didn't care about the fuse box any more. I just wanted to get out of there as quick as possible. My entire body was trembling uncontrollably, and I felt like I was about to pass out. Worst of all I felt dirty, as if I really had just committed some seedy act of sexual depravity. I felt like the lowest, dirtiest piece of filth, yet I hadn't even done anything! Imagine how unwholesome I'd have felt if I *had* looked.

I pushed the door open, just a crack, and checked that the coast was clear. The entrance hall appeared to be bereft of bright-coloured party frocks. There were still quite a few people walking to and from lunch, but there was no reason I should seem suspicious to them, so I slipped through the doorway and strode as quickly and as casually away from the theatre as I could.

I'm not a peeping pervert. I'm a very nice boy. I'm not a peeping pervert. I'm a very nice boy, I constantly reminded myself.

All I had to do now was find my rehearsal group. We had thirty minutes left before our lesson started. They were going to slaughter me.

3rd Period
Theatre Studies

By the time I'd found my group and dragged them back to the theatre (I made up some elaborate excuse about having to dash out for a toilet break and, when I came back, Eleanor and her group were just leaving), we had just enough time to do two and a half rehearsals before the rest of our class arrived for the lesson. Everyone was so engrossed with their projects that even fifteen minutes into it no one had noticed that we were still missing a Connie.

'Has anyone seen her?' asked Zack worriedly, after I pointed out that, once again, we were without a teacher.

'Has she even been in today?' I asked.

Right on cue the door swung open and in stumbled Dave Kross, carrying a stack of boxes, which he dumped at the back of the auditorium before disappearing back through the doorway. When he reappeared he was carrying a video camera and a tripod. He put them down in the centre of the stage, brushed himself off and addressed the class.

'Daahlings! Oh darlings, a circle, please,' he commanded with a clap of his hands.

Everyone looked kind of perplexed to see the short funny English teacher in their Theatre class.

'Chop-chop!' he cooed. 'We're already running late!'

With these last words he grimaced, like a little kid awaiting a bollocking. Man, he'd only been there one minute and he was already more fun than Connie.

Everyone brought a chair to the stage and made an ill-formed circle around Dave.

'Well,' he said, rubbing his hands together in an uncanny imitation of every drama teacher that ever lived, 'as you can see, I have undergone a rather impressive sex change and some dazzling plastic surgery to look like that stunning sex god of an English teacher – what's his name, the best-looking one?'

'Tony Trimble?' suggested Em, to rapturous laughter, even from Dave. (Tony Trimble was an English teacher who retired last year. He was about sixty-five and looked like he had been dead for ten years.)

'OK, OK, I should have seen that coming,' said Dave in his normal voice, 'what with the snake-tongued ice maiden being in this class 'n' all.' He gave Em a friendly wink. 'Now, before we get into a war of words I'll explain what's going to be happening. Connie can't make it in, so obviously I'm here to cover, and, those of you who are in my Lit class will be glad to hear that she will be taking that lesson for me tomorrow.'

Half the class groaned in disappointment.

Pansy Andy Gay Clay's hand went up into the air.

'Are we still doing our performances?' he asked.

'Your performances are going ahead as planned, which I

shall be filming on this here audio-visual apparatus so that Connie may watch them at her leisure, over and over again, spotting every minuscule mistake and scrutinising every minute detail and theatrical error . . . before she marks them. So, no pressure!'

'We're being marked on them?' asked Zack incredulously.

'I don't know,' shrugged Dave, 'I'm just being evil.'

I didn't really care if we were being marked or not. I'm kind of familiar with Connie's level of marking now, so whilst everyone else was flapped and panicked, I felt reasonably relaxed and self-assured that what we were working with was a fairly solid B grade.

How wrong I was.

Last Break
Hanging Out

In my weird week of things either going extremely wrong or extremely well, my performance fit perfectly into the former. I had been slightly over-confident about our little mime due to the fact that, unlike most plays, we didn't have any lines to mess up. Except for me, of course.

Yes. That's right. I spoke in our mime . . .

I SPOKE IN OUR MIME!

'Excuse me' is actually what I said. Excuse me! Those two words will probably haunt me for the rest of my life. I made such a fool of myself. I ruined the whole thing and it was not funny. How hard can it be to not talk? I doubt if we'll even get a C after that.

Still, of all the terrible things that could happen to me today, I guess my bad luck landed in a fairly harmless place.

The second our lesson finished I ran for cover in the toilets. The school toilets play an important role in my life. I could not write an essay about 'Myself' without mentioning the school toilets. I hate the school toilets. Yet at the same time they are my salvation. They are where I go when I've been sweating like a cow (didn't want to keep picking on the pigs) and when I need to spray my pits, or, if it's real bad, I pop into a cubicle, wash my pits with damp hand towels, deodorise, then change my T-shirt. The toilets are also the only place in school with a mirror, which is handy when you've just arrived after a ninety-minute bus journey with a head full of bed hair. And, of course, the toilets are where I go when I've been sat behind Eleanor in Physics and haven't dared let a fart out the entire lesson. Obviously I have to carefully manage my toilet visits to be at times when nobody is around (imagine the rumours if anyone were to see me walking out of a toilet cubicle carrying a bunch of soggy hand towels).

Fixing your hair is also something that needs to be done in private (unless it is literally a quick pat and fluff). There are some who will happily stand in front of the mirror (there is only one mirror, you see, none of this fancy mirror-above-every-sink malarkey) and style their hair with pout and pose included, but they are usually too popular to get abuse about how poncey and womanly they look. If someone comes in when I'm doing my hair, I cleverly pretend that I'm checking the non-existent stubble on my chin, or removing invisible chives from between my teeth, before making a prompt exit and returning later to carry on what I had begun. It's not easy being complex, which is probably why the school toilets can also be the bane of my life. Exhibit A: I cannot dump. I have never sat down on a public toilet in my life. Perhaps I might consider it if the cubicles were immaculately clean, with disinfectant seat wipes, some of those paper seat covers they have in films, and proper walls and doors that actually reach from the floor to the ceiling instead of hanging a few feet above and below. What kind of privacy is that? A toilet needs to be in its own little room with a powerful extractor fan and a good can of air freshener, not in some flimsy little makeshift box that allows for disturbing sounds, unholy stench and unwelcome visuals of tensing feet draped in underwear. Privacy and cleanliness – is it really too much to ask for in a bathroom? Clearly our school toilets meet neither of those requirements, which is why I have had more than a few uncomfortable bus rides home (oh, the bumps!).

Exhibit B: No privacy = no piss. If someone is stood next to me at the urinals then I cannot piss – I don't know why, I just can't. Maybe it's because I don't feel comfortable standing next to another guy when he's got his nob in his hands. If he's stood two urinals away that's fine, at least then there's something to separate us so that our elbows don't touch, so that the steam of his piss doesn't drift up into my face, and so that I don't get his backsplash up my arm. Call me old-fashioned but I just prefer it that way. Picking the correct urinal is crucial. Getting the wrong urinal can not only result in having to stand next to another pisser, it can sometimes mean being *sandwiched between two of them!* Can you imagine? You should always go for a urinal at the end of a row (either end is fine, but furthest from the door is usually preferable). If the aisle seats are taken then it is fine to go in the middle as long as you are sure to leave a gap of at least one urinal between each pisser. (An exception to this rule is if there are less than five urinals in a row and the end two are taken – then, just use a cubicle. Do not opt to stand next to another man with his nob out. It is wrong, I tell you. Wrong, wrong, wrong.) I know I must sound kind of odd and maybe a bit compulsive, but it reassures me to be able to say that some people have it worse than me. There is a whole bunch of people who will walk straight past five empty urinals to lock themselves in a cubicle just to do a piss! This is a real comfort to me. These guys take the emphasis off my freaky habits and make me feel normal. Although their actions are strange, I would not deem them unacceptable. After all, they are keeping it private. What is _NOT_ acceptable, however, is the event that brought me to this entire toilet discussion, the event that just occurred during my post-Theatre-humiliation piss. This is what happened . . .

The toilets were completely empty, so I went to my usual (end urinal on the right) and hung my head in shame as I replayed those two terrible words in my head again and again – _Excuse me . . . Excuse me!_ What kind of idiot talks in a mime? Then in walks Zack, wilfully break-ing all the rules of men's-room etiquette. Not only does he start TALKING to me (er, hello? Nob out here!) but he does it from only THREE URINALS AWAY! Insanity! Why not go all the way to the other end? This now leaves three empty urinals, one either side of Zack and one to the left of me. Five seconds later my worst fear becomes a reality – Pansy Andy Gay Clay breezes in and there are only three options available to him: one of the two urinals next to Zack (that would serve him right), urinal next to me (please, god, no), or a cubicle (ideal). Before I know it his nob is dangling in the air just twenty-two inches away from mine.

Last Break
Hanging Out in the Bus Bay

'What a prick!' exclaimed James, choosing his words poorly after I told him of the horrific incident. 'Why go second from the left when he could be a whole extra space away? Unless he *wants* to see your nob!'

'You think he's a bummer?'

'Who, Pansy Andy Gay?'

'No, I think that's a... are you stupid? He's called "PANSY GAY"! *Zack* – do you think *Zack*'s a bummer?'

James grimaced and opened his eyes wide, in a *He's right behind you!* kind of way. Sure enough, to my horror, Zack was barely twelve feet away. Thankfully he was too engrossed in chatting up one of his slags to pay any attention to anything I was saying. But James didn't relax. His gaze was still fixed stonily on Zack.

'What?' I asked.

But as I turned to look back at Zack I got my answer. That was no ordinary slag that he was chatting up, it was Helena – the No.1 slag on James's list. She giggled and playfully shoved Zack's shoulder.

'I wish he was a bummer,' muttered James sorrowfully.

'I wouldn't worry about it too much if I were you,' I said in a big-brotherly way.

'Easy for you to say.'

'No, not really,' I admitted.

'Why?' he asked, kind of confused.

'*That's* why.'

James looked up to see what I was seeing – although Zack was sat with Helena, his gaze was locked on to something very not Helena, something very much Eleanor, who very much gave a friendly little wave to someone very much not me and very much Zack. Zack turned back to Helena, said a few brief words, then jumped to his feet and very much jogged over to Eleanor.

'You think he likes Eleanor?' James asked optimistically.

'I'm afraid so . . . very much.'

'Hey, why afraid?' he asked, sounding insulted. 'That's a good thing!'

'For you,' I said, now sounding as down as James had just twenty seconds ago.

'Oh,' he said, catching on. Then, at a highly inappropriate volume, 'Ohhhh . . . ! You like Elea—'

'SHHH!' I ordered.

'Shall we kill him?' he whispered.

'There's a type of jellyfish in Australia that, if it stings you, will kill you in minutes without leaving any physical or chemical trace whatsoever.'

'Seriously?'

'Uh-huh, that's what I read anyway.'

'Cool, they should use that in a film.'

'That's what I always thought.'

'But just because he's talking to her doesn't mean *she* likes *him*,' reasoned James.

'True,' I said, feeling uplifted by James's wisdom for nearly two whole seconds, 'but this is Zack Pimento we're talking about. Even the girls that think he's a cheeseball still end up going out with him.'

James grimaced in a way that said *Sorry, mate, but you've got a point.*

'What do they see in him?' he asked rhetorically. 'Do you think that if we acted as camp and hyperactive as him then all the girls would like us, too?'

'Maybe you should give it a go,' I suggested. 'Either that or act like an arrogant wanker who treats his girlfriend like crap and tries to start fights with people every five minutes, so that his girlfriend is constantly having to shout, *Leave it! It ain't worth it!* Those kind seem to be just as popular.'

'Yeah, and . . .'

James trailed off and his face turned a nasty shade of grey as he stared into the distance.

'You all right?' I asked.

He swallowed, looking like he might be sick at any moment, and then the rev of a motorbike engine caught my attention, just as it did everyone else's in the bus bay (which I'm sure was the intention).

Oh crap. All of a sudden the threat of someone like Zack seemed like piss in a pond compared to what had just rolled into the bus bay. It was the single most crushing thing any unrequited school boy can ever encounter – The College Guy. But this was doubly worse, this was an older guy with a motorbike. In those few seconds I witnessed all of James's hopes and good feelings being churned through that beefy exhaust pipe and shat out into the air like lead diarrhoea. College boys – guys with proper bristly stubble and guys with their own wheels are things that no fifteen-year-old can ever compete with. Not only did this particular harbinger of misery have all of the above, he also appeared to have something else that James will apparently never have – Helena. As he removed his helmet and rammed his sweaty tongue down Helena's throat, I nearly threw up just out of sympathy for my heartbroken friend. This turd on wheels looked like the epitome of twat. He had a pinched and bitter face that said *What you lookin' at?* without even trying. He seemed to be completely the opposite to the type of guy you'd expect Helena to go for. Rather than being 50% geek and 50% cool, like you'd imagine a boyfriend of sexy, sensible Helena to be, this guy was 100% dickhead. He looked like a drug dealer who'd tasted too much of his own medicine and now thought the universe revolved around his balls. His malnourished face wrapped itself around Helena's and his black-ringed eyes glared intensely into her closed ones as she ran her hands through his mank greasy hair. The worst thing was that when she climbed on to the back of his bike, it didn't take much imagination to guess what they would be doing when they got back to his place.

I've never wanted to protect someone from what they were seeing as much as I did right then. I felt so sorry for the little bugger. I mean, I know James probably doesn't love her like I love Eleanor, but he was seriously infatuated with her and now she was as good as dead to him. And that's exactly how devastated James looked – as if he had just seen her die right in front of him. The air felt grey and heavy as the motorbike pulled away, leaving a sombre silence lingering in the bus bay. I felt a very urgent need to say something reassuring, but everything I thought of seemed trivial and clichéd. So I said nothing.

'That's – fucking – *it*,' said James.

His voice was blunt and determined, and for the first time ever he had said the F word without it sounding forced and unnatural. He almost had me believing that *that* really was *it*.

'We're getting her back,' he added.

Oh dear. I hated to be the one to tell him, what with his face being so tight and *I'm gonna kill someone*-ish.

'I . . . I'm not sure it would be such a good idea . . .' I began.

'Not Helena,' he said softly, 'it's too late for her, she's already ruined. I'm talking about Eleanor. We're gonna get Eleanor back. Now's the moment, Jack. I'll be arsed if we're going to let another cheese-dick sonofabitch take all the decent girls in this school.'

'Yeah . . .' I said, realising that, somewhere amongst all that rambling bollocks, he was talking perfect sense. If I was going to win Eleanor then I was going to have to do a lot more than sweet-talk fate into giving me a hand. I was really going to have to pull out all the stops.

'I just lost Helena to a nob-cheese cock-nugget wank-faced dick, Jack – we're not going to let the same thing happen to you.'

I think what he meant was that he didn't want to see *me*

lose *Eleanor* to a cheese-nugget cock-faced wanker, not that *he* didn't want to lose *me* to a nob-faced wank-faced cheese-nugget. I was tempted to lighten the mood by making fun of his melodramatic gibberish, but thought maybe it wasn't the right time, especially as he should have been feeling sorry for himself but instead he was thinking about *my* well-being. Right now he seemed to be more passionate about my goals than I was. I needed to adopt that same 'no bull-shit' mentality.

I *have* to, otherwise there's no way I'm going to achieve *anything* by the end of tomorrow.

'I'm going to get her,' I muttered in a daze of realisation. 'I *am*!'

'Shit yeah!'

'The gruff-nuggets of the world have shat on us for long enough! It's our turn now! It's our time to stand up and stand our ground, because we're not taking any more shit. And that cheese-cock Pimento can go suck his own dick if he thinks he can take my girl away from me!'

'Shit yeah!'

And for that brief moment in time we were not just two mediocre people who simply got swept along in the rest of life. We were rebels. We were soldiers. We were cool. Hell, we were almost black! Until . . .

'Oi!' boomed the unmistakable Scouse voice of Greg Harley, the stereotypical P.E. teacher who liked to think he was a drill sergeant and hated anyone who wasn't good at sport (which included me and James). 'Watch your bloody language!' he ordered, literally foaming at the mouth, as he frequently did.

'Sorry,' said James sheepishly.

'Sorry,' I agreed.

We held our breath and waited in hope that he wasn't going to issue us with detention. Finally he removed his hateful glare from us and walked away.

'Cocking nob-cheese wank-nugget.'

4th Period
Geography

I don't know why I even bothered going to my Geography lesson. I should have used the time to go to the library and start typing all this crap up (I've written a few pages more than I intended). Bunking off isn't usually my thing, I've probably only ever skived three lessons in my life (which is probably three times more than James and twenty times less than everyone else).

Unfortunately the idea of skiving Geography did not occur to me until halfway through the lesson, in which we were not only given a mass of homework for the weekend, but I also humiliated myself in the worst way possible. I'd rather not dwell on this for too long, I kind of want to forget about it as soon as is humanly possibly, so I'll be brief.

Em was late (twenty-three minutes). I was bored. Played that voiceover game thing by myself (the one where we make up dialogue for people outside the windows). No one outside except for Clive Cornish (wiggy hair, tweed suit) and Jane five-pints-moley-face Monroe having some dull Science conversation or something. I made up some mildly amusing immature dialogue for Clive that went something like –

'*Hello there! I must say, I do greatly admire your nipples!*' Moley-face Monroe shivered and tightened her jacket around her, which was impeccable timing – '*Eurghhhh*', she replied. '*What would you say to popping out for a spot of lunch some time?*' continued Clive. Moley-face Monroe shook her head and shrugged her shoulders – '*I, erm . . .*' '*Or maybe you might like to come for tea in my office and maybe I could . . . I don't know, maybe, umm . . .* (Clive nervously scratched the back of his head) *. . . you know . . . maybe I could, kind of, erm . . . pop my willy in your vagina?*'

It was only after I muttered this last line that I realised Maggie Dismal was stood directly behind me. She quietly took me out into the corridor (TWICE IN ONE WEEK?!), told me that she wouldn't stand for that kind of vulgarity in her classroom and that it was distasteful and extremely inappropriate to have those kinds of thoughts about teachers, so I lamely apologised and we went back into the classroom as if nothing had happened.

Hang on a minute . . .

Extremely inappropriate to have those kinds of thoughts about teachers?

No!

It suddenly occurred to me that Dismal, only hearing the end of my voiceover, may have thought that I was having an imaginary conversation between Moley-face Monroe and *myself*, and that *I* wanted to pop *my* willy in *her* vagina!

No! No!

And then another thought crossed my mind that made the bottom fall out of my stomach. *What if Dismal hadn't seen me looking at Moley-face Monroe at all . . . What if she only heard that last sentence and assumed I was talking to HER?!!!*

No! GOD! NO, NO, NO!!!

I have chosen to never write, speak, or even think about this ever again for as long as I live.

When Em finally arrived (I assume she gave Dismal some 'woman issues' excuse, which seems to work every time), I had to put up with her continual disgruntlement at me picking her second in Theatre. At least she was talking to me though. She was even kind enough to tell me that I shouldn't come in to school tomorrow because she'd heard that someone was going to 'tear a new arsehole' for me and that I was 'going to die' because I 'can't fight for shit'.

Her confidence in me made me feel stronger inside.

'What makes you so sure that I'm gonna lose this fight?' I asked, more than a little hurt at her lack of faith.

'I just do, OK?' she said uncomfortably.

That was the wrong answer. She was supposed to laugh, that's what Em does when I assume I'm better than I actually am. That was the natural response.

'How do you know?' I pushed, feeling a twinge of anger.

'Just leave it, all right, Jack?' she warned.

What the hell was wrong with her? Where was this hostility coming from?

'What's your problem?' I asked.

She took a while to answer, but when she did she did it with a big sigh, as if to say, *Well, if you must know . . .*

'I went out with him for a while, OK?'

I didn't know what to say. I couldn't . . . I couldn't speak. I turned away and attempted to copy down all the notes from the whiteboard but my hands were too weak to grip my pen properly, so I calmly began packing my things into my bag. We still had ten minutes left of the lesson, but I had to do something to keep me busy otherwise I thought I might . . .

'Ughhhh!' she sighed, exasperated. 'Now what?'

'When?' I asked, trying to keep my speech to a minimum.

'When what?' she demanded.

'You and him.'

I was going to be a baby and there was nothing I could do about it.

'It was months ago, all right? Not that it's any of your business.'

Her, too. She had gone and done the same thing that everyone else seemed to be doing lately – she had unveiled herself to be someone completely different to the person I thought she was, to the person she used to be. For some reason this hurt me more than anything else this week. I felt completely betrayed, more so than Cole turning to the dark side, even though I knew she was right – it wasn't any of my business.

'It was before I knew he was going to beat you up,' she added defensively.

It didn't matter. That wasn't the point. I wasn't entirely sure what the point was, but it had something to do with Em not being Em any more. Not my Em. Not nice Em. I wasn't sure I'd ever be able to speak to her again. *It was before I knew he was going to beat you up*! What was that? Could she have been more insulting? Well, he's not going to beat me up. Not any more. I'll make sure of it.

Every couple of minutes Em would toss an impertinent question my way, like, 'What's the big deal?' and 'Are you not talking to me now?' and all of a sudden that stupid old phrase *If you don't know now then you never will* made perfect sense for the first time ever. If she couldn't understand why this was hurtful to me then there was no point trying to explain because she never could understand.

And now I think I *do* understand – she's Em, the girl who was always there for me, the girl who maybe I was supposed to end up with when everything was all done and dusted, and now she's not there. She has completely removed herself from that equation, from my life. It was like when my parents used to own a caravan in Yorkshire and every now and then we'd pop up there for a half-term break or something. It was never the greatest holiday, and sometimes we would go years without going when there were better holidays to be had, but it was always there – good old reliable Caravan. Then all of a sudden we couldn't afford to keep it and just like that it was gone. I know it's shit of me to think of Em as a reserve holiday, but I can't help it, it's true and I'm being honest. I probably don't deserve friendship with someone who I think of in that way anyway, but . . . she was my safety net – always there, just in case.

Apparently I was wrong. She went out with Reaper. Not only did she go out with the sadistic sonofabitch, but this whole relationship happened without me (supposedly one of her best friends) knowing anything about it! Did she know him properly? Did she know what he was like? What is going on in my world? It seems so odd that the only two people I feel I can trust to not side with Reaper are the two friends I acquired only these last couple of days – James and Eleanor. They wouldn't betray me like that.

Neither of us had copied any of the notes from the whiteboard, so Em did her usual trick of pulling her phone out and taking a quick snap of them. I hope we're friends again before we have to finish our homework on this stuff (I have no camera on my phone, so usually get a copy of Em's pics).

'Excuse me,' Em said coldly as the bell rang and she squeezed past my chair.

Excuse me! That was a cheap shot.

Thursday Night

It's 1.13 a.m. and I can't sleep. I've done seventy-eight press-ups and I managed to do some weightlifting with two dumb-bells in one hand. That was over two hours ago and my adrenalin is still pumping like mad. So much for a good night's sleep. The strange thing is, it's not the prospect of facing Reaper tomorrow that's really gotten to me this evening – it's the fact that I'll be doing it alone.

FRiDAY

Judgement Day
The Journey In

Last night I was still awake at three a.m., laying on my back with my eyes wide open, listening to my MP3 player, shuffling through everything in the Heavy Rock genre. I didn't want it to shuffle through the songs, in fact I only wanted to listen to Muse, but unfortunately my MP3 player has a mind of its own (this is what happens when you put 'MP3 player' on your birthday list, but fail to specify any brand names). Finally, after refusing to play any more than the first twenty seconds of each song, the hard drive began making a whirring noise and it stopped working altogether. I think I fell asleep about two minutes later.

At a guess I'd say I got about three hours and fifteen minutes' sleep before Dad woke me up to get ready for school. If he'd known what lay ahead for me I think he would have happily let me sleep until I'd safely missed the bus. I love my dad. Jesus, it gets you kind of mushy and sentimental when you realise that you might die today. I'm feeling a bit bad that I've been writing this whole thing about myself and have barely mentioned my family. Too late now,

I suppose. Besides, it's not like I'm writing an autobiography of my entire life. I'm writing about this one week and I suppose my family haven't played a very big part so far.

It's amazing how awake I am right now. I had assumed and hoped that I would sleep the entire bus journey, but that doesn't seem to be happening. I feel sharp and alert, like I did yesterday morning. Maybe three and a half hours is the perfect amount of sleep for me, maybe it's the exact requirement for my body and brain to work at optimum performance. Or maybe I'm still pumped with adrenalin. Either way, I feel healthy. I feel *good*, and I'm not just saying this to sound macho or to trick myself into believing it, but I am genuinely not scared. Seriously! Not because I think that Reaper might actually turn out to be a chicken-shit weed, but because I've just come to accept that I may or may not get beaten up today, and being scared is not going to change a thing. I suppose I'm just used to the whole thing now and to be honest, I don't really care any more. Not wanting to sound too dramatic and self-pitying, but what have I got to lose? Unless Eleanor suddenly falls in love with me and then ten minutes later Reaper beats me to death in a *Romeo and Juliet*-style tragedy, then I can't see how a few kicks in the head are going to make much difference to the rest of my week. Christ, I sound morbid. I'm not meaning to though, I actually feel like I'm looking at this from quite a positive angle – whatever will be will be. Hakuna matata.

Yesterday was a cowardly failure day. I saw Eleanor get undressed (almost) but I didn't speak to her once. Not once! But today is the last day of this story and I'm going to make it a good one. I'm going to make it count. I'm going to face

Eleanor and let her know how I feel, not like a creepy geek who admits that he loves her more than anyone has ever loved anybody else before and that he has filled eight scrapbooks with sketches and photos he has been secretly making since he first saw her five years ago and that he thinks of her every night before he goes to sleep and has scratched her name into his stomach using a toenail clipping he suspects to be hers and that he fantasises about her pooing on his knees on every second Sunday of the month . . . I'm thinking of doing it more like Romeo would – calm, cool and honest. What have I got to lose?

The same goes for Reaper. I'm going to face him too, perhaps in not such a romantic fashion. He's a bully, a proper bully who uses his strength and intimidation to get what he wants. Well, I'm not going to let him intimidate me. I'm going to make sure he knows how much I'm not scared of him and if that means getting my head kicked in then I'm going to make sure he feels stupid for beating someone up just for saying they're a pussy (or whatever it was I said, it was so trivial that I don't even remember now!). I'm going to make sure he feels petty and desperate, because that's exactly what he is. He'll be sorry his foot ever met my skull.

Top Four Ways to Die

Still on the bus and my brain is getting too serious, so I am making a list to take my mind off things . . .

If I had to choose a way to die, like if terrorists kidnapped me and told me they were either going to kill me by slowly peeling my skin off with a pair of tweezers, starting with the scrote, or I could choose my own death, then my answer would be . . .

1. **Peacefully in my sleep (obviously)**
2. **Doing something fun like skydiving or something**
3. **Saving someone's life (at least I'd go feeling I'd achieved something)**
4. **Spontaneous combustion (it would be the ultimate shock ending). Imagine it, stuck in a queue at the Post Office, surrounded by miserable old people complaining about the weather, their health, the prime minister – and there's an argumentative arsehole in front who stinks of B.O. and thinks it's OK to bring his bulldog inside with him, whilst he blows smoke in everyone's faces despite the No Smoking**

signs – then you eventually get to the cashier and
she happens to be the most rude and obnoxious
person on the planet and you calmly turn round
and say, 'Excuse me, everyone!' then BOOM!
Your head explodes and everyone gets covered
in blood and brains. Obviously this would only
be carried out towards the end of a terminal
illness – I wouldn't waste myself on Post Office
queuees just for a laugh)

(Not sure that was the upbeat distraction I was looking for.)
'Hi!'

The chirpy little voice greeted me with such energised enthusiasm it made me jump nearly a foot out of my seat. I turned round, expecting to see the usual cocky little Bezzer-In-Training Tyler, who every once in a while enjoys pissing off as many people on the bus as possible, but to my surprise it was the scruffy little quiet Year 7 who sits at the front of the bus with his big orange hair bouncing around.

'Hello,' I replied dubiously. (You can't assume that a kid isn't intending to give you grief just because he has ginger hair, not these days. What is the world coming to?)

'Can I sit here, please?' he asked politely, pointing to the seat directly beside me.

'O . . . kay . . .' I said, even more dubiously, as I eyed the dozen or so empty two-seaters scattered all over the bus.

It bothers me – invasion of personal space. Why sit next to me when there are empty seats elsewhere? People do it in the cinema, too! Go sit somewhere else! It's the whole urinal-etiquette thing all over again.

'Shitting yourself, then?' he asked.

Does he seriously think I'm scared of him?

'About what?'

'The fight.'

'How the f— hell did you know about that?' I asked him. (I didn't feel comfortable swearing at an eleven-year-old, but at the same time I didn't want to look like a loser, so I had to do something to butch myself up a bit in order to counterbalance the lack of swearing. I had to do something cool, something rebellious, something macho . . .)

The mousy little boy eyed me with strange curiosity as I tried to hunch my feet up on to the back of the seat in front (that's what butch men do) but got my knees wedged halfway up and couldn't move (that's what big dumb losers do). I pretended that the uncomfortable, semi-balled-up-hedgehog position was what I was going for and stuck with it, despite the horrendous cramp and pain.

'Everyone f . . . ing knows.' He shrugged, considerately mimicking my non-swearyness, whilst taking his corduroy satchel off his shoulder and getting it tangled in his over-sized coat as he sat down.

'How the hell does "everyone" know?'

Is he a spy for Reaper?

'Dunno,' he shrugged again, 'maybe they don't, I'm just guessing they know because *I* know and I'm a nobody, so if I know then everyone else *must* know, mustn't they, really? Y'know?'

He spoke at about a million miles an hour and the further he got into a sentence the closer he leaned into my face.

'And how do you know?' I asked.

'Various sources, to be quite honest.'

'Like who?'

'Everyone.'

'Fine. No.'

'No what?' He laughed.

'No, I'm not shitting myself,' I told him.

'Seriously? I would be. In fact, I kind of am anyway, for your sake. Not because I think you're gonna die or anything,' he quickly added, 'but, you know, it's a fight. They scare the sh— out of me. In fact a couple of months ago Luke Fanning tried to start a fight with me – he's some nob-smeg in my year, who's, like, on a mission to punch as many people as he can, probably so he can turn them into his bitches and bum-sex them whenever he wants, like some big fat deviant who's been locked up for kiddie-fiddling or something and wants to set up his own bumming empire in prison or something, only he wants to do it in school, so he can appoint himself king of the arse bandits or something. So anyway, he tries to start a fight with me and, like, so, me being this super-hard killing machine that the military are keeping under wraps as a secret weapon against horses when they turn bad and try to take over the world, I f-ing run like the wind. I'm not joking, I ran through so many people's legs that by the time I'd reached my haven-like refuge of the library, I kind of expected to be wearing this delicately fash-ioned bouquet of minge and scrotum on my head. And, like, I stayed in the library for the rest of the day, except I was desperate to leave because that place absolutely reeked. And I, like, assumed it was that weird guy in Year 8, you know the one who has glasses thicker than a dead man's water melon and looks like he has to get his mummy to scoop his shit out with a 2B pencil . . .'

(Bear with me here, I haven't got a clue what the hell he was jabbering on about either, and you're getting the shortened version of it!)

'. . . and he, like, always smells like he holds the patent for the World's Most Potent B.O., and so I'm trying to get as far away from the smelly big cretin as I can, but, like, two hours later I go to scratch my bum, because it's itching like I've got worms or something, and, I'm not joking, I get sh— all over my fingers! It's like, *oh dear! I've shat my pants and rubbed my hand in it!* And then I look round the library and I notice that I've spread sh— all over the place. I am not joking. Everywhere I went, trying to get away from the putrid stench of death, I left a nasty brown smear. Man, I'm telling you, that library looked like the lesbian brigade had been in there all weekend with a year's supply of Mars bars.'

And that was the end of this insane little boy's story. I would like to think that he made it up, but the sad thing is, there was actually a day, a few months ago, when the library was closed for the entire afternoon because someone had apparently shat all over the place.

'I thought that was just some made-up rumour or something!' I said, barely believing what he had just confessed.

'No, it was definitely me,' he assured me. 'How did you know about it?'

'Everyone knows.'

'It's not the fifteen minutes of fame I've really been hoping for but, hey, can't complain really.'

He was weird. Yes. But I couldn't help but find him kind of brilliant.

'I'm probably going to try my best not to shit my pants,' I reassured him.

'Good,' he nodded, 'I would not recommend it. It's severely wrong.'

He rambled on about a bunch more bollocks that I have to admit went completely over my head (the kid has only just started secondary school, whereas I'm almost leaving, and he uses words that I've never even heard before!). He jabbered about comic books, *Judge Dredd*, *2000 A.D.* and these live role plays that he goes to where everyone dresses up like Orcs and warriors and gets together to act out some little virtual battle or something. It makes no sense to me. I later divulged that I have set myself some goals to reach by the end of the day (I didn't tell him what they were), which excited him even more and somehow inspired him to talk even faster.

'I do the same thing!' he blurted with genuine excitement, as if he had just discovered that I was his long-lost brother. 'I set myself a bunch of goals every day and keep a diary of everything that I do. It's, like, you have to! Like, I really do try something new every day!'

'OK. Like what?'

'Like, today I've got to say "Conjuring dumplings fallidgery fladgery".'

'What?' I snorted.

'Yeah! But you've got to say it to a teacher, not just any random nobody, and you get bonus points if you can, like, blend it seamlessly into a conversation without anyone calling you on it. If you end up getting bollocked then it doesn't count. You should do it too! It's amazing!'

'How the hell am I supposed to say "Flangery dumplings—"'

'Conjuring dumplings fallidgery fladgery,' he corrected me.

'How the hell am I supposed to say "Conjuring dumplings fallidgery fladgery" to a teacher without them thinking I'm absolutely mental?' I queried.

'I dunno, like, if you're in an Art class and they're doing a critique on Richard Nobblyknees' painting and they're like, "Oh gosh, it's very of the Renaissance period, don't you think?" and then you say, "Oh my golly yes indeed, I find it vaginally reminiscent of conjuring dumplings fallidgery fladgery, in a post-demographic hinderneggle where pointillism met cubism in the face of the colour brown . . . and red", and they're like, "The reds! Yes, the reds, they're intensely oblique!" Like that. It's like . . . it's easy!'

'Yeah, maybe for a demented fruitloop. I'm sure you can get away with telling teachers that you dropped your flooglewotsit in Benny McTittypants' codswallop, but unfortunately people are kind of accustomed to the stuff coming out of my mouth as being vaguely on the right side of sane!'

'I see,' he said, looking hurt.

'What?' I said defensively.

'Ha!' he barked. 'You just did it!'

'Did what?'

'You just said "flooglewotsit in Benny McTittypants' codswallop" and managed to blend it into your sentence without me thinking anything of it!'

'OK. Yeah.'

'Welcome to today's challenge,' he said, with a smile and a handshake, like some obnoxious tour guide.

'Great, another challenge for the day. Just what I need.'

'Splendid,' he chirped.

And before I knew it he was gone, back to his lonely spot at the front of the bus. I think this kid may be some kind of genius. I also fear that his head may one day explode.

And that was it. We were at school. He didn't tell me his name and I didn't tell him mine, but he certainly helped pass the time and did a good job of distracting me from my impending doom.

As the bus approached school I was prepared to see a welcome party similar to the one I saw yesterday, only this time I was expecting Reaper to be there and for a fight to ensue immediately. My heart began to race, but still, I don't think it was fear, just adrenalin. The bus pulled in and, sure enough, there was a group of people waiting in the bus bay. I took a moment to enjoy being pain-free and in one piece – maybe for the last time.

Registration

I stepped off the bus and straight into the path of those who awaited my arrival. This was not the group of people I had been expecting and it was not the reception I was preparing myself for.

'Why did you come in?'

'Are you insane?'

'Come here!'

Juicy boobs squished me from every angle. After hugging me like they had just found out I was dying of some terminal illness, Eleanor and Em locked their arms into mine and walked me into school. They were worried about me! *Eleanor* was worried about me!

'I only just found out this morning!' said Eleanor, reprimanding me. 'Why didn't you tell me?'

'I dunno.' I shrugged, genuinely wondering what the answer to this question was. 'It didn't really come up, I suppose.'

'You shouldn't have come in,' said Em seriously.

I was glad that she wasn't holding any grudges against me but I couldn't honestly say it was mutual. It still annoyed me how certain she was that I'm a complete wuss.

'I'd be curled up in bed like a big gibbering wreck if it was me,' said Eleanor, doing her best to be cheery in a situation she clearly considered to be very grave indeed.

This is cool – if I do die today I really think these guys would properly sob at my funeral. That makes me feel good inside.

'I'm not going to spend my life hiding from bullies,' I told them gallantly. 'If he doesn't find me today then he'll just find me some other day when I'm not expecting it. At least this way I can be prepared.'

'Well, we'll stay with you all day,' said Eleanor in a way that, looking back on it, I can only describe as *flirty*! 'We'll protect you, won't we, Em?'

But Em was still not taking the optimistic approach to this.

'It doesn't matter if you're ready for him or not,' she said sternly, ignoring Eleanor's reassurances. 'He'll get you when you're not ready anyway, that's the way he is—'

'You mean a coward chicken-shit?' I asked, butting in.

'Yeah, exactly that.'

'Nice taste in men you have,' I said, unwisely reopening old wounds. She scowled at me for a second and I fully expected her to either blow up in my face or turn on her heels and walk away, but whatever anger was bubbling inside of her she swallowed back, refusing to sink to my level and making me feel thoroughly twattish.

'You need to tell someone,' she said.

'Like who? A teacher? What are they going to be able to do, supply me with a permanent bodyguard? Even if they manage to keep him off school property, which is practically impossible, then he'd just wait for me outside school.'

'But you have to do something, Jack, he's supposed to be really hard!' said Eleanor worriedly.

'Gee, talk about boosting morale.'

'Sorry,' she giggled. 'But seriously . . .'

'Yeah, seriously, this isn't funny,' warned Em. 'He could kill you, Jack.'

'Shit . . .' Eleanor quietly gasped, as if the reality of the situation suddenly hit her.

'He's not going to kill me,' I assured them in a frustrated sing-song voice.

Shit. He isn't going to kill me, is he? It only takes one good blow to the head to give someone permanent brain damage, but . . . bollocks. These two are making me nervous!

'Look,' I said as we stopped outside my form room, 'I'm going to be fine.'

'We're just worried about you, Jack,' said Eleanor warmly.

I looked back into those big glacial eyes and they drew me in. Our eyes locked for a moment then, instinctively, I went with the moment and gripped her supple fleshy waist in my copious hands. Her passionate gaze told me to continue. My pulse surged like a galloping stallion and I pulled her close. Her juicy lips fell open and I found my mouth melting into hers in a steaming eruption of reciprocated lust. Our bodies were pressed so tightly together that her heaving chest consumed my own racing heart and for one fleeting moment I felt as if our bodies were fused together as one orgasmic being.

'Are you OK, Jack?' said Eleanor, snapping me back to reality with a disappointing thud. 'You look like you're going to cry!'

'No, I'm not!' I laughed nervously. 'I was just thinking about something.'

'What?' asked Em.

'What?' I replied, confused and flustered.

'You were thinking about food again, weren't you?'

'Erm . . .'

What the hell was she talking about?

'I can tell by the way your tongue was wiggling!' she insisted.

Em usually seems like she knows exactly what I'm thinking nearly all the time, to the point where I begin to wonder whether she's using the Force to read my mind. However, I am pleased to say that at that particular moment she was a little wide of the mark.

'Once Jack fell asleep on the bus home and woke up doing this . . .' Em mimicked someone eating from a fork with their eyes closed.

'It's true,' I confirmed to Eleanor, 'I did.'

'No way!' She howled with laughter. 'That's fantastic. I *so* wish I could have seen that!'

'But no, I wasn't thinking about food just then,' I added.

Why did I say that? Now they're going to want to know what I really was *thinking and I'll have to make something else up!*

'Then what were you thinking about so energetically with your tongue?' asked Em, with a suspicious glint in her eye.

See! What did I tell you?

'Something slightly more serious,' I informed her, with the lofty gravitas of someone who has learned to live with the ever-haunting possibility that certain death could be lingering around every corner.

And at that moment my eyes picked the worst possible time to glance at Eleanor's baps. It was a lightning-fast lapse of self-control and I'm sure she didn't notice, but I get the feeling that Em did. In fact the way Em was staring at me gave me the impression that she had now accessed the day-dream vault in my brain and was in the process of replaying my *Eleanor Kissy Kiss* project. I stared back at her and did my best to look inside her mind.

You're using the Force on me, aren't you? my brain asked hers.

'You really do look like you're going to cry,' Em replied (with her mouth). 'Are you sure you're all right?'

'Yes!' I insisted. 'I'm not a complete quakebuttock, you know!'

Yes! (Quakebuttock is a new word I learned weeks ago and have been meaning to slip into conversation ever since.)

'All right, all right. Jesus. Come up the field later, OK?' ordered Em. 'It's the safest place.'

'OK.' I smiled like I was humouring my mum when she tells me to put my jacket on (which I hate) if I get too chilly (is it just me that still gets treated as if I'm seven years old?).

'Ten minutes?' said Em, checking her watch.

'What, now? I've got a lesson!'

'So have we, but this is important!'

'I know it is, but what good is skiving our lesson going to do? He's more likely to get me up the field than in the middle of a lesson, isn't he? Plus, if we all go up the field every time someone threatens to beat me up then we'll all fail our exams and grow up to be mumbling imbeciles.'

Em took a moment to consider this.

'OK,' she sighed, 'but straight after lessons, yes?'

'Definitely.'

'OK.' She leaned forward and pecked me on the cheek. Eleanor did likewise . . .

Holy shit. Stay calm! Four lips and four boobs all touching me at once!

David Cameron! Winston Churchill! Margaret Thatcher!

My two favourite girls ever were making a Jack sandwich and there was a very real danger of a frankfurter getting thrown into the filling (and I think Eleanor's a vegetarian).

1ˢᵗ Period
Art

I spent my entire Art lesson with my emergency MP3 player on (the £5 piece of crap I got two Christmases ago that only fits twenty-two songs on and has been used as a memory stick for the past twelve months, so now only has six songs left on it), and continued my painting of a Welsh seafront, with a wry smile permanently plastered across my lips.

Eleanor hugged me! She actually hugged me!

OK, so it wasn't a soft and sensual 'I love you' kind of hug and more of an 'I'm related to you and I think you're going to die'-type thing. But hey, a hug's a hug and any physical contact with the girl of my dreams is more than most people get, right? Hell, I bet most people don't even get to *meet* the girl of their dreams.

I also spent a large portion of the lesson mulling over that little fantasy that had played through my head . . .

What if I had *kissed her?*

If Em hadn't been there I might actually have done it, and I'm not sure she wouldn't have reciprocated. It may even have gone exactly as I'd imagined. It could have been my chance! I am a complete coward. I mean quakebuttock. No . . . in fact that's not quite true, I am only a semi-coward, because it seems I am brave enough to come to school and face the prospect of getting totally messed up by a strange psychopath, but I'm not quite brave enough to kiss a pretty girl. So I'm not a complete coward. I'm just a dick. A small, floppy, woman's dick.

First Break

Things between me and Eleanor, I mean Eleanor and I (is that right?), seemed to be going pretty good (or well) and school hadn't even officially started for the day! The first five minutes of my final school day of this story (and possibly my life) went better than I could possibly have planned.

Sympathy – it is probably the greatest accelerator of non-platonic bonding known to man (is non-platonic the right word? There must be a proper word for it but I can't think of it right now). I always thought that parents dying-in-horrific-accident was the ultimate sympathy situation for getting girls to swoon for you, but it seems that just the *threat* of getting beaten to death works just as well, with the added bonus of not actually having to lose a parent figure. It would be even better if the threat of being beaten to death wasn't quite so real. Damn! Why didn't I think of that before? Starting a fake rumour about getting hunted down is way better than slipping a fake pervy love letter in someone's bag. (I wonder what happened with that. I'd forgotten all about it until just now. Maybe she still hasn't found it.) You know, for all the attention and affection I could milk from this, a punch in the face or two might actually be worth it (just as long as it doesn't result in a slight case of death or brain damage or wonky nose for the rest of my life).

This was the best I had felt since I'd gotten myself into this situation. I stood in the Art room in a happy daze and painted blotches of colour on to my not very good seascape. I was feeling completely content with everything, except for one little regret that continued to nag and gnaw in the back of my head – *Why the hell didn't I go up the field with them?!* The opportunity to spend all day with Eleanor had been handed to me on a plate; she was prepared to skive her lessons just to be with me and I had turned her down! Two beautiful girls who were clearly in the mood for making Jack sandwiches had offered to spend the day up the field with me and I said no. What's wrong with me?

Em and Eleanor were already waiting for me when I came out of my lesson. They weren't fussing about me so much any more, which was kind of disappointing, but they did choose to link arms with me as we all walked up the field together in considerably high spirits. We sat ourselves down with Dwight and a couple of other nameless Metallers, and I began to worry, as I remembered that the field stays relatively empty until at least eleven a.m. If Reaper did decide to come and find me up here this morning, not only would I be out of sight from the school, but I would be almost unprotected in terms of Metaller numbers. However, the second my bum hit the grass, Dwight said something that relieved my concern.

'What's all this shit about some prick thinks he's gonna kick your ass?' he asked with angry concern. (I appreciated his consideration, but it *was* kind of annoying how he said 'ass' instead of 'arse' – he's not American! Or is this just a 'grass/grarse' pronunciation-divide-type thing?)

'Yeah, some dickhead called Reaper,' I told him fairly casually, but making sure to not hide my trepidation (I needed Dwight to know that I was in need of back-up).

'You heard of him?' I added.

'What kind of name is Reaper?' he asked in disgust.

Exactly the kind of name I bet you wish people called you, I thought, but obviously did not say out loud.

'A cock name,' I said instead.

'You're telling me!' he laughed. 'I wouldn't sweat it, mate, he sounds like a complete pussy.'

I wasn't entirely sure how to take this remark. Was he really trying to belittle Reaper and therefore boost my confidence, or was he merely implying that if I don't go through with this on my own then I am a double-complete-pussy? I think he must have seen the worry in my eyes because he smirked and added, 'I'll sort him out if he comes up here.'

But the well-practised and choreographed super-cool drag he then took from his cigarette told me exactly what he was actually trying to say. His squinting eyes, jutting jaw and distant gaze meant the same thing as when any other wankface does it – *I'm a slimy twat and I am going to steal your lady friends!*

The sonofabitch wasn't intending to protect me at all, he just wanted to act like a hero in front of Eleanor and Em.

'See?' said Eleanor. 'You've got me, Em *and* Dwight to look after you now!' and she put a hand on Dwight's shoulder.

'Cool,' I said (which of course translates as *GODDAMN BASTARD BOLLOCKS!*).

Once again they offered to skive their next lesson for me but, to my surprise, I declined again. Maybe it was because I was pissed off that Dwight was clearly now the alpha male in Eleanor's eyes, or maybe it was because my next lesson was English, but I no longer felt like staying up the field. We arranged to meet back up there at lunch and I headed off to my lesson on my own. I didn't know if they were going to their lessons or not, but I had a sneaking suspicion they were going to stay up the field with Dwight, whilst he perfected even more examples of 'How to get girls and influence them' (all things I could do myself if I could stoop to being that sleazy).

2nd Period
English

'All right?' asked Cole as he waited for me outside the English room.

'All right,' I replied apprehensively.

I stopped in front of him and waited to follow him into the classroom, but he didn't move. He just stood there looking kind of ill.

'Look,' he said, unable to meet my eyes, 'maybe we should just go Xbox.'

Despite what it sounds like, 'Go Xbox' isn't actually homo-jive-talk for 'Go have bum sex'. It actually means we go back to Cole's house and play video games for the rest of the day.

'What, now?' I asked.

'Yeah.'

What the hell was going on here?

'Why, you got Reaper waiting outside for me or something?' I asked.

'No!' he said with disdain. 'I just thought you might want to avoid getting your stupid brains kicked in.'

This was not said with concern and it made my blood boil.

'Yeah,' I agreed, 'I do – and maybe if your new friends weren't such a bunch of wankers I wouldn't have anything to worry about!'

'Well maybe you shouldn't have called him a pussy then!' he retorted.

Was he defending these arseholes? Was he actually saying that I deserved to get my head kicked in for joking about someone being a pussy?

'Maybe I shouldn't have called him a pussy!' I retorted. 'Calling him a pussy is letting him off lightly, because if he's such a cock-sucking arsehole that he wants to beat me up just for calling him a pussy, then calling him a pussy is almost complimentary! He's more than a pussy! He's a rancid dribbling cock stain on the shit-stinking rim of *your* pussy!' The words tumbled from my gob before I had time to think about whether it made any sense.

Cole finally looked me in the eyes.

'You calling *me* a pussy?' he asked, deadly serious.

'Yes. I am calling you a pussy. Are *you* going to beat me up now?' I asked, then instantly regretted doing so when I realised that he looked as if he were seriously considering it. My entire body tensed up as I prepared for the punch in the face that was inevitably going to follow.

'He's gonna fuck you up so bad,' he muttered as he stormed past me, shoving me hard against the block of lockers, before he barged through the fire doors and down the stairs.

All of a sudden I was scared again. I had a horrible feeling that Cole would now do everything in his power to help Reaper hunt me down. I decided to seek refuge in the English room, but just as I began to open the door I saw who was sat at the teacher's desk. Connie. The sight of her actually made me jump back in shocked disgust, like someone who was about to take a bite of a sandwich only to find a slug hanging on to a piece of lettuce.

'What the . . . ?!'

Connie was supposed to be covering Dave's *Lit* class – not this one! Not *English*!

'Sod this.'

Connie turned to see who was lingering outside the door and I bolted aside to avoid being seen. Unfortunately that did not quite go as planned. Getting shoved into the lockers had caused my bag to get hooked up on one of the catches, so when I tried to scoot away from the doorway I did in fact go absolutely nowhere. Connie looked me straight in the eyes and our gazes locked. The little hamster that powered the treadmill in my brain was close to having a heart attack as I frantically tried to decide whether to free my bag, enter the room and endure what would undoubtedly be eighty minutes of pure torturous boredom, or whether I should make a run for it and face the consequences another day.

This may be the final eighty minutes of my life.

The decision was simple. I made a dash for it in the opposite direction to my previous attempt, so that my bag would unhook itself – but still my bag did not budge. It wasn't just caught up on a locker – it was caught up *in* a locker. The impact of me hitting the lockers had caused one of the doors to dent inwards and by sheer crap luck one of the buckles on my bag straps had managed to punch through the tiny opening that this dent had created and anchor itself there. I was firmly glued to the spot. I quickly slipped my arms free of the bag straps and gave my backpack one almighty tug. The lockers rocked back and forth ominously, but the bag remained trapped. Closer inspection revealed that the plastic buckle had actually cracked inside the locker. One more tug and it should snap, setting me free. I adopted a power stance and pulled with all my might. It worked! The buckle snapped off inside the locker and my bag swung free. It was not all good news though. A wave of terror sloshed over me as I watched the huge bank of lockers slowly begin to topple forwards. It was as if it were happening in slow motion, like a massive tree falling in a forest. I desperately threw myself against the towering block of metal in an attempt to push the lockers back, but it was too heavy. At that moment the door to the English room opened and Connie stepped out into the hallway.

'What in god's name is going on?' she barked, under-standably shocked at the sight of puny little me being swallowed whole by the giant metal beast.

'My bag got trapped!' I grunted. 'And I . . . Help!'

With my feet wedged against the opposing wall I had somehow managed to keep the lockers at a forty-five-degree angle, but they were too heavy to push back up and were slowly compressing me one inch at a time. If I let them go they would crash straight into my legs. Then came the hor-rific sound of a rolling drinks can . . . not any rolling drinks can, mind, this had the unmistakable glug and splosh sound of a *half full* rolling drinks can, and it was rolling off the top of the lockers straight towards my head.

There was nothing I could do. I had no free hand to bat it away and I was unable to move even an inch to the side. I watched as the can gambolled towards the edge of the locker-top and I braced myself for cold, wet, sticky impact. The can did not drop though. It jarred against the rim of the locker-top and stopped dead. The brown liquid inside it did not. It gushed out through the spout and leapt at my face like a big wet alien. I twisted my head back and . . . amazingly the damage was minor! I got a little splash on my chin but that was it. I checked my T-shirt – clear! Bad luck, good luck, bad luck, good luck – was this pattern going to stick with me for the rest of my life? Aside from the fact that my arms were trembling and I was in very real danger of getting more than a little crushed, this wasn't actually as bad a situation as it could have been. Until . . .

'Help!' echoed Connie, calling into the classroom rather than assisting me herself.

I heard the entire class jump to their feet and rush to the doorway to see me quivering beneath a wall of lockers with a puddle of not entirely un-piss-coloured liquid around my feet. A chorus of gasps and giggles erupted, rather predictably. As if it was not humiliating enough, I then had to swallow my final drop of pride as who should come rushing to my aid but Zack!

'It's too heavy,' I tried to explain to him, 'we'll need more people.'

But we didn't need more people at all, because, with what

seemed like very little effort, Zack propped the massive bank of lockers back against the wall with a loud SLAM!

'Thank you, Zack!' applauded Connie, patting him on the back as he heroically returned to the classroom with the rest of the cretins.

'Thanks, Zack,' I chipped in, panting for breath.

'Now what happened, Jack, are you OK?'

Yes, I was OK. I was shaken up, humiliated and exhausted, but I was OK.

'My arm . . .' I groaned, thinking fast.

My response was born from an attempt to save face – there was no way Zack could possibly be that much stronger than me unless I had seriously damaged my arm! I gripped my wrist and doubled over slightly. I felt like a five-year-old. But the ploy paid off in more ways than one.

'Right,' said Connie, trying to get to grips with the situation, 'will you be able to get yourself down to the medical room whilst I settle the class down?'

'Yes,' I replied, a tad too hastily.

'OK then, darling, off you go. I'll be down in five minutes, all right?'

'OK.'

And I was off. I felt bad that she was being so nice to me. She called me 'darling'! That was kind of weird, wasn't it? It felt wrong. I'm sure she calls me darling all the time in Theatre class, but it sounded different now, like she was my mum or something. My conscience suddenly went into overdrive and I pictured her rushing down to the nurses' room and being overcome with worry when she found it empty. I decided to do the right thing. I dashed to the nurses' room (which was empty, by the way – it always is) and left a note on the door – *Connie, taken Jack to A&E just to be sure* and signed it with a flourishing nonsense scribble-signature. There, my conscience was now clear. One lie to rectify another – see, two wrongs *do* make a right!

2nd Period
Not English

The hallways were empty and I was in serious danger of being caught out of lesson by a hawk-eyed, hall-patrolling teacher. I headed for the field as fast as I could, making sure to take a route that would not lead me directly into Connie's path. I was hoping that Metallers' Corner wasn't as deserted as the school hallways had been.

Unfortunately the field was not deserted enough. Just as I rounded the corner of the Arts building and came on to the field I noticed three people sat on the edge of the long-jump sandpit. They turned and saw me before I had a chance to quietly back away. Bollocks! It was Cole, Tim and Tampon and they were positioned directly halfway between myself and Metallers' Corner. I continued walking despite the burning urge to turn back. There was no way I was going to give them the satisfaction of seeing me scared, which is exactly what I was – scared shitless – especially as they now knew exactly where I was, for when Reaper wanted to find me.

'Yoohoo!' whooped Tampon, waving enthusiastically at me from the sandpit. I ignored him and continued on my path straight towards them. This was going to be torture. As if sensing my discomfort, Tampon jumped to his feet and did his best to make it worse.

'YEEE-HAAAAA!' he shrieked as he came charging towards me, trying to look as much like a lunatic as possible, with his arms helicoptering all around him. I could hear Tim chuckling obediently and Cole laughing heartily. A hot rage began to stoke inside of me, as if a dormant anger had somehow been ignited by the sound of Cole's laughter. Tampon was running straight towards me and I knew that he was wanting me to react in some way – tell him to piss off, walk in a different direction to avoid him, punch him – but I did nothing except continue in a straight line and stare at the little twat with complete indifference. Unfortunately this did nothing to diminish his enthusiasm for taunting me and he continued to do so whilst running alongside, pushing his face as close to mine as possible. Even though my hands were shaking with a mixture of fear and rage, and even though it was the last thing on earth I felt like doing, I forced a wry smile. It was a smile that hinted I knew something Tampon didn't, something that made me not give a crap, something that gave me the balls to smile like this – an Indiana Jones smile. A screw-you smile.

I'm not sure what exact effect this had inside Tampon's head, but it appeared to both scare and enrage him at once. He stopped his stupid dance and pulled away, but his big twatting grin was still plastered across his merkin face. I don't know what a merkin is or if it is even a word, but it describes Tampon perfectly – the merkin-faced wanker.

'Funny, isn't it?' he urged. 'Funny! Yeah? Yeah? Yeah!

HA!' He turned to Cole. 'He's laughing!' Then back to me: 'What you laughing at, pissy pants?' Then to Cole. 'He's pissed his little pants! HA! Look!'

He stopped and pointed, then doubled over in manic hysteria.

'You pissed your pants, you pissy-pants bitch!' he howled.

I was desperately trying not to fall for this, but he sounded so sincere I couldn't stop myself from slyly checking my jeans . . .

'You pissed yourself!!!' he repeated.

And, sure enough, there on my crotch was a big wet stain. 'PISS! PISS! PISS! You pussy!'

It appeared I hadn't been as lucky as I thought at avoiding the cascading drinks can after all. How had I not noticed? My entire English class must have seen this! And, in fairness to Tampon, it did look very much like piss.

'You pissed your pants!' he roared, right up in my face.

I stopped walking and so did he. The two of us stared at each other, inches apart. Silence boomed all around us until I finally spoke.

'Yes, I did.'

And I was off again, closely aped by the Tampon tit.

'Are they brown yet? Have you browned your little pantyhose? Yeah? Yeah? Yeah?'

(I decided this was a rhetorical question and chose not to answer.)

'I think he's scared,' he said to Cole as I walked past the long-jump sandpit. Cole tried hard to hide his laughter, turning his grinning mouth down at the ends and facing away. Tim, on the other hand, was positively revelling in the excitement, rocking back and forth in fits of giggles. Somehow it was Tim's reaction that really got to me the most – what had I ever done to him?

Tampon finally decided to quit harassing me and jumped into the sand instead.

'I'll let Reaper know where you're hiding – up the field, round the corner with all The Metallers that are too chicken-shit to protect you. Right. OK. Bye! Bye, pissy-pants pussy! Bye!'

I only hoped that The Metallers round the corner had heard Tampon and were now enraged enough to prove him wrong. Holding my bag strategically in front of my sticky crotch, I sauntered round the corner and was pleased to see a fairly large gang of black-clad, greasy-haired devil wor-shippers. They had music playing pretty loud, so I guess they hadn't heard any of Tampon's ranting, but that didn't really bother me. There were enough of them up here to intimidate a small army, let alone one person. I sat myself down, pulled out my notebook and, once my hands had stopped shaking, I began writing and didn't stop for a break until right about now.

2nd Period
Not English (but English)

Someone somewhere behind me had the hiccups. Hic-cups. That is the right spelling, isn't it? I've read books where it's spelled 'hiccoughs', which is stupid. Who calls them hiccoughs? No one! It's a hiccup! Is 'hiccough' pronounced 'hic-coff', or is it just a stupid way of spelling hiccup? Maybe somewhere in the world people do call them hic-coughs (probably posh people). Anyway, I was desperate to divulge my very own foolproof cure for hiccups and I needed a way to shoehorn my discovery into their conversation, so I began with . . .

'Do you call them hiccups or hic-coffs?' I turned round and bravely asked a random bunch of Metallers, who I only half knew.

'What the fu-*hic*-uck? Who the hell calls them hic-coffs?' replied the actually-quite-pretty hiccupping Year 10 girl with red and purple streaks in her hair and a stud in her nose.

'I don't know!' I replied defensively. 'That's why I was asking. I've seen it spelled in books as hic-coff.'

And there goes my 'only posh people call them hic-coughs' theory, because I know for a fact that this girl, Marina, I think her name is, is one of those common breeds of Metallers who comes from an extremely well-to-do family and only dresses like this as some lame form of teenage rebellion. She looks odd because she wears all of this scruffy crap, but it's all immaculate and extremely expensive scruffy crap. (Apparently, according to Em, her big black biker boots cost over £200 and her belt was £105 – that's more than I have spent on clothes in my entire life!)

'Do *you* call them hic-coffs?' she asked me, with a poorly hidden *hic* thrown in at the end.

'No.'

'Do you?' she asked the blond guy sat next to her, again followed by a *hic!*

'Nope,' he replied.

'No one calls them hic-coffs. It's bullshit,' she concluded.

Wow. I'm glad we cleared that up. She may be pretty, but she's got one hell of an attitude problem (probably *because* she's pretty . . . and rich).

'I think it's spelled like hic-coff but it's still pronounced hic-cup,' added another guy sat in their little huddle, who, though I hate to say it, does look like the kind of person who has an answer for everything (thick lenses in his specs, styleless mop of hair, vacant expression, serious acne – this does make me a Nazi, doesn't it?). He looks like he should wear a tank-top and an anorak and carry a thermos flask around with him, except he seems to have had a slight run-in with Satan – his thick black hair is almost down to his shoulders, he wears ripped black Slipknot T-shirts, and instead of a flask he has a Fender Strat guitar.

A posh rich bitch and a chess club nerd – if The Bezzers ever took the time to get to know any of these 'animals' up at Metallers' Corner they would probably die laughing.

'That's what I was wondering,' I said to the Geek of Darkness, 'but you can never tell, really, can you – I mean, the amount of different pronunciations for different words.'

And I turned back to my notebook to continue scribbling away.

'Like what?' said the Rich Hiccupping Bitch.

I turned round to check that she wasn't talking to me.

'Huh? You talking to me?' I asked, since she was staring straight at me.

'Ye-essssssss,' she sang, with a quaver of impatience (it was either a quaver or a hiccup, I can't be sure).

I took this to mean that she *was* talking to me.

'Sorry, what?' I asked.

'I said, like what?' she repeated, being purposely vague.

'Like what, what?' I puzzled.

'Jesus Christ . . .' She sighed impatiently, as if she were having to explain herself to an idiot for the fifteenth time. 'You said something about different pronunciations for different words, right?' She cocked her head and raised her eyebrows.

She was beginning to piss me off.

'Right,' I confirmed.

'And I said, "Like what?" . . . *hic!*'

'Oh. Right,' I muttered unenthusiastically. I would have

liked to have bitten back with an *If you'd made yourself clear in the first place!* argument, but unfortunately her near-perfect face and razor-sharp attitude were just too intimidating for me to cope with, so I held my tongue . . . well, sort of.

'Rich Hiccupping Bitch!' I muttered to a side camera somewhere.

'What did you just say?' she asked, genuinely looking as if she couldn't believe her own ears.

'Scone and scon?' I said hopefully, crossing the imaginary fingers in my brain.

She stared blankly at me. Was she going to buy it? Of course not. *Scone and scon* doesn't sound anything like *Rich Hiccupping Bitch!* The ever-deepening frown lines above her nose were early warning that she was not buying it. Her jaw began to jut forward and her face reddened. I could sense an imminent attack. I had to act fast. I did the only thing I could do, the only thing any sane person would do – I pretended to suffer from a very severe nervous twitch.

'Chuckeh-pe-behhh!' I grunted loudly through my nose.

I am undoubtedly a genius. It was surely a noise that, to the untrained ear, could easily be mistaken for the words 'Rich Hiccupping Bitch!' There was no way she would question me now. Nervous twitches, like all disabilities, must always go pretend-unnoticed.

Of course there was one thing about Rich Hiccupping Bitch that I had not taken into full consideration – she was a bitch.

'What the hell was that?!' she snarled in disgust.

I stared at her blankly. I didn't have a clue how to respond. Should I keep up the twitchy pretence? Should I be offended? Should I ignore it?

'And *sked-ule* or *shed-ule*?' I said, hoping to throw her off.

'*Sked-ule*, definitely,' her two friends chipped in, eager to draw the focus from my unfortunate affliction.

'But *scone*?' said the blond guy. 'Only snobs say *scone*!'

'No, they don't!' retorted the Rich Hiccupping Bitch. '*I* say *scone*!' (Which proved his point perfectly.) '*Scon* is way posher! And wrong!'

Internally I had to agree with the Bitch, I too say *scone*, but I was unwilling to publicly take sides with her.

Words That I Am Uncomfortable Saying
3.   **Scone (makes me feel posh)**
2.   **Scissors (makes me feel like I have a bad lisp)**
1.   **Excuse me (makes me look stupid in a mime)**

'There's no comparison!' insisted Blond Guy.

'OK, how do you pronounce this,' said the Bitch, scribbling something on her hand with a biro. She raised her hand to reveal the word: 'Bone'.

'It's a completely different word!' scoffed Blondie.

'How do you say it?' she insisted.

'It's a completely different word!'

'How do you say it?'

'Bone – but it's a compl—'

'Oh! Oh! Oh! Booeewwwwwwn?'

'It doesn't mean jack-shit!'

'And this?' She scribbled something else then revealed the word.

'Lone!' said Blondie. 'But—'

'Not "lon", then?' she asked. 'Or what about this?'

Once again she raised her hand to show the word 'Cone'. More and more people were drifting our way to take part in the debate. A dozen people were now all throwing their opinions about.

'Cone, but your argument doesn't make any sense!' spat Blondie.

'So how come if you put an S in front of cone it all of a sudden becomes *scon*? *That* doesn't make any sense!' exclaimed Rich Bitch, now having to shout to be heard above the jeering audience.

'What about this though?' said the Geek of Darkness, raising his own hand to show the word 'Gone'.

Rich Bitch was stumped.

A clear majority of angry spectators were leaning towards *scon* as being the correct pronunciation, and I did not have the courage or inclination to side with a bitch who was as rich and hiccuppy as the Rich Hiccupping Bitch. And I was definitely not going to share my 100%-guaranteed cure for hiccups with her either, so I slowly edged away from the fray, re-entered my notebook and once again became a non-person with no opinion.

Everyone else was now so caught up in the pointless debate that they did not notice the most unusual occurrence that was taking place at the bend of the field.

Something seriously bad is about to happen.

2nd Period
Visitors

There, where the fence makes a very definite forty-five-degree turn to the right, where it is generally considered that the field officially becomes Metaller territory, are three people very much out of their element . . . Cole, Tim and Tampon are heading this way.

Skaters do not mix with Metallers. They don't generally mix with Bezzers either, they are their own breed. Most importantly, Skaters do not come up the field. Tampon does not come up the field.

Why is he here?!

My heart is beginning to pound and all I can imagine is that they are coming to tell me that Reaper is here for me, and then he too will soon appear around that corner. None of them are looking at me. My paranoia hits the turbo-boost and my adrenalin kicks into overdrive. Just as I convince myself that this is the end I realise that Cole and Tampon are actually keeping a fairly wide berth from all The Metallers, and Tim is even further afield. It appears that they're walking right past and are heading for the far corner. This only alleviates my worry by a fraction – as long as they're up here then things are not good. What the hell are they up to? Are they here to keep an eye on me? Or maybe they're . . . holy crap . . . what the hell is that noise? It sounds like a hundred people heading this way! How many people has Reaper brought with him? I'm dead. I am absolutely dead. Dead shitting meat.

Everyone up here has fallen deadly quiet as they listen to the approaching herd of heavy footsteps and garbled talking.

'Pussy Fencers!' Dwight calls after the Year 8s that have just scarpered over the fence and away from the approaching onslaught.

'Shhhhh!' someone hisses at Dwight, 'Who the hell is it?'

'Who gives a shit!' says Dwight, lighting up a cigarette just for added rebel status.

'Art class,' mutters someone else. 'They came up last week, looking for twigs and shit to draw.'

Annnnnd . . . breathe.

It's amazing how that one sentence, uttered by someone who I don't even know, has managed to save me from the brink of a heart attack. My pulse begins to slow, my lungs re-engage and the blazing sweat that's been erupting from every pore in my body ebbs away.

Art class still isn't ideal though – it means teachers, and teachers plus skiving up the field equals suspension or detention. I have to admit, jumping over that fence is beginning to seem increasingly appealing. Unfortunately I can't bring myself to do it. I don't even have the guts to be a quakebuttock.

Hang on . . .

There's something wrong about the sound of this class.

Something very wrong . . .

'That's no Art class,' I mutter.

'Why?' asks one of Dwight's no-name friends.

'Because . . . that's why.'

I was about to say 'Because I don't hear any girls', but I didn't have to. The Art class, who clearly were nothing of the sort, were now here. A chorus of whispered *Shit*s and *Fuck*s bounced around The Metallers as they watched the large group of thugs emerge around the corner.

Shit and, indeed, fuck.

This does not look good.

This looks like trouble.

Serious. Shitting. Trouble.

2nd Period
Visitors – Bad

Bezzers . . . lots of Bezzers. Probably about twenty or more.
They stopped on the corner and made a strange formation in
which they tried to look casual whilst clearly discussing
something that had them all on edge. They repeatedly
glanced over towards us whilst they planned whatever it was
they were up there to do. What *were* they up there to do?
Were they friends with Reaper? Had Tim and Cole led them
up there to me? Was Reaper with them? Was he huddled
somewhere in amongst them all? Not wanting to stare, I nervously eyed them with occasional sideways glances. They
were definitely looking my way. They were making shifty
and obvious observations of something in my general direction. Everything in my stomach seemed to digest at
super-speed and drop straight down into my bowels. I could
feel hot, horrific diarrhoea bubbling up inside me. I couldn't
take it. I had to know who they were looking at. I bit the
bullet and took a full-on look in their direction.

Shit! One of them looked directly at me! But . . . hang
on . . . he *nodded* at me. A nod! A nod from one of these

guys is like getting a hug from an angry policeman. A nod is as close as The Bezzers can get to being affectionate. For an outsider to receive a nod from a Bezzer is like receiving a knighthood from the Queen, it's like being given immunity from the cops, it's like being a Made Man, like in *Goodfellas* (only I hope not in the same way as Joe Pesci). I got a nod. I am safe. I am untouchable.

The hot soup in my bowels began to cool and thicken into a soft pâté. They were not there for me. Closer inspection of their gazes proved this point. They were definitely not checking out anything in my immediate vicinity. They were looking beyond me. More of them caught my eye and they too acknowledged me with a nod, even the ones that hate me did! I didn't get it. Why pretend to like me all of a sudden? It seemed like maybe they were actually nervous about something.

The fearful mutterings of The Metallers was giving way to proper conversations and they started pretending that The Bezzers were no more bother than a few pesky flies, but no one really took their eyes off them and no one really stopped talking about them.

'What they doing here, Jack?' asked Dwight.

'Dunno.' I shrugged, wide-eyed.

'They're your buddies, aren't they?'

'Not really, no.'

They weren't my buddies, but I understood what had to happen. What with me being the only one sat on the fence between the two gangs, the only one receiving genial nods from The Bezzers, it was expected of me to now be the go-between guy. My cowardly eagerness to please everyone, to not fully pick one side, had now gotten me right in the thick of it. I could now feel the pressure of all The Metallers waiting for me to go and talk to The Bezzers. If I was hoping for The Metallers to stand with me against Reaper then I was going to have to do this for them. Before I knew it I was getting to my feet, doing my best impersonation of a calm person as I strolled towards The Bezzers.

What the hell am I doing?

Bezzer heads turned my way and all eyes watched cautiously, like a pack of lions that have noticed a stranger entering their territory. Sweat began to gather rapidly under my arms. I was horribly aware that not only were all Bezzer eyes watching me but all Metaller eyes were too. I had to force my legs to move because it seemed like they'd forgotten how to do it by themselves. Every joint in my body began to protest and I had to fight to stop them from locking. I fear I may have ever-so-slightly resembled C-3PO.

'All right, Jack,' Ed quietly said with a smile and a nod as he departed his gang and walked out to meet me halfway. It was like we were generals of opposing armies meeting for negotiations on a battlefield (except this 'halfway' conveniently happened to be about twenty feet from my guys and only three feet from his).

'All right, Ed,' I replied. 'What's going on?' I made sure I added a tone of excitement to my voice to disguise my trepidation.

'We're gonna batter that little Tampon freak,' Ed admitted with a cheeky smirk.

Oh, thank Christ. Again, my chicken-shit engine shifted down a gear and my bottom felt a whole lot less quakey.

'Cool!' I managed to force a laugh.

Ed and a couple of his friends laughed with me, except their nerves caused them to laugh a little harder than seemed normal.

'He 'ates the little prick as much as we do!' laughed some little pig-faced twat.

'You haven't got a problem with that, have you?' asked Ed, as if genuinely asking my permission.

'Do what you like with him, I couldn't care less,' I said, finding their gangster-like bravado rubbing off on me. 'What did he do?'

'Got his bum-chum to beat up Kev's little brother,' Ed said, now turning suddenly serious.

A flash of pure evil seemed to flicker across Ed's eyes. It was a fleeting glimpse of excited rage and, for the first time ever, I saw a part of him that I had heard of but never believed could really be true – he was a bloodthirsty maniac. He's always seemed almost completely normal to me, but I can see now that Ed probably isn't too different from Reaper – the thought of beating people up excites him.

'Shit,' I said, suddenly even more serious than Ed as I realised that the 'bum-chum' he was referring to must be Reaper, which meant . . . *Reaper is here and he's already found his first victim. I'll be next.*

'When?' I asked, hoping that maybe this all happened a few days ago rather than minutes ago.

'Just now, like, twenty minutes ago,' Ed said, looking extremely grave, 'put him in hospital.'

Oh shit. He put him in *hospital*? Suddenly, any hope that Reaper might not be so rough completely evaporated.

Reaper is here, in school, and he's come to beat two people up. One of them is ME and the other is now in HOSPITAL!

Crap. I could feel that soup beginning to heat up again.

My only hope now was that these guys did a job on Tampon, causing Reaper to choose to hunt *them* down instead of me. Surely beating up Reaper's 'bum-chum' supersedes calling him a 'pussy'? Or is personal pride more important to defend than a friend's face? I really cannot claim to be up-to-date with what requires bloodthirsty retaliation these days. Reaper beat up Kev's little brother because Kev's little brother beat up Reaper's little brother (or did he spit on his sister? I can't remember). Beating up people's little brothers must be one of the most common instigators of warfare. Whoever said that hairstyles are the cause of 99% of wars is an idiot. So why do I deserve to get beaten up? I've got sensible hair, I stay away from everyone's little brothers, and I'm not even religious! This whole thing is messed up! Ed must have seen concern in my eyes and tried to ease my worry.

'He's all right, though, just needs some stitches on his eye or something,' he reassured me.

'Oh, cool. That's good.'

Yeah, great! What do I care? I'm glad the little twat's in hospital! Kev's 'little' brother is six feet of pure shithead. He's started so many fights that it was only a matter of time before someone hit back.

'Well,' I shrugged, 'go for it, man.' (I wonder if I sounded as phoney as I felt.) 'I'm not going to stand in your way.' (As if that would stop them anyway.)

'Cheers, man,' said Ed, with an emotional pat of my shoulder that oozed testosterone and camaraderie.

'Good luck,' I added as I turned and walked back to The Metallers.

Good luck? *Good luck?!?* What the hell was that? Why was I wishing them good luck? They were two dozen guys come to beat up one single merkin-faced twat and I'm wishing them luck! They don't need luck and they certainly don't deserve it! I hope that no one else heard me say that because it is one of the stupidest things I have ever uttered.

Good luck my arse.

It's not that I like Tampon, I hate the little wanker, but what I hate more is that I just condoned what could potentially be his murder. Twenty to one!

As I made my way back towards The Metallers something amongst the trees caught my attention.

'Psssst. Jack!' came the extremely loud whisper.

What the hell was *he* doing here?

2nd Period
Badder

Tim was by himself, hiding behind the largest tree he could find.

I drifted towards him

'What you doing?' I asked, wondering why he was hiding behind a tree instead of hanging out with Cole and Tampon. (Of course when you put it like that it's entirely obvious what he was doing   I wish I too were brave enough to hide behind a tree.)

'Look at this!' he chuckled excitedly.

I wandered round to his side of the tree to see a large swollen notch in the tree's trunk.

'It looks like a fanny!' he giggled.

'Yes, Tim,' I agreed, although, having never seen a lady's special area before in my life, I wasn't entirely sure. I sincerely hope he is wrong.

'And look over there!' he said, pointing at another tree about twenty yards away. 'It looks just like a nob!'

'Mmmmm,' I mused, finding it hard to not at least smile at Tim's odd and ill-timed sense of humour. 'If you say so.'

I was actually kind of shocked that he even had the nerve to talk to me, seeing as not fifteen minutes ago he was having a good old laugh at my expense. But thinking about it, Tim isn't really someone who is able to grasp tricky concepts like loyalty, pride or friendship. He really just looks out for himself and doesn't quite realise that other people think less of him for it. He probably didn't consider that laughing at me whilst someone tried to humiliate me could be seen as rude, he was probably just laughing because the idea of someone pissing their pants made him laugh. He's kind of blissfully ignorant, and because of that fact he manages to get away with being a disloyal little coward – and we accept him and forgive him for it. It's something I really should consider taking up.

'Anyway, I'll see you later,' I told him.

I wasn't feeling much like forgiving him at that moment. He could sit this out by himself, like he deserved. There was no way I was going to hold his hand.

I sat myself down amongst The Metallers, who were also doing a good job of pretending not to care or be scared about what was happening.

'What the hell's going on?' whispered a plump girl whose make-up looked like it was applied by a blind dog with no nob (let's call her Lorraine).

'They're here for that Tampon guy,' I explained.

'All of them?' she asked in disgust.

'Dunno,' I shrugged, shaking my head with worried eyes.

'What are they going to do to him?'

'Dunno!'

'Christ's sake. I know he's a little prick, but all of them? That's out of order! That's bang out of order, man.'

'That's what I told them,' I lied (I've never said the phrase 'Bang out of order' in my life), 'but unless we want to start gang warfare there's not much we can do to stop them. I mean, he's not even one of us.'

Once again the words left a bad taste in the mouth. We can't protect someone from a severe battering because *he's not one of us*? *I'm* not even one of us!

But plump no-nob-dog-face-make-up girl (apparently we're not calling her Lorraine after all) didn't have time to reflect upon the shite that had gushed so hideously from my mouth, because The Bezzers were on the move. They had advanced from their post on the bend of the field and were sauntering towards us. Towards Tampon.

I say 'sauntered' but I suppose 'swaggered' would be a more appropriate word. Their shoulders swung like catwalk models', their arms hung unnaturally far away from their bodies as if they were carrying large tins of paint, and they all proceeded to spit in two-second intervals through their taut, scowling mouths (where do they get so much phlogm from, and how come none of it ends up on their chins?). The synchronisation was astounding. It was as if they had all attended the same 'How To Be a Wanker' finishing school. I couldn't help picturing them all hanging out in Ed's back garden, practising their bad-boy choreography in time to the *Grease* soundtrack, whilst Ed's mum kept them regularly topped up with cupcakes and lemonade.

Despite my imaginary comedy interlude, the prospective conflict sent my pounding heart up into my throat. Even though I knew they weren't coming for me I couldn't help shitting it. What for, though? For Tampon? Who cares? Then again, no one wants to be in a situation where there is a high potential that someone's skull might implode. You know that scene in *Platoon* with the butt of the rifle? It felt like I'd be watching that again for the first time, only slightly more real.

I've always been a bit of a wuss when it comes to conflicts – no matter how big or small, they always shit me up. But at least this time it didn't just seem to be me – everyone looked terrified. Especially Tampon. As I looked at his wide eyes it finally occurred to me what he and Cole were doing up the field. They weren't there to intimidate me or keep an eye on me, they were there for exactly the same reason as I was – protection. They had come up the field because they were scared and hoped that we might prevent Tampon getting torn to shreds, and here we are, in equal numbers to The Bezzers, just sitting around doing nothing to help, just watching.

'Oy!' Ed called out as he brought The Bezzers to a standstill just a few feet away from me, and about twenty yards away from Tampon.

Tampon ignored him and continued talking to Cole.

'Oy! You little fuckin' Tampon piece of shit!'

The entire gang of Bezzers burst into stupid hysterics.

'What?' replied Tampon, seemingly annoyed that they had interrupted him.

'Come over here!' called Ed, in a calm kind of way that implied his only intention was to have a nice little chat.

'No!'

Good answer! I seriously don't think I'd have thought to say no. It seemed that Ed hadn't considered that reply either – he looked kind of stumped. The gang didn't seem too sure of what they were supposed to do next. They mumbled anxiously amongst each other and I heard the words 'cheeky wanker' and 'kick his ass' before Ed cleared his throat and smiled. It appeared he had something clever to say, something more persuasive.

'Come here!' he repeated louder.

Nice tactic!

'What for?' came Cole's voice.

They want to tickle him with strawberries, you idiot!

'We just wanna talk to him,' replied Ed.

'About what?' asked Tampon

'You just got your boyfriend to beat up Gellar, didn't you?'

'No.'

He's on a roll!

Once again this answer stalled Ed for a moment.

'Then come over here and talk about it then.'

There was surely no arguing with such common sense reasoning!

'No.'

It gets them every time!

Ignoring the fact that I hate him, I was beginning to like the little wanker. But Ed wasn't so impressed.

I was beginning to wonder why *they* didn't just go to *him*, and it seemed Ed was thinking exactly the same thing. He turned to his gang of brightly clad Neanderthals, muttered something, then began leading them all towards Tampon at a leisurely march. They stopped and gently billowed around

him, like a large cloud enveloping a small hill. Through a
few gaps in their congregation I could see that Tampon had
not budged. He remained leaning back against a tree, one
arm resting across his knee. A handful of The Metallers got
to their feet, cautiously observing, like a bunch of badly
dressed meerkats. I couldn't be sure whether they were
rising in preparation to intervene or to run away.

Ed began talking but I couldn't hear a single word,
until . . .

'*So what's he doing putting a little kid in hospital?*' he
roared at the top of his voice.

So that was it. Ed would be able to justify anything he did
to Tampon just as long as he remembered that Tampon was
responsible for a 'little kid' being put in hospital. He was
obviously glossing over the fact that the 'little kid' in question was actually the same age as Tampon, twice the size
and probably responsible for putting a dozen real little kids
in hospital himself. But, no matter how immoral I found this
whole load of shite, I couldn't help thinking that Tampon
probably had this coming. After all, I myself may get beaten
to death today thanks to him.

'What the fuck did you say?!' shouted Ed.

This was going to be the start of it.

'WHAT THE FUCK – DID YOU SAY?!!'

And then it began.

2nd Period
Baddest

Ed spat in Tampon's face and, as Tampon's hand went up to deflect it, in came Ed's boot. That first sudden kick was the signal for everyone else to join in. And join in they did. Every single Bezzer dashed forward and kicked like mad. My view of Tampon was now completely blocked, but I didn't have to see it to know how bad it was. The impact of twenty foot kicking a body resonates through the ground like the rumble of an earthquake. I could feel the vibrations of it in my chest. It was like listening to a stampede. I swallowed back a throatful of sick.

The Metallers and I all seemed to utter the same gasp of disgusted horror at what we were seeing – *fucking hell*. Yet none of us moved. We all stayed glued to the spot, paralysed with either fear or shock – probably both. I can't imagine anyone wanting to mess with The Bezzers in their current state. They were beating away with such horrific ferocity that they were having to hold on to each other for support, like rugby players in a scrum. They kicked and they kicked and they kicked.

They'll stop now.

But they didn't stop.

I have to do something. Someone *has to do something!*

But still no one was moving.

They'll definitely stop now. If they don't then I've got to do something.

But they still didn't stop and I still didn't move.

It had probably been about ten seconds since the kicking began, but each of those ten seconds contained a dozen vicious kicks and every one of those kicks seemed to last ten seconds each. I didn't want to imagine the damage they must be doing to him.

I've got to stop them. They'll stop soon though, won't they? They won't actually kill him, will they? Christ, this is fucking horrible!

I suddenly realised that I too was on my feet. I don't even remember standing up. I took a step forward, preparing myself to put a stop to it. But what was I going to do? How could I stop all of them? They would probably turn on me, right?

To my relief some of them stopped kicking. A few of them paused, stepped back slightly, then . . .

Oh fucking Jesus . . .

They were actually stamping on the guy. STAMPING ON HIM! With all their might!

FUCK!

They weren't going to stop.

I took another step forward, I couldn't just stand by and let this continue. I had to do something. My conscience was screaming at me to help. Christ. This was it, I was actually going to say something . . .

'THAT'LL FUCKING DO!'

And that was all it took. Just three words shouted at The Bezzers and they stopped. I think maybe they, too, were somewhat disgusted by what they had done. I think they were waiting for someone to stop them. *Hoping* that someone would stop them, because none of them wanted to kill him, but none wanted to be the first to back down either.

I hope they felt sick inside for what they had done. I hope they felt as sick as I did – but I don't think they did. I don't think anyone did. They are all who they are and maybe nothing can change that, but I am me, I'm supposed to be a good guy, I'm supposed to be the hero of this story and I will never forgive myself for letting that carry on for as long as it did. But what makes me sick most of all, what is still making me feel sick just thinking about it, sending chills down my spine even now, is that, although I was the only person up there who was on speaking terms with The Bezzers, those three words that finally put a heroic stop to the hideous barbarism were not spoken by me. Nor were they spoken by Dwight. Nor Cole. In the end, the only person who had the guts and morals to stand up to these guys was the four-eyed chess-team Geek of Darkness.

I hate myself for that.

Lunch Break

Jesus Christ and all the little orphans, it HURT! The side of my head felt like it should be swollen to the size of a tennis ball and gushing with blood, but, to my surprise, as I touched it, it didn't feel any different to normal. So that's what getting punched feels like. Well, that's what getting punched with an arm bone feels like. It didn't knock me over or out, which is a good thing, but then again my attacker had just been beaten to within an inch of his life. Still, I could quite happily go the rest of my life without going through anything like that again. Unfortunately that is probably unlikely. I am not looking forward to the sequel.

I wrote down everything that had just happened whilst I waited outside James' German class. When he came out he was suitably sympathetic/enraged when I told him my news.

'What an absolute tit! Why did he hit you?!'

'Because he's a twat-faced wanker!'

'What did you do though?'

'Nothing! We were just checking he was all right and he was screaming at The Bezzers to come back and finish him off and I told him to shut up, but so did everyone else, and he just totally lost it. I mean *totally* lost it. He was crying and bleeding and shaking and screaming, and everyone was trying to hold him back, but he was, like, twisting and squirming all over the place, like my cat when we try to get him in the box to take him to the vet's, and he half broke free and just leapt at me!' I explained at a hundred miles an hour, still shaken up.

'And he hit you?'

'Yeah! He tried! I started to duck, so he half missed, but . . . half didn't,' I said, pointing to the painful part of my head, 'and The Metallers all pinned him to the ground and were like, *Just leave, all right? You're making it worse!* so I just left and now I'm here.' I was still sporadically checking my head to make sure I didn't resemble the Elephant Man. 'I don't look swollen or red or anything, do I?'

James inspected the side of my head at a distance.

'No, not really. It's probably going to bruise like a bastard though.'

'What?'

'Well, your cheekbone looks a bit pink and the side of your head's a bit swollen, but you can't really see anything, it's all under your hair,' he added reassuringly.

'You sure?'

'Yeah! I mean, I can barely see anything and I'm looking right at it.'

'Cool. Thanks,' I said with relief. If I was going to have any chance with Eleanor today then I'd be much better off if I didn't look like I was growing a baboon's bum on the side of my face.

We headed down to the canteen and James treated me to

a cone of chips. It reminded me of being a kid, when I'd fall over and graze my knee and my mum would give me a sweetie to cheer me up. It was good to have someone to talk to because it drew my attention away from the tight throbbing above my ear. I seriously needed to grow a pair of balls and fast. Tampon had just been kicked half to death by an entire platoon of vicious Bezzers and he was feeling good enough afterwards to have a stab at me, whereas I, on the other hand, had just been on the receiving end of his half-arsed swing and was now struggling to even function. Come to think of it, it was probably the actual ordeal that had me shaken up more than the physical pain. Yeah, the pain wasn't really all that bad. It was about as painful as being hit in the head with a ball or something. In fact I've probably sustained far more serious injuries just messing around with a swing-ball tennis set and thought nothing of it. I suppose it was the fact that this pain was inflicted upon me by someone else, on purpose, with the intention of hurting me as much as possible, that made it seem much worse.

As we scouted around the canteen, looking for an empty table, I saw something that instantly made me forget about any petty aches and pains. This was far worse. Eleanor was sat at a table at the far end of the canteen, but it wasn't Em sat with her – it was Zack. They were giggling heartily about something and my paranoia decided that the *something* was me. This was terrible. As I watched the two of them having fun together, Eleanor did something horrific – she *laughed*! Not just any laugh though, this was the biggest laugh I have ever heard from her. It was possibly the greatest, most heart-melting guffaw that she has ever laughed in her life, and it was Zack that had evoked it. She threw her head back, stamped her foot and clapped her hands over Zack's. She was *holding his hands*!

James had clearly noticed this too and he turned to look at me as if we had just witnessed my cat being run over.

Some slag at another table was calling Zack over to her (she, too, had probably seen his love-in with Eleanor and had become insanely jealous – she was not going to give in until Zack went and paid her a visit). Now was my moment. Eleanor was by herself and a sudden surge of courage/stupidity took hold of me. I steadied my nerves. Took a deep breath.

It's now or never.

'I'm going in.'

Lunch Break
Seize the Moment

I set my sights on Eleanor and quickly began weaving between the dining tables to get to her. I didn't know what I was going to do or say, all I knew was that this may be my last chance to win her over so I had to act fast. Before I knew it I was stood in front of her and she was staring up at me.

I think I may be about to tell Eleanor that I love her!

'Hi!' she said, trying to smile through a mouthful of broccoli.

'Hi,' I replied, remembering to smile in return.

She waited for me to continue, to explain exactly why I had just rushed over to her, but I completely dried up.

Speak! Sit down! Do SOMETHING!

I sat down, probably ten seconds later than a normal person would have. Zack's pizza and chips sat temptingly close in front of me. Then, almost of its own accord, my mouth began to form words!

'Eleanor . . . this is going to sound a bit strange, but . . . I was just wondering if . . . do you think . . .'

'How messed up was that!' came a voice over my shoulder.

Oh Jesus.

I hadn't noticed Rich Hiccupping Bitch sat at the next table (who, by the way, was no longer hiccupping). She quickly slid her chair over to Eleanor's table with an ear-splitting *SCREEAAAACH* as its legs dragged across the polished wooden floor.

'You should have seen him after you left,' she continued, rudely ignoring Eleanor altogether. 'He went even more mental than before!'

'Oh right,' I said, trying to sound as uninterested as possible, despite being extremely eager to know exactly what happened. I didn't want Eleanor to keep hearing about the horrible things that went on in the background of my life, in case she began to think I was a completely unwholesome person who was constantly dogged by drugs and violence.

'First of all he just thrashed around screaming for a couple of minutes, while everyone held him down . . .'

'Who?' asked Eleanor, leaning closer, fascinated.

'Then he just kind of drooped on to the ground and cried for about for ever,' she continued, ignoring Eleanor like a bitch. 'Then, when everyone had kind of stopped holding him and began comforting him, he just flipped and started lashing out and trying to punch *everyone* – he actually punched that fat girl with dodgy make-up in the tit!'

'Seriously?!' I asked, forgetting to not be interested.

'Yeah, and then he absolutely mutilated part of the fence, like, completely kicked it down, then walked away into someone's back garden!'

'Jesus. What did everyone else do?' I asked.

But she didn't answer. I'm not even sure she heard me say anything. She just sat there staring at me as if she were waiting for a rabbit to pop out of my mouth or something. I gave her that sideways stare, a *hello?* kind of thing, but she just looked at me with even more dubiosity (a made-up word, I know, but it works). I gave Eleanor a quick glance to check that she too was witnessing the Bitch's weirdness. And then it hit me . . . she was waiting for me to twitch!

Shit!

I couldn't! I couldn't do that twitch thing in front of Eleanor. She'd think I was an absolute mentalist! But Rich Hiccupping Bitch looked like she was ready to pounce with a tonne of raging accusations. Eager to avoid a scene, I reacted in the only way I could.

'I said . . . what did everyone – THNEH! – do?'

It was one of the worst things that has ever happened to me. As I twitched my head to the side and forced that ungodly grunt from my nose, that ungodly grunt did not come out alone – it brought a snotty green friend out with it and that snotty green friend landed smack-bang in the middle of Zack's pizza and chips.

Rich Hiccupping Bitch snapped out of her deep hypnotic state, tried (and failed) not to keep looking at my snot, then jumped to her feet.

'Anyway . . .' she said.

And then she was gone. And my loud twitch hung in the air above the table. And my dollop of snot hung across two chips on Zack's plate.

'What happened?' asked Eleanor, managing to look me in the eyes.

I'm not sure if she meant *What happened up the field?* or *What the hell happened with your nose just then?*

What can I possibly say to make this not quite so awful?

'Hi, Jack, mind if I have my seat back?' asked Zack, appearing beside me.

'Sure! Yeah. Sorry.'

I jumped to my feet. Then paused.

What do I do?

I have never been up against such a moral conundrum in my entire life. Do I apologise to Zack and explain? Do I sneakily try to remove the evidence? Or do I just walk away? Of course the correct answer would be to apologise, then buy him a new lunch, but this wouldn't be possible for two reasons – 1. I had no money; 2. I didn't like him. But, considering what Eleanor would think of me if I just walked away, I knew I had to do one of the above. Unfortunately my panicked little brain couldn't decide which option to choose, so I did all three.

'Sorry, Zack, I . . .' But there was no way to finish that sentence.

I reached into Zack's lunch and took the tainted artefacts. Zack looked slightly dismayed to say the least. He stared at me. I stared at him. Then, not wanting to look as if I was just stealing his chips to throw away and be spiteful, and without even thinking about what I was doing, I automatically put the chips in my mouth.

It was not the taste of cold salty snot that mortified me the most, it was the fact that I had just done all of this in front of Eleanor. How could she ever want to kiss me after this? Then, just as I thought she could not find me any more disgusting, Eleanor chose that moment to glance at my crotch. I would like to be able to tell you that she was checking out my legendary fake package, but I fear that what she was in fact seeing was the piss-like stain surrounding my ball area. The situation was beyond explanation. No number of excuses, no matter how genuine, could ever make this right.

'Seeya later,' I muttered.

I turned.

I walked away.

I wanted to die a little bit.

3rd Period
English Lit

There was a part of me that felt too ashamed to ever show my face to Eleanor again, and there was another part of me that felt I may as well tell her *everything*. After all, it couldn't really get much worse. Knowing that the first option was an impossibility (how could I spend the rest of my life with her if I was never going to show my face to her again?), it left me no other choice. There was only a matter of hours left before my time was up – I had to let Eleanor know how I felt about her and I had to do it now.

At first it seemed that our seating arrangements couldn't have been any better – I was sat right between Em and Eleanor. (Eleanor had chosen to sit next to me, so clearly my chances weren't completely blown. For all I knew she may not have even seen the snot! In any case, this was Jack sandwich Part Two.) But then disaster struck. Zack decided to abandon his usual seat at the other end of the room and plonked himself down in the empty seat next to Eleanor.

Nothing says 'I love you' or 'I'm gagging to nob you' like an impromptu seating rearrangement. Within seconds the two of them were nattering away again, probably continuing their engrossing conversation from lunchtime. The only part of Eleanor left for me to adore was the back of her head. I began to rack my brains for something to say that might draw her attention away from Mr Perfect over there, but unfortunately I was rudely interrupted by Em's constant questioning about Reaper – had I heard if he was in school yet? Did I hear about the guy that he put in hospital this morning? (At least I got a great big squishy-boob hug from her when she told me how scared she had been that it might have been me.) I explained the whole Tampon incident and how he got kicked half to death then went mental at me, and how I was assuming that, yes, Reaper was probably in school somewhere, looking for me. Maybe 'looking' wasn't the correct word, more like 'waiting'. If he had been looking for me then he clearly wasn't trying very hard – it was hardly as if I'd spent all day hiding from him. Anyway, the point is that all this talking to Em didn't give me any chance to spark up a conversation with Eleanor and steer her attention away from wank-features. In fact I couldn't help feeling that maybe Em was monopolising my attention for a reason. As nice as it was to be a Jack sandwich again, I couldn't understand how, this morning, Em and Eleanor had been inseparable, and now they were completely ignoring each other. It did cross my mind to ask Em what was going on, but I know better than to delve into the bitter labyrinthine politics of female relations. Plus, Em looked like she was in one of those moods where one wrong question could send her spiralling into a major flip-out.

The classroom door swung open and in strode Dave,

wearing a suit jacket over T-shirt and jeans. He was only seven minutes late today but it felt twice as long because I'd spent the entire time worrying that we might have Connie again. Em tutted and sighed in a very loud way, then pulled her books from her bag.

'What's wrong with you?' I asked her, then immediately cringed in case I had just triggered that whole spiralling flip-out thing.

'Him!' She gestured towards Dave, as if it was obvious.

'What about him?' I asked, confident that she wasn't ready to blow just yet.

'What do you think?'

Again, I had to rack my brains, as she'd said this in a way that implied there was an obvious answer here.

'I dunno.' I shrugged, feeling utterly ignorant.

'Well, he's late again for a start,' she said sharply.

'So what? He's always late, but he still teaches us twice as good as any teacher that turns up on time!' I rallied in Dave's defence.

'I take that to mean that you haven't heard yet,' she said loftily.

'Heard what?'

And at that moment Dave clapped his hands together and the class fell obediently silent. All teachers seem to have a knack for stopping my conversations just as they're about to get interesting.

'Can I have your attention, please,' he called needlessly, as everyone's attention was clearly already his.

'I'll tell you later,' whispered Em.

For the next twenty minutes I continually pestered Em at

every opportunity to tell me what the hell she was talking about. Finally she relented and wrote her answer on a piece of paper, then, as she did with all her secret notes to me, she folded it into a neat little origami-type pyramid-triangle thing and held it out. But as I reached for it she swiped it away and held up a cautionary finger –

'Patience!'

She picked up my bag, popped the note inside it, then put the bag down on the other side of her chair, out of my reach.

'Later!' she whispered reproachfully as I groaned my disapproval.

I'm feeling a bit guilty. For the first time in my life I am not paying attention to Dave's lesson. So far I have spent the entire time either pestering Em, watching Eleanor, or writing in my notebook. I shouldn't feel too bad about the writing, I suppose – after all it is English homework that I'm doing for Dave. Em seems to be paying just as little attention as me, because she has just got her phone from her bag and taken a photo of the whiteboard to save her from having to copy everything down into her book.

At last! Eleanor has finally broken away from her despicable love-in with Gruff-Nugget over there. 'Gruff-Nugget', it suits him! I really think it's going to catch on. Anyway, I don't want to miss my window of opportunity by writing non-stop. A good yawn and a stretch and a groan should be sufficient attention-grabbing material . . .

'You all right, chipmunk?' she asked.

It worked! That was so subtly manipulative I could

almost be an honorary girl for the day! Incidentally, chipmunk is now amongst my favourite words, along with –

1.   **Ffestiniog (there's a place in Wales called Blaenau Ffestiniog – it sounds made up. Also sounds funny. 'Ffessssss-TINNI-OG!')**
2.   **Crustacean (it feels nice coming out of my mouth – crust-AYY-shion)**
3.   **Fallopian (same as above – emphasis on the O)**

'Yeah, bit of a headache,' I lied with a sigh.

Please understand, ordinarily I hate people who do what I just did. I'm sure it seems like nothing, just a little white lie, but it's so much more annoying than that – it's fishing for sympathy and affection in the worst possible way, by using 'leading answers'. I don't think that 'leading answers' is an actual phrase, but that's what I call it. There's a guy in my class, Leigh, who does it all the time and no one else seems to be wise to it except me. He's always miserable and he's always moaning and no one but me seems to understand why – it's because it gets him attention. Leigh is the king of 'leading answers'. A good example of his expertise would be a conversation like this:

Me: How you doing, Leigh?

(An ordinary answer would be 'All right' or 'Not bad', but Leigh always manages to give an answer that leads you into asking him more questions.)

Leigh: Not very well really.

(See what I mean?)

Me: How come?

(Ordinary answer – migraine/lost my homework/nob fell off, etc.)

Leigh: It's May 13th.

(So now you have to ask what the story is . . .)

Me: What's May 13th?

(An amateur manipulator would now answer something like, 'It's the anniversary of my dog's death', or 'It's my birthday', maybe, but Leigh is a master and he knows exactly how to keep you reeled in.)

Leigh: I don't really want to talk about it.

Genius! He actually manages to trick people into caring!

As much as I despise his tactics, these are desperate times, so I am forced to take desperate measures. Unfortunately I have too much respect for myself and for Eleanor to attempt the maximum sympathy milkage of Leigh's standard, so I've opted for the old reliable rookie headache sympathiser.

'Do you want some paracetamol?' Eleanor asked.

'Nah, I try not to take them,' I replied, like a true hero.

'Awww,' she cooed and returned to her book.

DAMN IT!

Why did I go for the lame old headache sympathiser? It was an amateur move and it yielded amateur results. I should have milked it all the way! I could be curled up on her lap right now if I'd done it properly. Instead I get 'Awww'. *Awww?!* She gave Gruff-Nugget over there nearly two solid hours of her undivided attention and all I get is *Awww*? I can't leave it at that. It's time to get out the big guns and take a dangerous shot in the dark.

3rd Period
English Tit

'You OK?' I asked Eleanor with worried eyebrows.

Oh the sly and devious genius of it!

'Yeah,' she replied with zero ambiguity.

Bollocks. That wasn't the answer I was looking for. Try again. Here goes . . .

'Your *ear* OK?' I asked.

It was a risky move.

'Yesss . . .' she replied, confused. 'Why?'

Now for the counter-attack.

'Zack hasn't talked it off then?' I said light-heartedly, careful not to sound too petty or bitchy.

'Oh no, it's fine,' she said with a smile.

Crap. It wasn't working. I'm no good at this! I was getting very little attention and I was in danger of putting her on the defensive, in favour of Zack.

'Just be careful, OK?' I said, protectively.

Actually no, I didn't say it 'protectively' – I said it down-right melodramatically. I sounded like a badly acted character in a badly written soap opera!

Tone it down, baby. Keep it cool.

Christ! What the hell was Barry White doing in my head?

He's right though. You've got to chillax.

Was that Michael Caine telling me to 'chillax'? *Get these people out of my head!*

'Get them out!'

Oh dear. I do believe I said that out loud.

'What do you mean?' she asked.

Shit.

'About what?' I demanded nervously.

'You want me to be careful about what?' she said, now almost on the full defensive.

Phew, obviously she hadn't heard that 'Get them out!' thing.

'I just don't want to see you get hurt is all,' I said with a worried smile. Oh my god, I was spiralling into a world of eternally shit dialogue!

'By Zack?' she said, all traces of defensiveness dropping from her face to be replaced by surprised amusement.

What did this smile mean? Did it mean 'No chance – he's a repulsive little wart!'? Or did it mean 'Zack is far too adorable and sensitive to hurt anyone!'?

Yes, by Zack! I wanted to scream at her. *He's not as sweet and innocent as he pretends to be! He leers at people! Leers! He was gagging to get into Helena's knickers, and as soon as she was out of the picture he wanted to get into yours. Don't trust him. He has a cheese-dick and gruff-nuggets! He doesn't care about you, he only cares about your bra and panties. I, on the other hand, couldn't care less about your bra and panties, it's what's inside them that matters to me.*

Whoa! That sounds different to how it played out in my head. Maybe it's not such a bad thing that I don't always speak my mind.

'I just don't want you to become another rumour to add to his reputation,' I said.

Sometimes the words that come out of my mouth are so . . . Maybe I should give this whole 'talking' malarkey a knock on the head.

Eleanor turned to me and looked me in the eyes with an expression so serious that it nearly stopped my heart.

'You haven't heard, have you, Jack?' she asked softly.

No. I hadn't heard. Why was I not hearing any of the things that everyone else was? What exactly had I missed? Actually, I wasn't sure that I *wanted* to hear! The way she asked, as if she too were in a crappy soap opera, playing a doctor who was about to tell me that my wife hadn't made it. When someone asks a question like that, the answer is always going to be the thing you want to hear least in your life.

'Heard what?' I asked grimly.

There were surely only two possible answers — either Zack had a terminal illness and would be dead in six weeks (why is it always six?) or something far worse . . . She's already in love with him. Unfortunately one of these outcomes was far likelier than the other. I was too late. I knew it. I could see it in her eyes. I could . . .

'OK, eyes on the board, please, everyone!' Dave called to the class. Again! It's like my life is stuck in a loop. I wasn't sure whether to curse him or thank him. Dave's timing was either perfect or extremely unfortunate.

Eleanor tore off a piece of paper and, just as Em had done, she began to write her news down in a note, then she, too, folded it into a neat little origami-type pyramid-triangle thing (a trick she had obviously learned from Em) and handed it to me with a pained smile. The dejavu (don't know how to spell it) of the whole situation was beginning to freak me out. Except this time round I was not desperate to read what was written on that note – in fact I felt completely the opposite.

The thought of what might be written on the piece of paper between my fingers made me want to run out of the room and sob like a great big girl. After all I'd been through to try to get her to fall in love with me, and now all my hopes and dreams could be dashed to hell with a single stupid note. Or maybe not! The unrealistic optimist inside me wondered if perhaps she had written something completely different on the note, maybe she'd confessed her undying love for *me*!

It could be possible, but that only leaves one solution to this problem – I must never read that note. As long as I never know what is written on that piece of paper then it can never inform me that Eleanor and Zack are now an item and it can always hold the possibility of her confession of love for me. Call it superstition, call it escapism, call it lunacy – whatever it is, you can't deny the logic.

That folded piece of paper suddenly felt like a very important historic artefact and I needed to put it in a safe place to protect it from ever being exposed to any other human life form. I extended my arm and reached the piece of paper across to Em, who looked at me quizzically.

'Bag,' I whispered.

She picked my bag up and held it out for me to drop Eleanor's note into. *She actually held it out for me!* The fool. As I let go of Eleanor's folded page something caught my eye – there it was, Em's note that I had been so desperate to read. It was wedged between my English and Geography books. I wasn't quite so fussed about what it said right now, but as I saw it staring out at me, I couldn't resist. As quick as a flash I shot my arm into the bag and, before Em knew what was going on, I had the note pinched firmly between my finger and thumb. Realising what I'd done, Em reached for the note, but I whipped it back out of her reach and then . . .

. . . it was gone.

3rd Period
English Shit

'Thank you, Jack,' said Dave as he casually sauntered past during his speech about whatever it was he was talking about and effortlessly plucked the paper from my fingers.

Em's face turned grey, then very rapidly to furious-red. We both watched Dave's actions very closely. I wanted to see where he put it, so I could sneak it back later, but Em seemed more concerned about whether or not he was going to open it up and see what it said. Dave slipped the note into the inside pocket of his jacket.

'Sorry!' I mouthed desperately, hoping to douse the burning glare that was raging out of Em's eyeballs like a white-hot inferno. 'I'll get it back!' I whispered with fierce reassurance.

But how? There is no way I can sneak it back, not now it's dangling in front of Dave's left nipple!

'Jack, I'm serious . . .' she began, barely able to speak, 'if he reads that . . . !'

I didn't need to know what was written on that paper to know how vital it was to Em that Dave did not read it. She was absolutely frantic.

'He won't read it!' I told her. 'It's Dave! I'll just ask for it back later, OK? It'll be all right.' Even though I sounded convincing I found it hard to believe that anyone would have the will power to not take a peek at that note if they knew how desperate I was to get it back.

'I'm not joking, Jack,' she growled, shaking her head.

She was so worried that she looked like she could be sick, which made me so worried that I felt like *I* could be sick.

'OK!' I whispered, slightly too loud.

'Jack!' called Dave, making me jump. He shook his head shamefully and furrowed his brow, clearly disappointed that his most loyal and trusted student could interrupt him twice in one minute.

'Sorry,' I muttered sheepishly.

Em didn't say another word. She barely even moved. I could feel the contagious tension radiating from her like steamy sweat from a raging bull. I decided it would be best if I kept my head down from now on. Dave finished explaining his thing about iambic pentameter or something and the class resumed the general hum and buzz of a working classroom.

Now that Em wasn't talking to me it at least gave Eleanor a chance to get a word in.

'Anyway,' muttered Eleanor, taking advantage of the general hubbub to continue our pre-note conversation, 'I don't think it's Zack you need to be worried about.' She kept her eyes on her work, like a spy initiating an undercover dialogue.

'What do you mean?' I murmured back, mimicking her inconspicuousness.

She answered by reaching into her bag and pulling out yet another note, which, after checking that Dave couldn't see, she carefully handed to me under the table.

What the hell have I started with this stupid note-giving thing!

I sneakily opened the A4 page to see a typed message. I saw the phrases *I want to do you like a dog* and *pump you till your knickers catch fire* and I didn't have to read any more. The letter was signed 'Zed' and it was written by me just a few days ago.

'I found it in my bag this morning,' she added.

You know the phrase 'my heart was in my throat'? Well, for the first time in my life I actually understood why that phrase exists – I actually felt like my heart had lodged itself somewhere in my neck. The pulsing in my throat was so powerful that it was making my breathing wobble with each heartbeat. I knew I wouldn't be able to speak even if I tried. I sat there and pretended to read the letter that I myself had written.

'Jesus!' I said, managing to quell my trembling voice whilst frowning in disgust at what I was pretending to read. 'Who the hell wrote this?'

I wanted to hear her answer less than I wanted to read her note to me.

'I think it's kind of obvious, don't you?' she asked knowingly.

Oh Christ, this is the end.

'No!' I insisted innocently. 'Why should I?'

'Because it has a signature,' she said calmly.

What?!

'What?!'

Please don't tell me she recognises my handwriting! I tried so hard to make that signature look different to mine!

'Zed!' she said. 'I mean, how many people could that be?'

Exactly! That was the point! So why did she say that it's not Zack I need to worry about?

'Not many, I suppose,' I said, wondering where the hell she was going with this.

'Not many?' She sounded surprised. 'More like *one* person!'

'Yeah, I guess.' I laughed nervously. 'Who do you think it is then?'

She turned to look at me as if she couldn't believe I was being serious.

'Are you being serious?' she asked.

See!

'Ummm . . .'

I don't get it! I think she knows it was me! I think my game is up. I think I better explain . . .

'I . . .' I cleared my throat.

'Zed!' she said.

'Huh?'

'That Benjamin Zeddenaia guy in the sixth form!'

What are these words that flow from her mouth?

'Zed!' she clarified. 'Ben Zed.'

There's actually someone called Zed in our school?

'Is he new?'

'Six or seven years ago maybe,' she said, as if I were an idiot. 'How can you not know?'

'Why should I?' I asked, still paranoid that she was on to me.

'He's about six-foot-five, with dreadlocks down to his backside and his name is Zed,' she explained. 'How could you miss him?'

I do fear that I may have inadvertently incriminated an innocent student as being a sexual deviant.

Should I confess? Should I tell her it was me?

It was the right thing to do and I knew it. But I'm just not that good a person. Once again my dark side prevailed.

'He sure is one sick puppy,' I muttered, then folded the paper back up.

'Tell me about it!'

Thankfully she didn't seem too disturbed by the whole thing. I just hope that she doesn't take this note to the principal and get this guy expelled.

Last Break

'Well?' James said expectantly when he and I met up in the men's room at afternoon break (it wasn't a date or anything).

'Well what?' I asked.

'Did you tell her you love her and you want to rub her buttocks with a slippery fish and tickle her nipples with Jelly Babies?'

'No. Not yet . . . The timing was bad. I'm not sure it was such a good idea anyway.'

'Me neither,' admitted James.

'She wouldn't stop talking to that Zack twat,' I added.

'Well . . . she might change her mind about him,' he said confidently, making his way to a urinal.

'I wouldn't be so sure,' I said, waiting for the conversation to end before I unzipped, 'but she seemed to have something important to tell me about him.'

'What, that he's got a dick made of cheese?'

I reached into my bag, pulled out the folded paper and handed it to James.

'I don't want to know what it says,' I told him.

Whilst James read the note we both used the pause in

conversation to take a leak (him in the urinal on the far left, me in the urinal on the far right, of course). James suddenly stopped short, breaking off mid-flow (doesn't that sting?). His face dropped in horror.

'What?' I asked, breaking my own rule about talking whilst pissing.

'Holy shit,' he said, absolutely petrified. 'Take it. Quick!' He passed the note to me before continuing his piss with desperate speed.

'It's messed up, man,' he muttered fearfully, 'seriously messed up.'

'Should I read it?' I asked.

But James didn't have time to answer. The bathroom door opened and someone walked in.

Screw it, I thought, deciding not to wait for James's answer and taking a quick peek at the note.

Holy – shitting – arse-cheese!

It was certainly not what I had expected. It made every inch of my skin crawl. I could barely believe my eyes. I had to read it again just to be sure . . .

He wanks himself off in the toilets before every single lesson!

Whilst my tiny little brain was struggling to comprehend what I had read and why Eleanor had written it to me, the someone who had walked into the toilets unzipped himself at the urinals beside me. *Right* beside me.

'All right,' said Zack.

I'm not sure this is possible, but I'm almost certain that at that precise moment my willy actually shrunk. It was the most uncomfortable twenty seconds of my life.

'The sick bastard,' droned James as we marched out into the playground towards the tennis courts. 'Why the hell is he tossing himself off in the men's room four times a day?'

'Why do you think?' I said, exasperated. 'Didn't you see where he was stood?'

'Where he was st . . . ?' James's expression went from one of pure confusion to one of total realisation. 'He's a bummer!'

'He's as bent as a bent stick,' I confirmed.

'That's so weird.'

'No, it's not,' I corrected him. 'It's absolutely buggering-well brilliant!'

James looked at me dubiously, trying to work out exactly why this excited me.

'Er, why?'

'Because that means I have no competition for Eleanor! There is no competition! It's just me!'

'Oh yeah,' said James, finally catching on. 'But if he's gay then why is he always leeching on to the girls?'

'For the same reason that girls hang around with other girls,' I said. 'He's one of them!'

'Oh man . . .' James drawled, still in disbelief. 'But still . . . in the men's room?' He shuddered.

'I know, kind of messed up,' I pondered in disgust. 'Who would have thought that Zack Pimento's a big cheesy arse-bandit that likes to spend his spare time whacking off in the toilets?'

'Dude.'

'Do you think he spies on people through the cracks in the cubicle doors?' I said.

'Dude, shut up.'

But it was too late. Helena was back from her College-Boy shag-fest and, as luck would have it, she just so happened to be walking only a few feet away from James and me. I hoped that she hadn't heard me, but the evil death-glare she shot my way convinced me otherwise. She stormed off in the opposite direction.

'Shit,' I said. 'I didn't know she was there!'

'Me neither,' said James. 'I only just noticed as you said it.'

'Shit.'

'Meh, so what?' said James. 'What's she gonna do?'

He had a point.

'True.'

Before long we had wandered back inside and were now on the first floor outside the staff room.

'What the hell are we doing here?' asked James, seemingly unaware of how he'd even gotten there.

'It won't take long,' I assured him, 'there's just a little something I need your help with.'

As I casually strolled past the staff room door I peered through the window and there he was – Dave Kross. Just as I'd hoped, he was not wearing his jacket. This meant his jacket was probably in his office and, unless he had already removed it from his pocket, so was Em's note.

Most of the teachers had their offices scattered around just outside the staff room and Dave was no exception – his was right next door, and I prayed that his jacket was in there, alone. I walked tentatively over to the office door, which had the name plate 'Dave Kross, Head of English' on the front and I gave a knock, just to be sure that it was empty. After three seconds of non-response I turned the handle and peeked inside.

'What the hell are you doing?' hissed James.

But I was too preoccupied to reply. Just a few feet in front of me sat Dave's chair, and hung on the back of it was his jacket. I could be in and out in a matter of seconds – but suddenly a gush of paranoid panic surged through me –

What if Dave comes out of the staff room and straight into his office whilst I'm still in here?

'James,' I said, standing in the open doorway, 'if Dave comes out of there in the next ten seconds then make sure he goes back in. Whatever it takes. OK?'

'What?!'

I didn't hang around to hear his protests. I slipped straight into the office and the door clicked shut behind me.

Last Break(ing and Entering)

I darted across the room, directly to Dave's chair and sunk my hand into his inside jacket pocket . . .

Empty!

My heart almost stopped.

Wrong pocket!

I thrust my other hand into the *left* inside pocket and, avoiding stabbing myself on an open biro, my fingers curled around a piece of paper.

Thank god!

But my fingers knew something was wrong before my brain did. I pulled my hand out to reveal a crumpled till-receipt.

Shit! Shit! Shit!

I double-checked the pocket. There was definitely no more paper in there. I double-checked the other pocket. Then I checked the side pockets, then fumbled stupidly with the breast pocket until I realised it was sewn shut. The note was definitely not in any of his jacket pockets. I checked the floor, in case it had fallen when I had pulled my hand out, the way stray £5 notes do if I don't put them in my wallet. No luck. I checked his desk, which was completely

covered in paper, none of which happened to be the piece I
was searching for. Then, to my horror, and making me jump
almost straight out of my skin . . . the bell rang.

That was it. I had to get out of there, note or no note. But
as I dashed to the door I spotted the waste paper basket.
There, wedged between a plastic sandwich box and a wad of
tissues, was Em's note, still in its original pyramid formation. He hadn't opened it! He probably didn't even realise it
was a note and not just some rudimentary origami. The fool!
I grabbed the paper, along with an accidental handful of
snotty Kleenex, stuffed them straight into my pocket and
darted back to the door.

I don't know exactly how it happened, but somehow, as
I had been crouched down at the bin, my broken bag strap
had connected with the corner of Dave's coffee table and, as
I stood up, the table came with me. With a huge crash the
table dropped back to the floor, scattering the carpet with
coffee mugs, papers and plant-pot soil. There was no way
the people in the staff room next door would not have heard
that. Just as I was about to dart from the room and leave the
mess behind me, I noticed something that made my stomach
drop to my feet – my bag was too light. I turned back to the
crap-strewn office floor, and there, scattered amongst all of
the coffee-table crap, was the entire contents of my bag –
books, papers, sweet wrappers, T-shirt, deodorant,
banana . . . I was screwed. I scrambled to my knees and
stuffed everything, whether it was mine or not, into my
broken bag. When I was sure that I had gathered any incrim-
inating artefacts I clutched it tight (making sure to hold the
tear closed) and shot back to the door. But I did not leave.

On the other side was a gaggle of voices. My hand hovered, trembling, over the door handle as I strained to hear what was being said.

'I don't know!' I heard James say innocently. 'I just turned round and saw someone running out of Dave Kross's office and down the stairs.'

'Boy or girl?' I heard a teacher ask.

'Boy, I think,' replied James, 'but they had their hood up.'

I heard running footsteps as more members of staff gathered to see what was happening. Then I heard Dave's unmistakable voice.

'A hooded top. What colour?'

'Errr, black, I think.'

Nice work. Almost half the school owned a black hoodie.

But it wasn't all nice work. I understood what James was trying to do – to send the staff, who were obviously investigating the humungous crashing sound, on a wild goose chase away from Dave's office. But there was no way they were all going to give chase without someone checking to see what had happened in here. The second that thought passed through my head I heard footsteps approaching at a rapid pace.

This is the end.

There was nowhere to hide – no closet to climb into, no bed to crawl under, no curtain to sneak behind, just Dave's desk, chair and the upturned coffee table. I was well and truly screwed. And then the handle suddenly turned beneath my fingers and the door swung open towards my face. I instantaneously shot aside and flattened myself against the wall behind the door. The door kept coming, closer and closer, until – THUD! – it rammed into my toes and jolted to a halt. The game was surely up. The door remained pressed firmly against my feet and I heard Dave's voice inside the room.

'Christ,' he muttered. Then, shouting back out to the other staff, 'They've taken something!' The door swung away from me and I was completely exposed. The door slammed shut and . . . the office was empty.

'What did they take?' someone asked outside the office.

'I don't know, but they've taken something,' a very agitated Dave replied.

I was alone. I finally allowed myself to inhale a carefully controlled breath, being mindful of my volume. And just as I was beginning to think that I might get away with it, I heard the most horrifying noise of my life – it started with a jangle, then a scrape, a clunk, and it ended with a very definite CLICK. The door was locked. I was trapped.

White-hot panic erupted from my stomach and towards my throat. I swallowed back a bitter mouthful of vomit. This was the most scared I had ever been in my life. I was locked inside a first-floor office, which I had just ransacked and vandalised, and now half the teachers in school were on the hunt to find the perpetrator. When they finally came back – which would no doubt be fairly soon and possibly with the company of a police officer or two – I would be caught red-handed, and there was absolutely nothing I could do about it. This time the vomit came without warning and, far from being able to swallow it back, it sprayed all over Dave's carpet. It was the cherry on the icing. As I looked down at the horrendous mash of what was very clearly chips and ketchup mixed with stomach acid, something else erupted from my mouth.

The laugh burst out with as much restraint as the puke did – there was nothing I could do about it. The only way my brain could manage to process such a magnitude of bad luck was simply to laugh. What else *could* I do? I couldn't stop! I slapped my hand over my mouth to muffle the torrent of guffaws, but it was little help. I had just puked on a teacher's carpet! I was in so much shit! I had to stop laughing and find a way to get out of there, but I couldn't concentrate – it appears there's only a certain level of awfulness the mind can cope with before it just gives up. And then something suddenly snapped me out of it – it started with a jangle of keys . . .

Luckily I had some reserves of common sense and it kicked in like a shot. In an instant I had raised the office blinds and was at the open window. I climbed on to the ledge and, without even a second thought, I stepped off.

4th Period
Little Pricks

I'm just going to give you a few moments of believing that I am an Action Hero God who jumped from a first-floor window before I mention that, due to the school being built on a slight hill, the first floor, which is a good thirty-plus feet high at the front of the building, is actually only about eight or nine feet off the ground at the back. Needless to say, Dave's office is at the back of the building, so it was kind of like jumping from the top of a basketball player (although that didn't stop me from collapsing in a heap on the flower beds as I landed). I jumped to my feet and, much to my surprise, came almost face to face with James. James, however, was slightly more surprised.

'HOLY SHITTING SHIT!' he cried, jumping back about six feet and falling over.

'Hey,' I said casually, 'did you know there's a guy in our school called Zed?'

An immense sense of pride began to swell inside of me: I had just pulled off a line that was so comically cool and well-timed it was worthy of one of Will Smith's better films.

At least that's what I thought.

James stared at me with the most confused/shocked expression I have ever seen outside of a cartoon. He looked me up and down and took a minute to take in the situation before he managed to speak again.

'You've got a stick in your arse.'

(End sense of proud action movie coolness.)

I twisted round to check my bum and, sure enough, there was a big thorny twig attached to my right buttock with its claws stuck deep in.

'Oh shit.'

I tried to brush it away but the stick put up more of a fight than I expected. It stayed exactly where it was, thorns embedded deep in my jeans (and obviously my bum cheek too), and now some had come off into my palm.

'Oh shit,' I repeated, with a hint of a whimper, as I noticed a small patch of blood slowly begin to spread across my back pocket.

I will attempt to make the following as brief as possible . . .

Men's room – toilet cubicle – two minutes later . . .

'Oh man that hurts!' I whispered (all of the following is in hushed voices).

'Keep still!' laughed James. 'You've got a prick in your arse!' (not as hushed as I would have liked).

'Ha ha! Very funny! Just hurry up, would you?'

'Trust me. This is far worse for me than it is for you.'

'Good! Be quick!'

'Oh Christ!' he said in disgust. 'You're bleeding all over me!'

'Get it out!'

'Bend over a bit more. Not that much! Shit! I'm not going to be able to sleep tonight!'

'It really cocking-well hurts!'

'Done.'

'Really? It's all out?'

'Yes! Now get your arse out of my face.'

Exit cubicle and reveal a small Year 7 kid standing outside in slack-jawed horror.

'Mention this to anyone,' said James, in a casual yet threatening voice, 'and I'll tell every girl I know that you've got a nob like a chipolata.'

We left it at that and vowed never to bring it up again. I fear we may have somewhat overstepped the boundaries of men's-room etiquette, resulting in the two of us being scarred for life and a small boy who will probably never bring himself to use the school toilets ever again.

Eager to begin a fresh topic of conversation, I explained to James why exactly I had gone into Dave's office in the first place. I reached into my bag and retrieved the ill-gotten note that I had not long since stolen from Dave.

Except I didn't. I retrieved *a* note, but it wasn't the one I pulled from Dave's bin. This was an altogether different note . . .

4th Period
E Note

I did not have a clue who the note was from or where or when it got put into my bag. It was not folded in the Em/Eleanor fashion, but as I opened it I definitely recognised the handwriting.

McDonald's 4 p.m. E.

That was it. That was all the note said – McDonald's 4 p.m. E.

'Shit,' whispered James.

'Why shit?' I asked.

'Do you think it's from Reaper?'

'It's signed with an E!'

'So?'

'"So" what? It's signed with an *E*!' I reiterated to the idiot. 'Why would Reaper track me down, drop an invitation in my bag, then sign it with an E?'

'A trap. He could have got anyone to put it in your bag.'

'Not very likely, though, is it?' I asked rhetorically.

'Who's been at your bag today?'

'I don't know!'

'Is it definitely from today?'

'Yeah. I don't know!'

'Have you noticed anyone messing with your bag at all this week?'

'No. Yeah, Em.'

'Well there you go. You said yourself she used to be friends with him. It's a trap and she's in on it,' James said conclusively.

'Genius! Orrrr . . . I'm just clutching at straws here, a bit of a wild stab in the dark . . . it could be a note frommmm . . . Em? Maybe?'

'Yeah. Fine. That's exactly what he wants you to think,' argued James, sounding hurt that I wasn't buying into his conspiracy theory.

'Or Eleanor! It could be from Eleanor!'

'Didn't she already give you a note today?'

'So did Em.'

And then I remembered the note, the one Em had put in my bag, the one I had been so desperate to read yet still hadn't unfolded from its original pyramid formation. What was the secret that had made her so hateful towards Dave and so scared about him reading the note? I was finally going to find out. I fumbled with the tight folds of paper, which in my excitement I tore a few times, then, eventually, I folded it out to read her message. I have to admit, I was more than a little shocked when I read those two short words . . .

He's GAY!

No way is Dave Kross gay! Why is he always flirting so much with the girls? Why does he seem like such a ladies' man? This is unbelievable! Not that I care, but . . . man! You think you know someone! Who woulda thunk – two gay people in one day!

All of a sudden he seemed like a completely different person. But, the more I thought about it, the more it wasn't the news about Dave that shocked me the most – it was the fact that Em was so appalled by it! I had no idea she was so bigoted towards gay people. I was sure she never *used* to be a Nazi! She used to like Dave almost as much as I did, how could she suddenly dislike him so much just because he likes men? Or was that it? Was I wrong? Was it possible that maybe she used to like Dave *more* than I did and *that's* why she was upset? Was Em in love with Dave? . . .

. . . What a slag! First she goes out with a tit like Reaper and now she wants to shag a teacher – I told you she wasn't right for me!

'Who's gay *now*?' asked James as he read the note.

'Dave Kross!'

'No way!'

'According to Em.'

'Is it catching or something?'

An idea suddenly came to me.

'Compare the handwriting.'

I held the three notes side by side (Em's one, Eleanor's one and the McDonald's one) and, sure enough, it was utterly inconclusive – they all looked similar and different in equal measures!

'Chances are it was *one* of them,' I theorised.

'Mmmm, or chances are it's from someone *pretending* to be one of them!'

He wasn't going to let it go.

'Well, I guess there's only one way to find out,' I said.

'What? You're not going, are you?'

'Yeah!' I said, as sure as if he'd asked me whether I'd squeeze Julie Quill's boobs if she really begged me to.

'Don't blame me when you get your head kicked in then. Don't say I didn't warn you.'

'I'll get there early and hide out, then see who turns up if it makes you happy.'

'Ecstatic,' said James dryly. 'Come on then.'

'Come on then what?'

'Let's go!'

'You're coming with me?' I asked.

'Why not?' he said, sounding offended.

'What if it is from Eleanor? What if she's waiting to pounce on me and rub her boobs in my face? She won't do that if I show up holding hands with you.'

'We're going to hide in the hedges, see who it is!'

'Oh you're sick!' I jested. 'Now you want to hide in the hedge and *watch* her rub her boobs in my face? First you fondle my buttocks in the toilets, now you want to watch me kiss a girl?'

'I thought we weren't going to talk about that ever again!'

'Starting from now,' I promised.

'Fine,' he said, pretending to be upset, 'go by yourself. But what if it isn't Eleanor waiting to rub her boobs in your face, what if it's Reaper waiting to rub his fist in your face? Even if it *is* from Eleanor you still have to walk a mile down the cycle path – the pissing territory of every psychopath in town. Chances are Reaper's gonna be down there anyway.'

'Good point,' I said, suddenly acting sober, 'maybe you should come.'

One of the great benefits of having James as a friend is that he's so easy to read. He's a decent liar when he tries, but in general day-to-day chit-chat he's an open book. Like, for instance: I could tell he really believed that the note was from Reaper and the idea of joining me on the long walk down the cycle path to McDonald's scared the crap out of him. Yet he was still willing to go with me. In fact he was making up excuses so that he *could* come with me. Do not take this the wrong way, but if James were a hot girl, he'd be the perfect match.

I cannot believe I actually just wrote that. Maybe it *is* catching.

4th Period
Life or Death

By the time we had finished arguing over whether James was going to his final lesson or skiving with me on my expedition to McDonald's, it was already too late for him to try and make it to class anyway (there's an ironic truth in the fact that if you turn up to your lesson twenty minutes late you are more likely to get a detention than if you don't turn up at all – something to do with teachers having only a two-day memory span), which meant he was coming with me.

As we made our way down the cycle path a huge dark cloud began to drift in overhead, threatening to obliterate the clear blue sky. The impending storm did not improve the trepidation that James and I were both feeling (picture the part in *Jurassic Park* where the glass of water shudders, then drag it out over a mile-long walk). We did our best to keep a steady flowing conversation to distract us from our worries. We talked about girls for a bit, about who James was going to set his sights on now that Helena was out of the picture with that cradle-snatching paedophile College Dick. We talked about how we couldn't wait to be genuine adults, not for any reason other than that older girls don't seem so obsessed with shagging older men, so we'd be in with a better chance of getting girls our own age. And if we do end up with younger girls it's not such a big deal – a thirty-two-year-old girl going out with a thirty-eight-year-old boy seems like nothing, whereas an eighteen-year-old going out with a twelve-year-old is too sick to even think about, yet it's the same age gap.

'Who's the oldest celebrity you'd shag?' I asked, desperate to avoid a lull in the conversation.

'Living or dead?' asked James.

'Why would you want to shag someone who's dead?'

'No, I mean . . . you know what I mean!'

'No. I don't. Living. You sicko.'

'OK fine, ummm . . . Madonna?' He answered as if it were some kind of test.

'Seriously?'

'Sheryl Crow . . .' He started counting them off on his fingers as if trying to recount a list.

'How old is she?'

'I dunno, forty-five, fifty-ish maybe.'

'OK, not bad, who else?'

'Sharon Stone – she's fifty, I think.'

'Is she still hot?' I asked dubiously.

'Yeah, I think so, maybe, I haven't seen her in anything for years.'

'Exactly.'

'Ermmm . . . oh, the mum from *Wedding Crashers*!'

'Jane Seymour?!'

'Yeah! She's hot!'

'She's about sixty!'

'I don't care. She'd so get it. That's it. Sixty. That's my score. What about you then?'

'I don't know, it's tricky. I mean, with make-up and lighting it's hard to tell exactly what they look like. Imagine waking up next to them in bright daylight, with no make-up and all the wrinkles. You know, in the real world, if Sharon Stone was stacking shelves in Tesco's, would you even look twice?'

'Would she be naked?'

'Why would . . . ? I'm not having this conversation with you any more. You're an idiot.'

'Suit yourself. You brought it up.'

Unfortunately it turns out I was accidentally telling the truth about not having this conversation any more — it ended there and then. And for a moment or two we were walking in complete silence. Not talking was bad — there was nothing to distract me from the paranoia that was bouncing about in my brain. The silence seemed to amplify each bounce, reverberating through my skull until it became a continuous ringing drone.

Maybe Em is secretly still going out with Reaper, or at least still in love with him, and she put that note in my bag as part of a trap. Or maybe Cole put it there. Or Tampon. Perhaps The Bezzers have found out something about me that they don't like and Ed put the note in my bag and . . . Ed? E? . . . Do you think? Perhaps Ed and all The Bezzers AND Reaper are waiting for me. Maybe they finally found out I'm not a kung fu master and they're going to deal out five years' worth of beatings that I have dishonourably

*avoided. Maybe the note is from some random pervert who
wants to violate me in the toilet with hamsters! Ergh, Jesus!
Stupid silence! Start talking again!*

The silly thing was, as long as there was a 1% chance that
the note was from Eleanor then I was going to make sure I
was at the McDonald's Drive-Thru at four p.m. I didn't want
to jinx myself by saying this, but deep down, beneath all the
paranoia, I had a good feeling. This week had been kind
of . . . special. It's odd that as soon as I decided to write an
essay about myself, my life suddenly got a lot more interesting. Good things started happening. Bad things started
happening. They seemed to be taking it in turns. Was it luck,
coincidence, or had I been unconsciously making these
things happen just to add some spice to my story? I don't
know. But I do know that it felt very much like this week
was going to end with a bang. I just hoped it was going to be
a firework bang, as opposed to a bomb-strapped-to-my-balls
type bang.

And then (as hard as it may be to believe) . . .

BANG!!!

(Seriously!)

The loudest clap of thunder erupted from the sky with no
prior rumbly warning. James and I both jumped out of our
skins and the sky lit up like a thousand paparazzi and their
flash-bulb cameras were hiding in the clouds. The rain
began to fall, gently at first but soon growing to the point
where the large splats of water were painful when they
smashed into my forehead. As the rain increased in power,
so did our strides, until the two of us were flat-out running.
Out of the corner of my eye I saw James fumbling with the

zipper of his hoodie. He looked like a little five-year-old the way he feebly wrestled that thing . . . and then he was gone.

I didn't see him drop but I sure as hell heard it. I hoped to god that the loud *crack* sound was just his hands slapping the rain-drenched concrete and not his head breaking against it. I turned in time to see him skidding on his face, his arms trapped beneath him, obviously unable to move from his zipper in enough time to break his fall. I lurched to a halt and dashed back to him as he jumped to his feet and clutched the side of his face. The blood trickled between his clenched fingers and I knew it was bad, but, bad as it was, I was eager to keep him moving, unsure of what had floored him. Worried that we were under attack.

He marched in small circles, doubled over, groaning and sucking sharp intakes of breath through clenched teeth.

'Shit, man! You OK?'

It was a stupid question. When someone is bleeding from the head it is usually a clear indication that they are very much not OK in a rather large way.

'No!' James managed to grunt between agonised groans.

'What happened?' I asked, keeping an eye on the hedges in case Reaper was the culprit.

'Aarrghhhh!' he replied.

He quickly checked his hand to see if there was any blood, but there wasn't much. From what I could see, though, it was only because he was applying pressure and the wound was fresh. It looked to me like it was ready to gush.

'Let me see,' I told him, still watching the hedges.

But he was too busy moving in circles.

'Let me see!' I demanded. He briefly relented, staring up to the sky and clenching his fists close beside him.

Raindrops and dappled blood covered one side of his face, making it difficult to actually see what damage had been done. It looked as though his face was badly grazed and I thought I saw a large swollen split across his eyebrow and down the side of his eye.

'Right. Back to school,' I ordered tersely.

'It's all right,' he groaned.

Obviously he would not have said that if he could see how much blood was washing down his face and on to his clothes. I didn't want to worry him by pointing this out though.

'It's not all right,' I said, turning him round and guiding him back towards school.

Selfishly, my top three worries at that moment in time were as follows:

3. James's face

2. An ambush by Reaper and co.

1. Being late for my appointment at the Drive-Thru

James didn't put up a struggle, and shuffled along with me in the direction we had just come from.

'You'll be late,' he said selflessly.

'I don't care, your face is my main concern right now, OK?' I lied selflessly. 'What the hell happened?'

But I didn't need to wait for his reply because the answer was right in front of me. If I had not seen it with my own eyes I would not have believed it, and I would forgive you for thinking it a mere work of fiction.

'You slipped on a banana peel!' I revelled, partly in disbelief, partly in awe.

'No way!' said James, taking a break from his groaning to appreciate the novelty of the situation.

'You slipped on a fucking banana peel!' I laughed, unable to help myself. 'I thought that only happened in silent films!'

'Me too,' said James, not making it as far as laughing but trying his best.

'Thank Christ for that! I thought someone had attacked you or something!'

'Apparently not,' he groaned, pulling his hand away from his eye and observing the pool of blood on his palm. 'Shit.'

4ᵗʰ Period
I Walk Alone

The hobble back to school was sickeningly slow and I couldn't help but continually check my watch. Someone had obviously seen us from the staff-room window because two teachers were running out to us before we had even made it across the car park.

'Oh dear,' said Clive Cornish in a sing-songy voice, as if James were a two-year-old girl, 'what happened here then?'

'He slipped . . .' I decided to save James's dignity and not mention the *on a banana peel* part. It's bad enough to get hit in the face by The Planet Earth (which is actually what happened if you think about it . . . weird) without having people laugh at you about it too.

'I'm OK,' said James, completely unconvincingly.

'You're not doing too bad considering you just got hit in the face by The Planet Earth!' I laughed, trying to inject some physiological humour into the situation.

Humour, apparently, was not what the situation called for and nobody even attempted a smile (either that or it just wasn't very funny, which is a strong possibility).

'Thank you, Jack, we'll take it from here –,' panted a flustered fat Maths teacher who has never taught me in her life and I hadn't a clue how she knew my name. (I don't even know hers! She looks like a Barbara, though. Or a Wendy.)

And, just like that, I was stood in the half-empty school car park by myself, watching two strange teachers walk my new best friend away to the school. All of a sudden I felt very alone. The thought of walking all the way down that yellow brick road (actually green and red tarmac) by myself was not so appealing (it's about a mile long). The sky was almost black. The warm summer air had given way to a cold, damp wind and the rain was hammering the concrete like a non-stop blanket of gunfire (wet gunfire).

I hesitantly turned back to the deserted cycle path. A foreboding presence lingered in every molecule of the atmosphere with a threatening hum and, as I once again set foot on the path, the grey clouds above me lit up with a series of sheet lightning and a bone-trembling rumble followed soon after. (This had actually been going on for about fifteen minutes, but it seemed all the more apparent now that I was on my own.) The hedge-lined path was completely deserted and I could not shake the feeling that I was being followed . . . watched . . . preyed upon. Keeping a sharp eye open for hedge-dwelling psychopaths and banana skins, I broke into a run and had no intention of stopping until I safely reached my destination. The winding path, the recesses in the foliage and the upcoming housing estate created dozens of hiding places that would be perfect for an ambush, and I accelerated to a sprint each time I passed such an area.

Shortly after the spot marked by a faint wash of blood and a squished banana, something caused me to grind to a halt. It was impossible to be sure (what with the noise of the rumbling sky, the splattering rain and my hammering feet), but I could have sworn I heard voices drifting towards me from beyond the blind bend ahead. I listened hard, trying to filter out all noises except vocal ones. There was nothing. It must have been my paranoia messing with my head. But, as I began to move off, I heard it again. Was it a shout? A scream, maybe? My racing pulse quickened some more and I could feel an asthma attack coming on. Stationary once again, I cocked my head and listened into the wind. Nothing. I silently slipped my hand into my bag in search of my inhaler, when—

'AAAAAAAAAARRRRRRRRGGGGGGHHHHHHHHH!!!!!!!!!!!!!!'

The shout was unmistakable. It roared from just around the corner.

Whoever it was, they were close. Very close. They were probably going to appear around that corner any second now. Abandoning any attempt to retrieve my inhaler I launched myself into the thick and brambly hedge to my right, but it was impenetrable, giving no place to hide. I dashed back on to the path and scanned the hedge for a nearby recess. I was in luck. Six feet ahead was a two-foot hole at the base of the hedge, which led straight into the adjacent field. Without a moment's hesitation I was lying in the mud and sliding myself through the opening. It appeared as though the passage had once been in regular use, but had now, for some reason, been abandoned and begun to overgrow. A moment later I discovered why. A brand new fence – wooden struts, firm wire mesh and barbed wire blocked my exit. I tried to slip down the side, between the fence and the hedge, but there was zero room, they were flush against each other and the hedge was too dense to negotiate.

Once again I heard the voice – a loud cry – this time followed by a chorus of laughter. There were lots of them, I would guess five or six, maybe more, and they were getting closer. Where I stood, crouched beneath the hedge, was a paltry hiding place. Not only did I stick out like a sore thumb, but I was also boxed in – trapped and exposed – at a perfect height for feet to attack. Another outburst of roaring voices erupted nearby. I quickly weighed up my options – *lots of feet in my head, no escape, hospital* vs. *scratches from a hedge, over the fence, freedom.* It was a fairly easy decision. I launched myself upwards and tried to ignore the pain as branches, twigs and thorns ripped and tugged at my flesh. As long as I kept moving, the pain was bearable, but it was when the dense brambles clung on to every scrap of my clothing and dug their claws deep into my body that I really began to panic. A flash of an imaginary war movie played through in my head – *a lone British soldier waiting in the deserted trenches, listening in terror as the approaching German voices grow closer and closer. He finally makes a dash for it, but becomes completely entangled in a rolling barricade of barbed wire. He scrambles for an escape, writhing and ripping as the Germans casually stroll up and playfully puncture him with their bayonets, laughing and jeering as he slowly bleeds to death, arm outstretched for the photograph of his wife and daughter that has fallen from his pocket.*

They may have put the willies up me but these arseholes weren't going to playfully stab me with anything. Blocking out the pain and out-muscling the brambles, I forced myself through. My hands found a wooden fence post, which I used to lever myself up, and once I was in motion I just kept on going. As soon as my waist was level with the top of the fence I threw myself forward, barbs puncturing my thighs as I gripped the long grass in my fists and dragged myself along the ground until my entire body was clear of the fence. I knew that my clothes and skin were in a mess, but to what extent I was not sure. The feel of the cold wet grass on my bare thighs told me that my jeans were completely shredded. Every inch of my body was soaking wet and I only hoped that it was rain and mud, rather than blood. It was only when I pushed myself to my feet that I realised the true hideousness of my situation.

Covered in mud. Soaking wet. Spots of blood. Clothes torn. TROUSERS ROUND MY ANKLES! And the owners of the loud voices just so happened to be on *this* side of the fence!

'Shit.'

4ᵗʰ Period
On The Run

The gang of cider-swilling Year 9 thugs that stood before me were not people to trifle with. Luckily I had the element of surprise on my side (note to self: crawling through a hedge with your trousers down is the perfect way to stun your would-be attackers). They were not six metres away, sheltering under a tree and gawking speechlessly at me, cider bottles in hand, as I pulled my trousers back up and retrieved my ever-diminishing bag from the barbed wire fence. Of course it only took a few seconds before their silence rapidly evolved into full-blown hysterics. There were eight of them. Three were actually rolling on the ground and clutching their stomachs they were laughing that hard, one was violently choking on a mouthful of frothing cider, and another, younger than the rest of them, stepped to the front and pointed his finger at me. He was horribly familiar.

'That's the chin-tickler that was getting buggered in the boys' room!'

The entire universe stood frozen in time whilst my

cerebral cortex processed the god-awful shitstorm I currently found myself splashing about in. I was completely
unable to move. My brain had stalled. I couldn't decide
what was worse – the fact that the little kid from the toilets
had identified me as a bummer to his maniacal colleagues,
or the fact that he referred to me as a 'chin-tickler'. My
mental conflict rendered me immobile. How had an insult as
perfect as 'gruff-nugget' been outshone by Tim's lame 'chin-
tickler'? It had shot to stardom in under a week! How could
this possibly be happening? Seriously!

The laughing and jeering insults were mere background
noise as I plodded past the screeching pack of uncontrollable inbreds. Even the spray of shaken-up cider being
aimed at my face was little distraction as I struggled to comprehend the inexplicable success of 'chin-tickler'. It was
only when a glass bottle flew before my eyes that I snapped
back to reality and realised that maybe I should be running
from these rampaging Neanderthals. Their hysterics had
quickly turned to rage, and more objects flew at my head.
What the hell was I doing?

Run, you idiot! RUN!

I ran.

My feet pounded the waterlogged field. Fear of these guys
finally set in. The faster I ran, the more I panicked.

They might all be right behind me!

I didn't dare look. I tried to listen, but something was
blocking my ears, something inside my head – a soundtrack
began to swell and there was nothing I could do about it. A
pack of cider-swilling animals were chasing me down and
all my brain could manage to do in assistance was sing *Run*

rabbit run rabbit run run run! over and over again. This was not helpful.

I ran as fast as I could. I pictured someone rugby-tackling me from behind, a bottle being smashed against my skull. Somehow my feet moved even faster. I pictured Reaper leaping out from the hedge and bowling me over. My legs were going so quickly they were in danger of overtaking me.

Run rabbit run rabbit run run run!

I took evasive action – swerving from left to right. My pursuers would surely struggle to catch a moving target. My feet slipped on the wet ground, but I was moving too fast to fall. Each stumble became my next step. I could see a large opening in the hedge ahead. The ground was growing increasingly uneven. My stamina was quickly deteriorating. I needed to get to safety fast. I wasn't sure how much longer I could keep running. Lungs burning. Thighs numb.

'Run rabbit!' I accidentally roared as I leapt through the opening in the hedge and back on to the cycle path, almost scaring an old woman to death and nearly flattening her dog.

'Sorry!' I yelled, without a second's pause.

And it was over. The music stopped, and I soon realised that no one was behind me. There was no rampaging mob. No flying bottles. They hadn't even attempted to give chase. The cycle track was silent apart from the distant hum of the road, the pitter-patter of rain, a few tweeting birds and the never-ending echo of me shouting 'Run Rabbit!' reverberating through eternity.

I felt like a tit.

I did not dwell on it for long though, as I had finally reached the end of the road. There, in front of me, standing high on the other side of the car park, like a Mecca for the obese, stood those golden arches – that big yellow M. I had made it to Oz. I was at the Drive-Thru.

I took a deep breath and prepared myself for the unknown.

It turns out no amount of deep breaths could have prepared me for what was to follow.

School's Out

As I drew closer, I was able to see a number of people filing in and out of the Drive-Thru, none of whom looked like Eleanor or Reaper. My feet took one last step from the coloured paving and I was officially there. I was in the car park of the Drive-Thru.

Why do they even have car parks? Isn't the whole point that you don't have to stop?

This was not the time to allow my mind to wander. Reaper could be waiting to pounce from anywhere. However, I couldn't see anyone who looked as if they were waiting for anything. Everyone was all too busy rushing to get out of the rain, which was still falling hard. I could only assume that my host was actually inside the restaurant. This idea sent an electric bolt of excitement through my heart — no psychopath waits inside a restaurant to beat you up! Restaurants are for romance and love, not for head-kicking-in. Come to think of it, note-sending is also not a typical pastime associated with face-pummelling. As far as I can tell, the crushers of skulls tend to be lacking in the subtle social etiquettes of sending invites to prospective victims.

As I began to weave my way through the parked cars

towards the restaurant, something caught my eye – something in one of the windows, something wet and beautiful and very much like . . .

Eleanor! It was Eleanor! Here! To meet me! And she wasn't going to kick my head in! My heart did a huge somersault inside my chest and I was practically skipping across the car park – until something brought me to a sudden standstill. The football seemed to come from nowhere. It hit the back of my head with such force that my chin jabbed into my chest.

'Fuck,' I grunted in shock and pain, certain that I heard something snap inside my neck.

I waited for the dramatic cries of apology and questions of my well-being from whatever stupid cock had kicked it. But no one said anything. I began to turn round to see where it had come from, when it suddenly hit me again.

BAM!

This time it got me square on the side of the head.

'Fuck!' I yelled reflexively.

My vision flashed white, then black.

This was no accident. Some twat was doing this on purpose.

Dazed and confused, I stumbled back between two parked cars to get out of the line of fire.

BAM!

Another direct hit. Right into the back of my head again!

Pain, confusion, dizziness, confusion, panic, pain, dizzy, feet . . . There was a pair of feet. They stepped forward and stopped in front of me. I looked up to see who it was and—

CRACK!

Straight in the mouth!

'Fuck!'

I raised my arms to protect my head, but not before another blow caught me hard on the cheek.

'Fuck!'

My entire head was ringing. What kind of magic football was this? My arms took a bombardment of blows as they protected my head, until one hit caught me in the ribs. I struggled to get away and stumbled into the side of a parked car.

My naïve innocence that made me think this might have been an accident was long gone. My stupidity in assuming it was a football was, for some reason, still lingering.

No one can move a football this fast! I thought to myself. *Maybe it's a tennis ball on elasticated string.*

As the blows continued to come, it slowly dawned on me that this person was not using a ball at all. They were punching me! With their real-life fists!

'You dick!' I yelled.

A sudden burst of panic shot through me as it occurred to me that I was being attacked. Some cock was beating me up!

'You prick!' screamed the cock. 'You FUCKING PRICK!'

I recognised that cock's voice.

No.

It couldn't be . . .

My McJust Desserts

'Zack?' I asked, lowering my arms slightly so that he could see it was me.

Who could he have confused me with? Who would Zack want to beat up that looks like me?

'You fucking prick!' he screamed in my face.

'Zack, it's me!'

He must be possessed!

The punches paused and I took this opportunity to sprint back a few yards, round the back of a parked car, out of arm's reach.

'What are you doing?' I asked him breathlessly, confused, still sure that this must be an accident, and that he would now apologise profusely.

'You fucking prick!' he shrieked, darting forward and giving me an almighty shove that sent me flying.

My legs struggled desperately to run backward and keep me upright, but they failed, and I skidded across the concrete on my bum. Straight away I got myself back to my feet, but thankfully Zack didn't take the opportunity to kick me in the head.

'Zack! What are you doing?' I asked again, desperately

trying to reason with him, hoping that if he heard me saying his name he might snap out of it.

'You're a fucking prick!' he screamed, saliva stretching between his lips and tears streaming down his face. He looked practically rabid.

I get the feeling he thinks I'm a prick.

'What the hell are you doing?' I demanded, raising my voice for the first time. It appears that when you're in a fight your brain doesn't have the ability to think up new things to say, so you end up muttering the same crap over and over again. I think that by this point I was quite aware of what he was doing – he was beating my bloody face in.

'You . . . !'

Was he trying to say something other than 'fucking prick'?

'. . . fucking prick!'

Apparently not.

'You . . . !'

Oh, hang on . . .

'. . . I'm going to fucking kill you!'

Change isn't always for the better.

'Why?' I asked, constantly stepping back as he continued forward.

'I know what you've been saying about me! I'm not a fucking idiot!'

'What?'

I pretended not to know what he was talking about, but I had a horrible feeling I knew exactly what he was talking about. I had a horrible feeling that Helena had gone straight to him after she had overheard what I said about him whacking off in the toilets.

'I know what you said, Jack!'

'I don't know what you're talking about!' I insisted, finally halting my retreat for dramatic emphasis.

'That's funny!' he said, suddenly regaining his composure, scarily fast. 'Because you only said it a couple of hours ago! Something about me being a pervert!'

'I . . . I wasn't *saying* that!' I decided there was no point in denying it. 'I was just repeating what someone else had told me! I didn't believe it though!'

He looked like he was struggling to think of what to say next, like maybe he had made a horrible mistake.

'That's not what it sounded like to me!' he retorted.

'You weren't there! You heard second-hand information about something I was repeating about second-hand information that I heard!'

It didn't make much sense but it was the best I could do under the circumstances.

'Well next time you go around spreading rumours, you might want to get your fucking facts right!' he fumed. 'I'm gay, OK? I'm sorry if that offends you, but it doesn't mean I'm a fucking pervert, all right?'

'I . . .'

And with one final shove, accompanied by another 'PRICK!', Zack eventually stalked away.

What the hell just happened?

I had made my journey down the yellow brick road, avoiding all manner of lions and tigers and bears, only to reach the end and get the shit kicked out of me by a friend-of-Dorothy! That's what just happened. I stood there in a daze, twelve feet from the entrance to McDonald's, before I realised that my face felt like it had met the ugly end of a meat grinder.

Quickly, yet calmly, I steadily made my way towards the restaurant (at least it felt like I was being steady, I was probably stumbling all over the place). I had to go and check out the damage to my face. I had a horrible feeling I was going to need a visit to hospital. Visions of what my face probably looked like began forcing themselves into my mind – deep cuts, snapped bones, shining great lumps of swollen red flesh – and as I weaved my way through the busy restaurant I began to panic. Adding to my fear was the thought that Eleanor might have left already, or, even worse, she might have just seen me getting pummelled by wimpy Gruff-Nuggets. I traipsed my demi-corpse into the bathroom and prepared myself for what I was about to see. My entire face felt swollen and numb. I slowly raised my head in front of the mirror and . . .

Oh my god.

Show Your Face

Was there something wrong with the lighting? Something wrong with the mirror? Was I really seeing what I was seeing?

I couldn't quite believe my eyes. There was barely any damage! I looked practically normal! Then again, fresh bruising isn't always highly noticeable, whereas in a day or two . . .

In a day or two my face is going to look like it has been playing pat-a-cake with a blind gorilla!

The longer I looked, the redder my face grew. I could almost see the welts swelling up before my eyes.

This is not good. I am going to look terrible.

The thought made me want to be sick. I clutched the taps on the sink and retched up a big dry heave. Nothing more followed. I began to hear the voices of everyone in school on Monday morning – *'Holy shit! What the hell happened to you?'*

If I don't tell them anything, then they can imagine some dreadful incident by themselves . . .

Of course!

If I keep quiet then everyone will assume it was Reaper

that did this and that I took my undeserved beating like a man. Brilliant! As long as Zack doesn't go blabbing his mouth off then I have a good chance of coming out of this as a reluctant hero, a downtrodden victim.

I rinsed my face in cold water for a while, which seemed to reduce the redness of my bruises (or increase the redness of the rest of my face, I couldn't be sure), making them barely noticeable. It wouldn't last long, though. If I wanted to go out and face Eleanor looking half decent then I'd have to move fast because in ten or twenty minutes they were going to be swollen red lumps.

I took a good look at myself in the mirror.

You're the good guy, I reminded myself, *not the baddie. You could have annihilated that cheesy gruff-nugget, but you let him off because he was crying. You are a good guy.*

Of course, in retrospect I am aware that my brain was talking utter bollocks, but I needed to do something to boost my self-esteem if I was to meet Eleanor in this state. The anticipation of seeing her raised my spirits. Just the *thought* of her was like a warm, comforting blanket around me.

Somehow I still had a sense of optimism inside me. I took a deep breath, stared at my reflection and looked myself in the eyes. I was ready.

I tried to quell my positive vibes, scared they might jinx me, but it was no good, I couldn't keep them down. A rousing soundtrack began to swell inside my head – *DAH, dah dah DAH, dah dah daaaaaaah . . .*

As soon as I realised it was the *Rocky* theme I quickly replaced it with something less cheesy – *On Her Majesty's*

Secret Service. You probably don't know it, but trust me, it's brilliant. You should seek it out (the music that is, not the film so much).

'Let's do it.'

The Pick-Up

I marched confidently out of the toilets, scanning for Eleanor's face as I ploughed a path through the fast-foodies. She was gone.

I stepped out into the car park, the doors swinging shut behind me. My girl was out there somewhere. I could sense her.

I felt like a cowboy. The cool breeze was fresh against my hot skin, and as the rain fell I allowed it to caress and soothe my bruises. I felt unstoppable. Where was Zack now?

The whistling from *The Good, the Bad and the Ugly* began mixing itself into my soundtrack, pumping my adrenalin even harder. Squinting my eyes against the rising shower of rain I tried to seek out that beautiful face. There were a couple of people rushing to their cars, some dashing past on their way home, one or two sauntering along without a care in the world, and just as I was beginning to give up hope, thinking she must have left already, I saw her.

There she was, waiting at the corner of the road, looking out amongst the passing cars. My heart turned to hot marshmallow and a warm smile tugged at the corner of my mouth. She looked so innocent and vulnerable, standing there alone . . . and wet. I took a moment to ogle her beauty before setting off towards her. Oblivious to my presence, she sat herself down on the low fence at the side of the Drive-Thru entrance and checked her watch. Poor little thing was probably wondering if I was ever going to show up. I began planning my moves, deciding what I should do when I reached her. I wanted to surprise her, but I wanted to play it cool at the same time, so I decided that I would silently sidle up beside her when she was looking the other way, then surprise her with a gentle, 'Hi.' She would respond by whipping her head round to see me, a grin would burst across her face then she would throw her arms around me. It would probably be the most romantic/cool moment of my life. I just hoped that my nob would die down before I got to her (I could kind of see her nipples through her top). *I can't believe that kid called me a chin-tickler!*

Wait.

Eleanor was standing up. A car pulled into the car park and she began to jog after it, her breasts bouncing in dreamy slow motion beneath her damp blouse. Her dad was here to pick her up already! I could not miss this opportunity. I couldn't let her slip through my fingers. I had to speak to her!

'Eleanor!' I yelled. But my voice was drowned out by a fleet of passing lorries.

I began to sprint for the car. There was no way it was getting away. I watched as Eleanor threw open the passenger door and jumped in. My legs pumped harder than ever before, my thighs instantly burning under the sudden exertion.

If she goes home now she'll think I stood her up – she'll think I don't care!

There was no way I was going to let this story have a tragic ending. I was going to make it! The car was still stationary! I lurched to a standstill outside Eleanor's window and, as I peered in, the sight that greeted me caused my stomach to leave my body. The driver of the car had his arms wrapped around Eleanor and his face was mashed into hers with a deep passionate kiss. It soon occurred to me that this was not Eleanor's dad.

GET YOUR DAMN HANDS OFF HER!!!

I wanted to scream. I wanted to throw the car door open and yank that dirty sonofabitch out on to the rain-pummelled concrete and stamp on his face. I would be her knight in shining armour.

Or maybe not.

I paused as I realised that Eleanor didn't appear to be doing any of this against her will. She wasn't struggling or kicking or making a fuss. She was kissing back. She was running her fingers through this guy's hair. My stomach lurched and I stepped back. Her fingers ran across his face, down his chest, then disappeared below. An icy chill ran down my spine and the uncontrollable throes of pure sadness began to take hold of my bottom lip, my flaring nostrils, my huffing breaths and watering eyes. I took another step back. Then another.

Please don't do this, Eleanor . . . Not you . . . not like this . . . please . . .

I could feel my world slowly coming to an end. The guy twisted himself round, practically forcing himself on top of my sweet Eleanor.

And then I saw the wanker's face.

Sick

My throat instantly choked up on retching sobs. I couldn't decide whether to vomit or cry . . . so I did both. I tried to walk away, but my legs were unresponsive. I continued to watch as there, in front of me, thrusting himself against my Eleanor, slobbering into her mouth, violating her young body with his filthy hands, was none other than Dave Kross.

My body began to shake violently. Dave pulled back from the kiss, whispered something to Eleanor, then opened the driver-side door. He was getting out! Suddenly my body remembered how to move again and I quickly darted behind a row of cars and flattened myself against the back wall of the Drive-Thru. Unfortunately the vigorous movement triggered more gag and I continued to throw up until there was nothing left and I was retching on bile. The tears, however, seemed never-ending. And just when I thought my life could not get any worse, something miraculous happened — it got twice as bad.

My body was hurled against the brick wall behind me. I was numb with shock. I grabbed at Dave's arms as he wrapped his hands around my throat and pushed his grimacing face into mine.

'You'd do well to keep your fucking nose out of other people's business, eh, Jack?'

I had nothing to say. I just wished that I had saved some of that vomit to spew straight into his face.

'You mention any of this to a single person and I assure you that you will fail your exams most fucking triumphantly, and then I'll get to work on draining every last drop of happiness from your waking life. Do you understand me, Jack?' He spat the words out with more heartfelt evil than I ever would have believed possible from him.

I wanted to tell him to do his worst, to let him know that there was no more happiness left inside me to take. *Like blood from a stone*, I wanted to growl in a Clint Eastwood kind-a-way. Unfortunately I was unable to say any of these things as his thumbs were crushing my larynx. I stared into the eyes of the man who had just taken everything from me. I'd had so many goals for the end of this week and in just a few seconds he had blown them all to hell. So much for him giving me a good grade. So much for Eleanor becoming my girlfriend.

But there was one goal he had not managed to take from me. There was one little thing remaining that burned in my heart like a tiny pilot-light and kept my soul alive. As he loosened his grip on my throat I looked him square in the eyes, took a deep breath and, with every ounce of dignity I could muster, I imparted these rasping words of triumph . . .

'Conjuring dumplings fallidgery fladgery.'

My week's work had not all been in vain.

Dave stared at me for a moment, clearly wondering how he should respond to this . . . and then he did it.

His head sped towards mine faster than I could comprehend. Too fast to dodge. His forehead collided with my nose and a sickening crack shot through my skull. The back of my head smashed into the wall behind me, and pain sliced through my brain like an ice-cold dagger. My eyes instantly filled up with stinging tears and there was nothing I could do to keep them open. I could feel warm blood gushing down my chin. I could taste it like salty metal in my mouth. I coughed frantically as I struggled to breathe. Blood was flowing heavily out of my nose and down the back of my throat simultaneously. It was impossible to take any air in without drowning on a lungful of blood. There was nothing I could do. I was about to choke to death on my own noseblood.

Then Dave did something that probably saved my life. His hands gripped firmly on my shoulders and he slammed his knee hard into my groin. My eyes were still shut but I could hear exactly what just happened. A throatful of blood shot from my mouth directly into Dave's face and, I assumed from his resulting spits, straight into his mouth too. Almost as good as a faceful of vomit! I dropped to my hands and knees and leaned forward, which allowed the majority of the blood to flow from my nose, leaving my throat clear to breathe (that was the life-saving bit). I gasped in large, choking gulps of breath and blindly spat mouthfuls of blood out on to the rain-drenched concrete. I was alive. I wasn't aware of any pain in my balls. Not yet. That would come later. I heard the sound of Dave's spluttering gradually diminish as he moved off in the direction of his car, then I heard a new set of footsteps approaching from the opposite direction, running.

Please don't let this be Reaper, I pleaded to any god that would listen. *I can't get attacked more than three times in one day. There has to be a limit on these things.*

Still unable to open my eyes, and now unable to stand up (ball-ache was setting in, it felt like a cord had wrapped my nuts to my guts and was slowly being pulled tighter and tighter), I crawled away from the approaching footsteps as fast as I could. I dread to think what I looked like. I was crawling around a car park in the pissing rain like a blind toddler on speed. But at that moment I didn't care. I just didn't want to get hit in the head any more.

Unfortunately the exertion was too much. I felt a heavy, hot darkness begin to fill my body and I knew that I was going to pass out. The owner of the footsteps arrived and my brain suddenly felt very heavy.

Fade to black.

'*For never was a story of more woe, than this of Jack and Eleano . . . r.*'

My Top Five Poignant
Observations of the Week

5. Grown men will always pine for the one that got
   away
4. Females will always pine for the unattainable
   male
3. People will always crave guidance, be it from
   parents, teachers or god
2. There will always be bullies
1. You're not a grown-up until you realise that
   nobody ever grows up

The Awakening

Even though I felt like I was going to puke my balls up, even though my face felt like it was swollen to the size of a beach ball and my nose had nails hammered through it, I was still very aware of two damp breasts pressing against the side of my ribs as someone threw my arm around their shoulders and guided me to a bench.

'Sit down here and let me take a look,' she told me.

I was able to open my eyes for a second at a time, catching fleeting glimpses of Em's ginger rain-soaked hair matted round her sticky-out ears; her worried expression as she examined my mangled face; her beautiful porcelain skin untarnished by make-up (a rarity at our age), and dappled with raindrops and freckles. Were those tears she was wiping from her big blue eyes or was it just rainwater? She chewed intermittently on her bottom lip with concentration or worry. It was suddenly very clear to me that I had been more of a dick than ever before. It was very clear that I had made a series of very serious mistakes. It was very clear that . . .

I passed out again.

*

I know! I'm sorry! It's all very convenient and reeks of Hollywood ending, and this story would be far more original if I just accepted that it was a tragedy and avoided any attempt at a Happily Ever After. But what can I say? This is the way it happened and there's nothing I can do about it. Yes, I know, I don't deserve her. She's too good for me. I'm a dick, she's a sweetheart and blah blah blah. Those things are going to change – well, not the bit where she's a sweetheart, but all the other bits.

'Hi,' whispered a voice, drawing me out from the black fuzz that enveloped my brain. It was a friendly voice, a worried voice.

I opened my eyes to see Em's face beaming down on me.

'You OK?' she asked, in what was probably her best attempt at tenderness.

You know when you wake up at someone else's house and it takes your brain a couple of seconds to work out where you are? This was like that multiplied by 8.2 million. As my brain recapped the day's events it also relived all the emotions that came with them – car park, fear, blood, vomit, heartbreak, Dave, Eleanor, failure, footsteps . . .

'Was it you?' I asked drearily.

'Was what me?' replied Em.

But I had already forgotten what I had asked. Where was I now? Red curtains, torn wallpaper, a faint smell of antiseptic.

'Am I broken?' I asked, pointing at my throbbing nose.

'Nope. Nothing. As far as I can tell. We'll take you to the hospital later though.'

'No, thanks,' I said. Hospital was the last place I felt like going.

'You don't have any choice. My mum's a nurse, don't forget. She'll drag you there by your nuts if she has to.'

My nuts. I wasn't really aware of the pain until she mentioned those words, then all of a sudden an intense wave of nausea washed over me.

'It wasn't Reaper,' I told her as I curled my knees towards my chest with a heavy groan.

'I know.'

'You know?'

'Ummm . . . yes,' she said, with an unmistakable twang of guilt.

'What do you mean, "Ummm . . . yes"?'

'Well, apart from the fact that Reaper got hospitalised by Gellar's dad . . . I kind of saw the whole thing with you and . . . Dave.'

'He's in hospital?' I sighed with a smile. Then, with a note of panic, 'What whole thing?'

She didn't see me get pummelled by Zack, too, did she?

'You looked kind of upset. I didn't want to interfere, and then . . . I can't believe he headbutted you!'

'Where were you?' I asked.

'Cycle path,' she answered. 'James told me where you'd gone, so I came to, err . . . protect you.'

'Thanks,' I said, feeling a little insulted. 'A girl bodyguard.'

'I meant I came to protect you from what you were going to see.'

'How did you know what I was going to see?'

'Eleanor told me at lunchtime. They've been meeting after school every Friday.'

'So why did I get a note?' I asked.

'What note?'

'This note,' I said, pulling my bus pass from my pocket. 'No, this note,' I corrected, showing her the *4 p.m. Drive Thru* one.

Em had no answer for this and I didn't need one – I quickly worked it out for myself. The note *was* from Eleanor, but it was not meant for me. I must have picked it up off Dave's floor with all that other crap.

'I'm a dick.'

'I know.'

'Why didn't you tell me earlier?'

'I'll do my best to make a habit of it. You're a dick.'

'No, I mean why didn't you tell me about Eleanor and *him*?'

And more importantly . . .

'Why did you tell me he was gay?'

'Who's gay?'

'Dave!'

'He's not,' she said, more than a little confused.

And once again my brain slowly caught on, as I eventually worked it out for myself. (Yes, I can see now that it was extremely obvious and I should have worked it out ages ago, but I had a lot on my mind, OK?) The note that I had swiped from my bag (and then Dave swiped from me) was not Em's note. I had blindly shoved my hand into my bag, thinking I'd grabbed Em's note, but had accidently picked up the very same note I had just dropped in there. I had put Eleanor's note into my bag, then pulled it back out again! So that means . . . Dave is not gay. Zack is. Zack does not whack off before every lesson. Dave does.

'That's why he's always late!'

Em nodded grimly.

'Sick fuck!'

Em continued to nod.

'No wonder Zack hates me.'

Em stopped nodding. 'What?'

'Never mind. Just, from now on, no more notes. They could get someone killed.'

'OK . . .'

Needless to say this wasn't making much sense to Em.

'Speaking of notes,' said Em, slipping her phone from her bag, 'you might want to take a look at the ones I snapped from the whiteboard.' For some reason she looked extremely pleased with herself. 'Might help get you a good grade.'

I got the distinct impression there was something she was not telling me.

SUMMARY

OK, let's face it, summaries are shit. They simply recap everything that you've already read and they always feel kind of '. . . *and the moral of the story is . . . !*' so I'm going to try to keep this as short and pain-free as possible. Firstly, I suppose I better recap –

I set out at the beginning of the week with two goals:

1. **Get the grade**
2. **Get the girl**

And as the week progressed, another two goals got thrown in there too:

3. **Stay alive**
4. **Say 'Conjuring dumplings fallidgery fladgery' to a teacher without getting bollocked for it**

OK, so numbers three and four went fairly well (unless getting headbutted and kicked in the bollocks literally counts as a bollocking . . . possibly). The first two are debatable. All right, so I haven't ended up with the girl I set out for and, well, actually I haven't officially even ended up with any girl – but I've just realised that, although I made that promise that it wasn't going to happen, I do actually quite like Em. A lot. And I get the feeling that she might feel the same way about me. So it's hopeful. As for getting the good grade . . . well, there are really only two possible outcomes here –

1. **Dave reads this essay from beginning to end, realises I have an ace up my sleeve and gives me the mark I deserve (surely at least a B–?), I get into film school, I make award-winning films and spend the rest of my life doing something I love . . .**
2. **Dave ignores the introduction that I'm going to write (he taught me to always write your introduction _afterwards_, that way you know exactly what it is you're introducing), which will warn him that 'To Not Read This Could Seriously Damage Your Health' and that his future happiness hangs in the balance. If he doesn't read, if he fails to spot the ace up my sleeve, if he gives me a bad mark purely out of spite, then he leaves me with no choice other than to take matters into my own hands.**

You've probably guessed by now that the 'ace up my sleeve' and the 'something' Em 'was not telling me' are one and the same. What you may not have guessed is that the 'ace' and the 'something' stem from Em having waited and watched in that Drive-Thru car park. Em did not just watch on in dumbstruck horror. She had her camera phone with her. And she took pictures. She took pictures of a teacher getting it on with one underage student, then beating the crap out of another one. Just read that sentence again. Yes. An *underage* student. Eleanor, like myself, is still fifteen (she turns sixteen in two or three weeks), which officially means that not only is Dave a twisted and immoral human being, he is also a rapist and a paedophile. Try to imagine the shitstorm magnitude of what would happen to Dave if this information and those pictures wound up in the wrong hands.

Of course I wouldn't wait for Dave to crush my future with a cripplingly bad mark and then proceed to blackmail him with those photographs. That's not my style. It's cheap. I would simply attempt to ruin his life, just as he has done mine. Those photos would go to every newspaper, every parent, every school governor, every police station I could lay my hands on. This essay would go to every editor, every agent, every publisher I could find and I would not stop until every last detail of this story ended up in the pages of a bestselling book, which would become a cult playground classic and would then be adapted into a lesser cult film (the film is very rarely better than the book). This route would, of course, also lead to a rich and illustrious career in the movies and would probably prove a lot easier and more enjoyable than five years of college and film school and then working my way up from the bottom of the ladder. In a way, I am now kind of hoping that Dave *does* give me a bad mark. His future now hangs in the balance, somewhere between a C– and a B+.

I suppose this really does bring me to the end. I began this story promising you no clever writing or character development. I guess I was wrong (not about the clever writing bit, but characters do develop, people change, there's nothing I can do about that). I started out the week not knowing who I really was. I spent five days pouring my innermost feelings on to these pages and agonising over what category of person I am. It turns out I don't really care any more. I am who I am. Screw the labels and categories. If I don't fit in that's fine with me.

THE END →

So now I lay here (on a *girl's* bed!) with Em's fingers inter-locked with mine and her thumb stroking the back of my hand. We haven't kissed, we haven't confessed undying love, we haven't even stared longingly into each other's eyes. The rain continues to drum against her bedroom window and I am content.

'How you doing?' she asks, laying herself down beside me and lurching with an unexpected hiccup.

'Pain,' I groan pathetically, not wanting to imagine the bruising on my groin.

'Anything I can do?' And she hiccups again.

'If I told you the 100%-guaranteed cure for hiccups, could you hold my balls?'

Now let me restart this chapter . . .

So now I lay here (on a *girl's* bed!) with Em's fingers kindly cupping my nuts and there are just three words on my mind:

3. **I've**
2. **got**
1. **nob-ache.**